THE BEST
AUSTRALIAN
STORIES
2011

THE BEST
AUSTRALIAN
STORIES
2011

Edited by
CATE KENNEDY

Published by Black Inc.,
an imprint of Schwartz Media Pty Ltd

37–39 Langridge Street
Collingwood Vic 3066 Australia
email: enquiries@blackincbooks.com
http://www.blackincbooks.com

ISBN 9781863955485

Printed in Australia by Griffin Press. The paper this book is printed on
is certified against the Forest Stewardship Council® Standards.
Griffin Press holds FSC chain of custody certification SGS-COC-005088.
FSC promotes environmentally responsible, socially beneficial
and economically viable management of the world's forests.

FSC
www.fsc.org
MIX
Paper from
responsible sources
FSC® C009448

Contents

Introduction

Cate Kennedy

It's been my pleasure again this year to plunge into piles of short stories, swim lap after lap through them and emerge dripping from the deep end with my selection.

I start with this lame metaphor for two reasons. First, because starting to write a story often feels like this – feeling our way forward awkwardly with an image, trying out its heft and shape to see whether it will bear weight – something David Mitchell, at this year's Sydney Writers' Festival, described as hesitantly stepping forth into the minefield of plausibility, testing the ground ahead as you go. The instinctual part of our brain starts its run, finding connections, either racing ahead of us like an advance guard, if the writer is having a good day, or setting down each foot with agonised uncertainty. We know we'll be redrafting later (*Plunge into a pile? Get the red pen ...*), or maybe jettisoning the whole thing and starting afresh.

The second reason is because this feeling of immersion in another element, which has characterised my reading of this year's submissions, has reminded me that this is the fundamental pleasure of reading itself. Reading is time spent in a conjured world, oblivious to ordinary demands, buoyant, afloat and finally rendered weightless. With hundreds of great stories to read this year, I spent a long time in the water.

Winnowing down my shortlist from the boxfuls I received resulted, as usual, in far more excellent stories than I had room to include, and I would like to thank all the writers who submitted stories in 2011. If their vitality and diversity of subject matter and style is anything to go by, the state of short fiction in Australia is alive and thriving. Thanks, too, to Denise O'Dea and the staff at Black Inc. for giving me the opportunity again to make this annual selection.

There are thirty-one stories in the collection this year, running the gamut from well-known authors to writers whose work I was encountering for the first time. I read from individual unpublished submissions, anthologies, literary journals and new collections. The stories ranged in word length from a few hundred words to works that could be classified as short novels, so clearly the concept of what actually constitutes a short story is also a living and shifting notion. Generally they fell between 1500 and 5000 words and authors explored an extraordinary range of subjects. From faith healing to growing tomatoes, from road trips to romance, it struck me again and again that, like life, it's not what you start with, it's what you do with it that matters. Stories about small, mundane things unfolded so beautifully and with such arresting imagery that they stopped me in my tracks and, conversely, stories with richly conceived plots and characters, that surged forward full of promise and dimension, occasionally lost their way. Some stories had been polished to a high sheen, some seemed barely proofread. Some strained for effect, some made their point with effortless grace and originality. All of them showed, in some way, the wonderful possibilities and constraints of the form.

Constraint can be a marvellous thing in fiction. The need for limitation demands that a writer learns to see exactly what needs to be there, and only that. Nothing teaches us what makes a story more effectively than the requirement to strip it of its inessentials, and a great short story is a perfect model of an author carefully weighing every word to fashion a miraculous whole that carries a rich, invisible freight. Such stories have a power like a depth charge, subtext roiling up to the surface at precisely the right moment.

This skill, I'm convinced, is learned in the doing and in the development of each writer's own idiosyncratic voice. The stylistic diversity of the stories contained here attests to how difficult it is to reduce this process to formula or aphorism. Just as a great meal is a different thing from a recipe, a fine story offers satisfactions on many levels. Allow me to drag the blackboard menu over.

Nicholas Jose's delicate handling of grief and the unstoppable rise of unbidden memory in 'What Love Tells Me' explores a terrain of family tragedy and loss similar to 'The Anniversary' by Deborah FitzGerald but makes very different stylistic decisions. Marele Day's slyly witty 'Ten-day Socks' and Marion Halligan's sumptuously gothic 'Shooting the Fox,' meanwhile, share a knowing humour but are worlds apart in subject matter.

Subtle layering of detail that seems casually incidental at first is found in Mark O'Flynn's 'Beneath the Figs' – skilful use of tone has you smiling right up until the story reveals its poignant underside.

I enjoyed the expertly handled shifts and balances in Joanne Riccioni's 'Duty of Care,' in which a past wrong drives the story along like an inescapable undercurrent, and Louis Nowra's 'The Index Cards,' a story which gradually unfolds from a stack of implication and rising dread. I am pleased to include 'Matter,' one of Miriam Sved's excellent AFL-themed stories, some of which have appeared in *Overland* and *Meanjin*, and Sharon Kent's 'Jumping for Chicken,' both of which delineate with great empathy the inner lives of their troubled male narrators. The utter despair of Mark Dapin's female protagonist in 'Visiting Day' is drawn with equal credibility and care.

Chris Womersley and Jennifer Mills are both masters of creating atmosphere and their stories here demonstrate how a short story's constraint and brevity – what John Marsden calls 'the eyedropper rather than the bucket' approach – can evoke tension and suspense.

When Rodney Hall's 'Silence 1945' appeared in the *Good Weekend* Summer Fiction issue in January this year, he was quoted as saying: 'Isolating a moment in fiction feels like walking into a forgotten room. At a glance you know everything that's there.' That isolating of a salient moment drives many of the stories represented here, including Penny O'Hara's 'Strawberry Jam,' which manages to pack an intensely felt realisation into less than a thousand words, and Karen Stanton's 'The Gills of Fish,' in which the moment of birth itself turns a souring relationship back on course. Julie Chevalier's protagonist in 'This Awful Brew' finds it when she suddenly castigates herself for her own credulity, as do the protagonists of the stories by Michael Sala and Sarah Holland-Batt as they recognise the scar tissue of old trauma. Gretchen Shirm's compromised mother makes an awful choice for her own child and is left to live with her decision and its hidden, unresolved effects.

Childhood and adolescence, in particular their unexpected and frequently unwelcome rites of passage, were explored to wonderful effect by many writers, and Leah Swann's piece from her impressive first collection *Bearings* mines this territory. Totally different again in tone, Nick Smith's 'Everybody Wins on Kid Planet' takes an afternoon at an indoor playground and skillfully morphs it to present a mordantly comic overview of the state of childhood itself.

'Izzy and Ona' by Favel Parrett shows the same economy and deftness in revealing the stakes for her juvenile characters here, in the distilled space of a short story, as she does in her highly praised debut novel *Into the Shallows*.

The twin dilemmas of failing elderly parents and/or demanding adult children on overworked, middle-aged protagonists featured strongly in this year's submissions – I fully expect to see a reality TV show soon, capitalising on this demographic zeitgeist – and 'Fifty Years' by Stephanie Buckle and 'The Sleepers in That Quiet Earth' by Debra Adelaide tackle this fraught subject with great style. Russell King, in 'The Road to Nowhere,' expertly skewers the expectations of more instantly recognisable protagonists as they set off in their spanking new motorhome to hilarious holiday disaster.

While many writers wrote of pregnancy and infants, nobody did it with quite the same playfully light touch and intriguing implication as Tim Richards in '(Favoured by) Babies.' Liam Davison's 'Space Under the Sun' poignantly explores the ethical dilemmas of gender selection in a terrain where there are no easy answers.

Karen Hitchcock's always-edgy prose snaps and crackles with energy in 'Forging Friendship,' while Kate Rotherham's subtle 'Shelter' works on a gentle register of suggestion and precision.

Catherine Cole's 'Home' also uses implication for impact, presenting us with a numbed refugee desperate for his daughter and grandchild to arrive by boat to join him in his patched-together life in Australia. For the reader, the knowledge of the catastrophe of the Siev X and other disasters like it hangs like a pall over this character's tremulous hope for peace and asylum – a perfect example of how a short story can carry a particular depth charge of subtextual implication solely by working on something the reader, but not the character, is privy to.

Finally, I was totally immersed in 'Blow In,' an unusual and sophisticated piece from Rebecca Giggs, one of four writers under thirty featured in *Overland 201*, a special expanded fiction edition curated by Kalinda Ashton and Samuel Cooney.

It's been my pleasure putting this final collection together, and I hope it's as much of a pleasure for you to read.

Enough whetting of your appetite, though. It's time for you to pull your chair up to the table, and start.

Cate Kennedy

Duty of Care

Joanne Riccioni

When it's just him and me, when I'm prodding for the pulse between the bones of his wrist, or strapping the cuff around his wasted arm to take his blood pressure, my own heart races with unspoken words. Sometimes I imagine spitting them, hot and shocking, into his face. Other times, when I'm calm, I want to loom over him and whisper them as an icy draft across his bared skin. Instead I give him his bed bath in silence and focus on the task at hand: I straighten his clenched fingers, watch them retract, tease them out again with my sponge. The right hand is more gnarled and seized than the other and the movement makes him grunt. So I uncurl it again and push my sponge between each arthritic claw, watching him flinch, listening again for the complaint gargling in his lungs. When I roll him over, his weight always surprises me, catching me in the small of the back. It's as if death, like some silty sediment, is already settling into his hollow bones. When I let go he rolls back neatly into his own shape imprinted on the mattress, the fossil of a grown man.

Some days I can't manage to turn him on my own. I call Manjit in to help me. She holds him on his side while I wash his back. His skin is almost transparent, so thin you could tear his arse with a broken fingernail. 'I hope you've been manicurrring,' Manjit says primly, rolling the R's. She's hamming up Shona, our nursing director from Dundee. Manjit plays her like Miss Jean Brodie's evil twin. 'Now little gels,' Manjit mimics through taut lips, 'I like to rrrun a tight shep. There's no rrroom for slovenly on my watch. I do things by the buke.'

Shona likes to line us all up to inspect our nails as if we're in boarding school. She comes back to check Manjit's twice, as if she might have somehow overlooked chipped red nail polish and a forearm of noisy bangles in every colour of the rainbow. 'Jesus, I reckon she thinks I'm some bloody checkout chick at the Caltex, just off the plane from Delhi,' Manjit snorts. She does that half-nodding, half-shaking thing with her head, like a Bollywood star. When I laugh he moans softly at the sudden sound. His mouth wrestles with the beginnings of words. 'Don't you start,' I tell him, as I begin the brittle operation of dressing him, grinding my teeth as I slowly thread his arms through his pyjama top.

Manjit smiles and strokes his head. His white hair is thin and wild and innocent as fairy floss above his ears. 'All right, Mr B. Toni's nearly done,' she coos. 'Then I'll bring you tea in your crossword mug. If you give me a smile I might even pop in an extra sugar. OK? OK, Mr B?' He manages an animated gargle. It could mean, 'That would be lovely, dear.' Or it could mean, 'Go to hell, you stupid bitch.'

Manjit doesn't care either way. Any response is a miracle with the end-stagers. I've seen her chase the life in them like some kind of Holy Grail. She's young. She still has the energy to talk to them as though she expects an answer, touch them as though she remembers who they were. Most of us in Acute have become slack with all that. It's easy to drop the pretence when you get nothing in return. We're too busy following Shona's manual of day-to-day maintenance: the correct method of spoon feeding, bed bathing, turning, strapping in, the temperature and blood-sugar monitoring. In between all that, who has the energy to talk or touch for no reason? No one but Manjit, anyway. Sometimes, not often, but sometimes, she gets the flicker of a brightened eye following her across the room, the locking of fingers around her wrist, a suddenly girlish giggle or snatch of half words, all where there was nothing before. She bites on her brown lips then and her smile is stubborn. She doesn't tell Shona or the doctors. What do such things mean in a patient who is slowly forgetting how to chew, how to swallow, how to breathe?

She looks up when she knows I'm watching. 'See, Antonella? See?' She blinks at me, like I'm complicit in her secret, like we're partners. But I look away.

*

Manjit brings Mr B's tea in a plastic beaker with a straw in the lid. She has put the plastic beaker inside a mug printed with a blank crossword. When I roll my eyes, she shrugs and says, 'Well? He likes it in his crossword mug. He drinks more.' She pushes the straw between his lips and I hear her murmur soft encouragements to him, like a mother to a child. When I wheel in the trolley from the meds room, Manjit says, 'Someone left him halfway through his bed bath last week. Did you know?' She catches the drips of tea on his chin with a flannel and doesn't look at me. 'Didn't they, Mr B? Poor thing.' She puts the mug down and begins to check the names taped to the plastic trays of pills on the trolley. 'When I found him he had no pyjama top on and a wet sponge on his chest. Blue as ice, he was. God knows how long he'd been like that.' She doesn't say anything else as she cross-checks the meds. The discordant ragtime ring of a piano drifts down the corridor as if from some haunted old-time music hall. I imagine the rows of ghosts nodding their grey heads in music therapy. She looks up and searches my eyes carefully, one and then the other. I turn away and take a pill tray from the trolley.

'Really?' I say with my back to her. 'Good job Miss Jean wasn't on that day, then.' Manjit stands still for a moment. When I face her, she opens her mouth and inhales as if she might continue the conversation, so I cross over to the next bed and say with a brightness that makes me feel sick, 'Look, Mrs Porteous, you get a purple one today. Your favourite!'

Maeve, strapped in her bucket chair, does not look up. She cowers bald and wrinkled as a fallen chick. You could almost cup her in your hand and see her heart fluttering under her skin, grey and translucent as her cotton nightdress. I look down at her twisted body in the chair and imagine scooping her up and cradling her across the shiny, disinfected floors, away from the strip lights and out into the fragile morning sun. I might leave her at the base of a tree covered in autumn leaves. Instead I put my fingers in Maeve's mouth and prise it open, slotting the pills into her like coins. I close her jaw around a beaker of juice and massage her throat.

'Maeve, my lovely,' Manjit says. 'How are you?' She takes Mrs Porteous's fingers, veined and blue as old china, and folds them over her own, the colour of tea. 'She's uncomfortable today, Toni. Don't you think?' She hooks a finger under the old woman's chin and runs a thumb over the muscles in her jaw, locked grimly as if wrestling some invisible force. Manjit is good at reading the signs: she understands the writhing, chafing hands, the whittling tongues, the rocking and huffing and humming. She can read them like Shona reads medical charts or operations procedures. I've taught Manjit these things. At visiting time families seek her out now instead of me to translate the secret language of the demented and dying. Manjit can show them the vacant stare, the slack mouth, the contorted, shaking limbs and retrace for them the father, the uncle, the mother that once was there.

'Do you think we should speak to the doctor about upping her meds?' Manjit asks. I busy myself with ordering the little trays of drugs, their Technicolor glory winking through the plastic, making everything else look pasty. 'Toni?' Her delicate brown hand is on my own, fat and ruddy as a butcher's. She wants more than a *yes* or *no*.

'I'm just tired,' I say. 'You know what it's like.' She doesn't, of course. She is too young and bright and full of hope to have felt the suffocating panic of the past, the gnaw of old resentments.

*

Sometimes when I'm to feed him his pureed pumpkin or potato I find some small job that needs attention. When I get back to him I take the spoon and stir up the food, making sure it's completely cold and unpalatable. Then I shovel small balls of it into his mouth and watch him grimace with the effort of swallowing, pulling down his bottom lip with disgust, and with greed because he is hungry. It is exactly how his mouth looked when it was just the two of us in his office, all those afternoons, all those years ago. That same grimace from the effort of landing the cane on my palm, hard and flush along the welt already pulsing there, like a plumped vein; that same tight repugnance beneath his nose as he looked down on me; that same hunger in his eyes as if he couldn't help himself. I remember the slow-motion walks down the corridor back to class, holding before me that strange object in the shape of my hand, waiting for the blood to blossom from the scars below like some exotic flower he'd just given me. I have to look away, then, away from his mouth smeared with pumpkin, because I have the taste of blood in my own.

*

By the aviary, at the cheap outdoor setting the staff use for their breaks, Manjit and I slip off our shoes in the sun. I curl my toes on the chalky plastic chair and look at my throbbing bunions and chipped toenail polish. Her feet are thin and brown, delicately veined, too beautiful for the bleached industrial paving. 'Mr B doesn't like you, Toni,' she says, tossing the words into the air, like a child teasing. I squint at her mischievous little smile for a moment, then I light a cigarette. 'He told me.' She laughs.

'Yeah, right,' I say and blow smoke down my nose.

'No, seriously. He flinches when you walk in the room ... and he wets himself. I'm always having to change him after you've been near him.'

I scratch at the psoriasis in the folds of skin behind my knee, psoriasis I haven't had for years, not since I was a kid, not since school. When I look at my fingernails there is blood underneath them.

'Yeah, well it's like Pavlov's dogs, isn't it?' I say and toss my ash into the pot of an umbrella tree. 'Except instead of food, he knows he's going to get a bed bath or a needle or a mouthful of pills.' When I see her frown, I add, 'Poor bastard.' She smiles wanly as if to say, 'Don't treat me like I was born yesterday.'

I grind out my cigarette in the soil of the pot plant and heave myself out of the plastic chair.

'Just don't,' she says. 'Not on my shift.'

My gut tightens and I reach for the psoriasis again. 'What?' I say.

'Just don't do that with your cigarettes. It's revolting.'

*

Shona finds us by the aviary.

'Mrs Porteous, bed five, has gone.' She glances briefly at her wristwatch. 'Twenty-five minutes ago.' Even announcing death Shona runs a tight ship. She wields her clipboard before her like she's some auditor for the Grim Reaper. Her lips barely move when she speaks and she blinks with rapid efficiency. 'Her records show a morphine increase that wasn't approved by a doctor and a DNR order not signed by the correct family members.' Shona looks at Manjit's bare feet and the cigarette stubs in the plant pot. We do not speak. 'This will have to be revisited in a staff review. You are aware of that?' We nod simultaneously, like children. Shona flares up, 'Oh, for God's sake, Kaur, get some bloody shoes on and see to Mrs Porteous before the family arrive.' She turns in the doorway to the ward and comes back to lift up Manjit's fingers, compulsively. Then she shakes her own hand free of them, like she would inconsequential coins or car keys. As she leaves she says with her back to us, 'And get those earrings out. You're not at the temple now, Kaur.'

*

When she has gone, Manjit rests her forehead on the table for a few seconds and I hear her breath against the plastic. But when she stands she is sure and elegant, slowly pulling down her hair and coiling it back into its clip in one smooth manoeuvre. She unhooks her earrings and looks at me. I lean sideways to scratch at my knee again but the folds of fat that gather at my waist stop me short. I straighten up and head to the door.

'Toni,' she says. She has already shaken off Shona's bullying and is back on the job. 'Mrs Porteous's family wouldn't sign a Do Not Resuscitate order. Don't you remember? They said they couldn't bring themselves to. You were there when I asked them. Remember?' I shrug and turn to leave. 'Antonella?' she says gravely.

'Yes, Kumari Kaur?' I tease her. She doesn't laugh. 'No idea,' I say finally. 'Let Miss Jean worry about it – she's the one on the power trip.' Then I say, 'Don't take it so personally.' But my voice sounds lame. I'm thinking of Mr B and wondering whether someone can be destined to hate another person the way others fall in love: irrationally, uncontrollably, obsessively.

*

His family visits on Sunday afternoons. A daughter, mainly. She's about my age, almost as fat. Sometimes she brings her teenage kids. They hover uncertainly in the aisles, all oversized clothes and open-mouthed absence, as if they too have forgotten who they are and why they are here. The daughter tidies his bedside cabinet and stocks it with Sorbolene and folded white handkerchiefs embroidered with his initials. They get stolen by the cleaning staff or by more mobile patients on walkabout from other wards. Every week she hopefully replaces them, thinking he has used them. It assuages her guilt, this one small service. One week she asks me about them.

'White handkerchiefs?' I say. 'No, I don't remember seeing any. Perhaps they're in the laundry.' I smile at her but all the while I'm sick with the memory of those little starched squares.

*

In the afternoons before the home bell rang he'd send for me. It was always worse at the end of the day, when everyone else had gone. I'd wait in the corner of his office listening to the squeaking of chairs and hurried feet in the corridors, the parting shouts on the other side of the closed door, while he leaned back in his chair, swivelling slightly, the newspaper in his lap pressed into a crisp rectangle around the crossword. He'd mumble the clues to himself as if he was alone and fully engrossed, but I'd already learnt how he liked to tease out the thrill of anticipation. I'd see the tips of his neatly trimmed nails turning white as he squeezed his pencil; watch the way he rolled his thumb excitedly backwards and forwards over the rubber bands he kept lodged around his knuckles; try not to notice the red lines where they cut into the skin on the back of his hand. His desk had the same brutal order to it: the immaculate leather writing set with fountain pen upright to attention; the glass paperweight of Pope Paul always to the left, his two fingers raised in stern benediction; the jar of fiercely sharpened HB pencils always to the right, behind the plaque of thanks from the Rotary Club; and at the very front, the clean line of the cane resting on a folded white handkerchief embroidered with his initials in deep blue thread. I'd wait, tracing the monogram, the letters almost hidden among the loops and curls, and I'd try to guess his middle name from that one clue, as if that single character might unlock the man behind the neat rectangle of newspaper, might make me understand the why and where of it all.

*

His daughter stops bringing the handkerchiefs. It doesn't matter anymore. I already know his middle name from the Do Not Resuscitate order in his records. She brings him orchids, prearranged in a coloured box with loops of ribbon. After a time, when she is at peace with her decision, when she has grown used to wishing for the end to come, she will bring cheaper flowers wrapped in service-station cellophane and busy herself arranging them in the ward vases. It gives her something to do and shortens the time she must look at him. She will read her book and pat his hand for the twenty minutes it takes to feel her duty is done, and she will not have to look at his crooked jaw, the hollow of his cheeks, the way his tongue worries a rotten molar. And when she is gone, I will skimp on his morphine and give him tea from his crossword mug, as Manjit likes me to. It's our duty – offering these small pleasures for as long as possible.

'Thirteen across, seven letters,' I'll say. 'A dish best served cold. Blowed if I know. I bet you know, though, don't you, Mr B?' And I will remember the way that Do Not Resuscitate order twitched on my open palm before skating like a dead leaf on a draft, up and up towards the strip lights and down under the filing cabinets.

Carrying On

Gretchen Shirm

It was the car idling in the driveway that woke her, the headlights on the wall through the frame of the old fig. The engine did not cut; it just purred, as if in a trance. Her eldest had taken the Mazda to an eighteenth birthday party. There'd been a run of them lately, as if all his friends were suddenly realising they were adults and their exams were over.

Tracee's friend Rhonda, from down the street, had said, 'You just have to let them go at that age,' the tip of her cigarette flaring as they sat together on Tracee's back step.

And that's why, now, Tracee doesn't get out of bed and move towards the wardrobe for her dressing gown; why she doesn't go downstairs; why she lies, staring at the wall, listening to the alarm clock tick out its steady rhythm as her heart knocks against her chest.

After the motor chokes, she hears the car door close and footsteps. She pushes off the covers and goes to the window, looking down to the driveway. Tracee sees his lanky body folded in half, looking at one of the headlights. A scrape, she thinks to herself. He's gone and had himself a scrape – just what he needs right now, before he gets his exam results, before he leaves for university.

Then he disappears from view and she throws herself back on the bed, as the back door shudders in its frame and the stairs creak. Her bedroom door opens with a yawn. It's been so many years since he came to her bed. Not since the separation, when all three of them used to sleep together in her bed, tossing like a boat every time one of them rolled over.

*

'But how do you let go?' Tracee had asked Rhonda, as she scraped the tip of her cigarette along the step.

'Oh, letting go,' Rhonda sighed. 'Letting go is easy. Letting go is just like walking around and pretending you don't see anything.'

Tracee's eldest boy was the school captain, and now they expect him to get dux, or that's what his teachers tell her. She knows she should be happy – any other mother would be happy – but Tracee worries that this early success will spoil him.

*

She stays facing the wall when she hears his breathy little sobs from the mattress behind her. And when she asks, 'What's wrong?' she does not take his shoulders and demand it of him. She asks him flatly, as if she doesn't care to know the answer.

'The car,' is all she catches through the straining in his throat.

The smell of alcohol on his breath drifts to her. He hasn't even bothered to brush his teeth. It's funny, that strange complicity between adults and their children; this I won't ask, as long as, whatever you do, please don't tell.

'Go to sleep. We'll worry about it in the morning.'

She says this, but all through the dark night her eyes are fixed on the grey wall beside her bed and she lies stiffly, conscious of the body of her son spread out on the mattress beside her.

*

In the morning, she's up before the boys. The sun is ready to rise, pink, like a damp mouth about to swallow the sky. She drives the Mazda up the driveway, into the garage, and steps outside slowly, bracing herself for the damage. But when she surveys it, there is nothing except a small dimple in the bonnet, where it looks as though something hit and bounced.

Then she turns the key in the ignition and the engine sniggers and turns over. She flicks on the headlights and they illuminate the back wall of the garage suddenly, as if it's a stage, revealing the lawnmower and the rake and shovels huddled together. She walks once more around the car and at the headlights stoops to see a brown smudge over the Perspex. She bends down and rubs her finger against it, but it doesn't lift, so she scratches it off – first with her fingernail and then with a key – until it has all flaked away, and she sweeps it up with a dustpan and broom. When she's finished, she stands in the garage for a moment, feeling the air thicken with carbon monoxide, the smell of it scratching at the back of her throat.

She leaves the boys to fix their own breakfast and drives into town. At the panel beaters, she says something about driving behind a semitrailer and a stone hitting the bonnet. The panel beater just nods, wiping his oil-stained fingers with a damp rag.

At ten, right on time, the ex comes to collect the boys, parking out on the street at the front of the house, as though acknowledging it is not his driveway anymore. The youngest clings to Tracee's leg: he is shy around his father, and this – of everything about the separation – is what pains her most. Travis has them every second weekend and for a week in the school holidays, but the youngest doesn't like moving between the two places. Travis leans against the car, the way he used to when they were teenagers, but the smile, the we-can-go-anywhere-smile, that is what is missing now. When Travis smiles at her, his smile is swallowed by his mouth, his lips one straight line in his face.

While they are waiting for the boys, they talk about their friend Charlotte, who is finally remarrying. They speak of it carefully, dancing around the details and stealing little glances at each other. It wasn't so long ago that Tracee visited his new apartment for the first time. It isn't new anymore; he's had it for four years now. It's a small, two-bedroom place, right near the beach. Neat as a pin, he used to say, as if quoting from a real-estate brochure. It has a small balcony and a galley kitchen. The boys like it, at least, because there is an Xbox to play.

'Where's the Mazda?' Travis asks, looking towards the empty garage.

'I took it to the panel beaters,' she says, ignoring the pull of her eldest's gaze. And then she repeats the story, word for word, the same as she told the panel beater.

'Will you be right without a car?' Travis asks, as if the very thought of it pains him. And all she can do is nod.

*

Sometimes, she thinks they could have mended things, Travis and her. But she was busy going to university and then, for a year or two, he had a new girlfriend – a woman with freckly skin and a heavy fringe. And now it's too late. Now they're like two old bones that can't knit back together again.

When the boys have gone, she sits out on the back step, fondling the almost full packet of cigarettes that she hides in her underwear drawer, where she knows the boys will never look. The eldest begged her to quit. She would die of lung cancer, he said, if she didn't give them up. They show them now, at school, pictures of tar squeezed from dead lungs like molasses and solidified fat clotting the aorta. In her day, there were no pictures: they just let you work it out for yourself. So she quit when the eldest was ten and she does not tell him about her occasional lapses.

Tracee strikes the match to the box; it flares and she holds it to the end of her cigarette. Beside the steps, hydrangeas bob up and down in the breeze like nodding heads. Every time Tracee looks at them now she has to remind herself to come back out to them later with the secateurs – they've grown thick and bushy. She draws in a lungful of velvety smoke, exhaling it evenly from her nostrils. She practised this as a teenager; the art of smoking a cigarette is all in the exhale, she used to tell her friends.

Around her mud wasps hover like jumbo jets, their dangling legs like wheels preparing for landing. It's not until the third breath of smoke that she starts to feel giddy, and it reminds her of when she used to smoke at school, behind the tin shed at lunchtime. On the step beside Tracee, their black and tan kelpie rests her head on crossed paws. Her ears prick at the thud of the Saturday morning paper on the front lawn.

Tracee takes a drag of the cigarette. From the corner of her eye, she sees something move in the grass. She blinks hard: sometimes the rush of nicotine plays with her vision. She walks towards it and stoops down. It is moving in short pulls, but even up close, she still can't make it out. Furry bands of orange and black and something attached to it, brown. Then it takes shape: it's a wasp carrying a huntsman. The spider is bigger than the wasp. She watches it labour over the grass, pulling at the weight of the spider, a load too heavy for flight. It stops at intervals, as if gathering its strength. The wasp carries it all the way across the lawn to the grille underneath the back step, where it disappears, pulling the spider in behind it.

When she can feel the warmth of the cigarette too close to her fingers, she drops it in her glass of water. Then she rubs her fingers on the grass, a trick she learnt as a teenager, so that her teachers couldn't smell cigarette smoke.

Tracee lets the dog through the back of the house and she skids on her nails across the wooden floorboards, down the hall to the front door. She scrambles down the front steps, diving for the wrapped newspaper like it's a moving prey. Tracee takes it from the dog's mouth and flattens it out on the kitchen table. On the front page there is a grainy image of the pedestrian crossing on the main street. A girl was hit by a car there last night and found unconscious by passers-by in the early hours of the morning. They rushed her to the hospital, the article said, and removed a small piece of her skull to minimise the inter-cranial pressure. There's a photograph of the girl above the article; she's in her school uniform and her unblemished face is smiling straight at the camera. Anyone with information is asked to contact the police.

Tracee recognises the girl from the supermarket deli, where she scoops chicken thighs into a plastic tub on Saturday mornings, her slack jaw working away at a piece of gum.

Tracee doesn't read the rest of the newspaper. Instead, she goes to the bathroom and squares herself off in the vanity mirror. She does this sometimes, when she feels herself slipping, to get hold of herself. She pushes her fingers into her skin and lifts it upward, trying to remember what she looked like before gravity started to take effect.

*

Later on, in the afternoon, when she and Rhonda have come back from their walk to the beach, she fingers through her old leather-bound yearbook. She had all her friends sign it on their last day of school.

The pages are now fragile and tea-stained. There are poems and tributes and friends who promised to stay that way forever. There is that poem she copied out, the one she liked, about foot-prints. About how there are two sets of footprints in the sand, and how there are places where there is only one set of foot-prints, and about being carried during the hard times. At the end of the poem, in her uncertain teenage handwriting, 'ANON' is written in capital letters.

*

Her boys probably wouldn't believe her if she told them she was popular at school. That she had friends, lots of friends. That she was the girl everyone looked up to. Not like now, since Travis and her separated and the boys have become the two planets she orbits in figure eights. She used to roll her school uniform up at her waist to make it short on her tanned teenage legs. She used to go to all the parties down on the beach on Saturday nights, where they lit bonfires from old driftwood. She used to walk behind the dunes with the boys who had wandering fingers and glance back over her shoulder to her friends, who watched her leave.

That's what happened one night with Travis: the nervous boy in their year, the one that they were all surprised she left with that night, that she chose. Then it was an early marriage and a difficult labour at nineteen, and then people stopped looking at her in quite the same way.

At thirty, though, she finally put herself through university. She studied psychology and now she has her own practice. Some-times she thinks she ended up this way, sorting out other peo-ple's problems so that she'd never have to confront her own.

*

Now her eldest has a girlfriend, Amy, a girl from school. She comes over for dinner occasionally during the week. Tracee likes Amy; she's quiet and polite and she crosses her cutlery over her plate when she's finished eating.

Tracee bought her eldest a packet of condoms one day and

when she handed them to him, the colour rushed violently to his cheeks. It had taken her a long time at the chemist to find a packet not coloured or studded or flavoured in some way.

'Mum,' he groaned.

'I just want to make sure you're practising safe sex,' she said. 'It's nothing to be embarrassed about. You're almost an adult now.'

He took them and walked to his room, shutting the door quietly behind him. That was before Rhonda had told her about letting go.

*

On Sunday afternoon, Tracee is upstairs in her bedroom, looking out from her window, when she sees the boys walk back up the front steps. Travis drives away with three toots of the horn. He probably knows she's up here, looking down. It's five o'clock: he's right on time.

She always seems to be looking out of her window at this time. There is something sad and inevitable about Sunday afternoons. She notices, out on the street, the old fig tree is starting to sprout leaves again. Soon, there will be little fig balls strewn all over their front yard.

The kelpie rushes to the boys, dancing around them in little circles, nipping their heels, guided by some innate sense for herding, back along the garden path and up the stairs to the front door.

*

That night, Tracee is reading to the youngest and they have almost finished *Charlotte's Web*. They are at the part where Charlotte's babies tell Wilbur they are leaving the farm, and the little one's eyes well with tears as Tracee reads it to him. He is teary, her youngest, he cries at the smallest things. He was young when they separated – too young, really, to have understood why Daddy had to go and live in another house and why Mummy just needed some time on her own. It was almost as if all the sadness she held on to about the separation seeped out through him.

She takes him in her arms and says, 'They have to make their own life.'

'But can't they just stay with Wilbur?' he says, between bursts of tears.

'No, they're going to use their webs to fly to a new home.'

Only the fact that three of them will remain at the farm stems the flow of tears. She stays with him, with the lights out, until his body starts to twitch and surrender to sleep. He always sleeps this way, with his head tucked under his arm, like a small bird.

Downstairs, Tracee stands in front of the fridge, looking for the milk. Then she sees the empty bottle poking out from the top of the bin. It is always a surprise to her, how much milk the two boys go through between them.

'Mum,' says her eldest from behind, in that croaking pitch his voice so often takes. She turns around and sees him in the cool light of the fridge. Lately, his nose and mouth look too big for the rest of his face, as if he hasn't quite grown into his features.

'About the car …' His voice is straining.

She closes the fridge door and the light goes out. Suddenly, they are in darkness together. She takes his hand and feels it tremble.

'Shhh,' she says. 'Shhh.'

And he leans in towards her and his two manly shoulders are shaking against her. Then she leaves him in the kitchen and walks upstairs to her bedroom.

*

A week later, she drives into town, past the pedestrian crossing in the main street. There are flowers taped up to the stop sign; the girl is still in hospital, quietly lying in an induced coma. They look so ineffectual, the colours are purple and pink, and they are all bruised and browning with age.

The wheels screech as Tracee turns the steering wheel hard, U-turns on the main street and drives home. In the backyard, she tramples over the flowerbed to the waratah and cuts through the woody stem with a sharp kitchen knife. She pulls off a forked branch with two waratahs brimming crimson at each end. Then she drives back down to the crossing and ties them up to the stop sign with an old piece of twine. They hang there like two throbbing hearts.

*

In the new year, early one morning, the three of them drive down to the post office, before the mail is sorted. Her eldest collects the crisp A4 envelope with his name showing through the cellophane frame. His fingers shake as he rips the envelope open.

He leaves three weeks later to study in Sydney. His father drives him up there – he borrows Tracee's Mazda for the trip, which is better for long distances. It has a smooth, flat bonnet now; you can't even see where the dent was. The little one is in the back seat; he's taken his pillow along for the drive.

After they leave, Tracee will be out on the back step again with the same packet of cigarettes, dragging the swirling, cancerous smoke into her lungs and holding it there, as if she is smoking out a wasp's nest.

Beside her, on the lawn, she'll see how her single set of footprints has flattened the wet grass. And then she'll think, as she starts to feel giddy, that mostly it doesn't feel like she's carrying; it feels like she's dragging, and not turning around to see what's left behind along the way.

Having Cried Wolf

Blow In

Rebecca Giggs

The feet were the first to break away. I put on weight quickly in the months following the fires, and so my feet spread out for balance. They reverted to feet from some human prehistory, all stiff hair and hide, the toes blackening. Whose feet are *these*? I looked on dumbfounded as they tried to stuff themselves back into the shoes at the end of the bed. Stamping around the hotel with that Neolithic gait, the unfamiliar, cavewoman pelvis; and whose feet had I dragged out of the aftermath?

When we were told it was safe to return, I didn't. I got in my car and drove straight to the city. For two days running I did nothing except eat, and eat, and eat. Sleepless at the all-night food palaces – hummocks of dumplings, tapioca milk and those edible ghosts that dangle in the tanks. But no matter how much I ate I couldn't get full, so I booked a room. Now, when I wake in the dark, I can no longer feel my feet. How women say, 'She's let herself go.' I've uncoupled them.

There's a lightness inside all this heft you can't measure. A buoyancy of accumulating fumes and heat that I'm fighting to weigh down. It threatens to slit me right open. The problem is, I am not fat all the way through. It's the empty parts inside me that are expanding, and so I have to keep adding kilos, layering on lipid thickness, to keep myself contained. But in the dark recesses of my body something is still on fire. There are embers that won't be put out. I can feel the flames crackling in my gullies and burning through the sawdust walls of my stomach. Every morning I am starving again. The pillow smells like cigarettes, although I've never been a smoker. I dream of Pompeii. Casts crouched speechless in the ash.

Sometimes, I don't think I will survive it. The sinister contracts of electricity in me will fail, wires fried, and I will have a stroke. I spend whole days staring at those dusky feet beyond my ankles, or into the distant traffic far below the window. Waiting and eating. But even looking down from above, I can't get things in perspective. Where are the edges of the burn? When do the fires end? I am not myself here. What I thought I left outside has become ingrown. The swallowed weather gathers fuel.

*

Today I am considering a cube of air on the other side of the glass as Paul Jarrow is directed over to the table by the maître d'. Paul has arranged this – a truce, a lunch. I'm reluctant. We're in the Cirrus Club, a few floors above my suite. Clouds mottle the light that falls into the plates and the music is featureless.

Paul is visibly nervous, even from this distance. This is because he is over forty and he thinks he knows what I am responsible for. Who I am responsible for. I don't mean he is mistaken, only that he has been misled. Which is an entirely different thing to say. Paul is marrying my daughter, Alice, tomorrow. It goes without saying that he intends to put the hard word on me – to wheedle, bargain or beg – until I descend from the upper levels of the Broadbeach Tower Suites and drive back into town for their wedding. Alice doesn't expect it, but he doesn't know why he shouldn't. He brings high hopes of brokering our reconciliation.

I know that Paul has been married before, without any children, to the pharmacist who works at the town chemist. He was a secret Alice kept from me for over a year, or, to put it another way, she was his secret, in the advanced CPR class at the Dugong Park Aquatic Complex. Alice confessed later that that's where they met: in the recovery position, trading breaths through a mannequin with a chest built soft for compression practice. Mouths slicked on British plastic.

Alice plays water polo. She wants to be an opera singer. My daughter reads science fiction and before all this, she worked weekends at the gardening centre with me. Alice is fierce. She is creative, she is impressionable. She is full of lungs. She is twenty-two.

And although Paul doesn't know it, Alice is a criminal.

Smiling too widely as he approaches, he catches his lip on a dry eyetooth. He surveys the table, chewing the lining of his cheek, and notices the open bottle. *Good*, he is thinking. Paul would like me to be a little drunk, a bit pulpy to begin with. We've all been through a great trauma. The communal drowning of communal sorrows might be one of the few things left to inspire community in any of us.

I know how that goes. And I won't say I'm above exploiting it. I told the staff where I'd come from, the macabre password, on the day I arrived at the Broadbeach. They knew it from the news coverage. By then, no one in the country *didn't* recognise the name of our town. The maître d' put a hand on my back and whispered wetly into my ear: how I am entitled to vices that expand the hotel's definition of responsible service. As he steers Paul Jarrow over to me now it is not beyond his imagination that Paul is here as *my* lover, summoned up from the back pages of a magazine. In previous conversations the maître d' has implied he can source things like this, things I have a need of 'in excess.' Drugs, presumably, and men. Those are only two examples of what he thinks I might need. Or deserve.

Paul kisses my cheek and grabs my hand awkwardly, clasping the thumb in a partial handshake. We've never been this close.

'Well,' he says, still holding some of my fingers in his fist, 'Mother of the bride, mother of the bride.' He shakes his head. Up close Paul has a certain thinness of expression, as of a rat looking in through a picket fence. But the maître d' seems disappointed. He gives an almost imperceptible nod and leaves the table. Now I wonder if that hand, rested cosily on my shoulder blade, conveyed a more complex message.

'In the flesh, Paul.' I turn my attention to this future son-in-law, much too old to be called that. *In all this flesh.* 'Calm the heck down, and sit down.'

*

Like all mothers who have their children after the time of mother-hood is expected, when Alice was born I was petrified. She came into our lives late, but tiny and early, at a time when no one else we knew had a newborn. The first few weeks were unspeakably awful. Delivered premature – *premmie*, the word inappropriately cute for the rawness of her small body – she was placed into a ticking humidicrib at the hospital. Alice. Horrifying and precious, mammalian and wired. We didn't name her for the Lewis Carroll books, and yet she arrived trapped in that electrical wonderland, the disembodied grins of the nurses scything above.

When Tom went anywhere near our baby girl he was scared witless that she might die. In white beds and pacing the blue hallways I brimmed with self-loathing. The nurses insisted there was no trigger for an early labour, but the conviction wouldn't dislodge – it was my fault. Impatience, unease and condemnation. I raced through a list of culpable acts while our daughter stayed untouched, every organ matched by a machine. The little argonaut.

Finally the day came when they lifted Alice out of the crib. Her heart thrummed against my collarbone like a bug in a jar. We took photographs of her hands set with their impossible fingernails. She was ours, after all. The living thing we switched on. She yawned once, and we were hers.

Later on, everywhere I looked I saw lethal, poisonous, maiming things, and for her part, Alice was intent on getting to them. It was more than what you'd expect – what's under the sink, or on the road. Everything Alice reached for was something I knew you shouldn't give to a child. I'd be baking in the kitchen or digging the flowerbeds, but she would not be distracted by the cooing singsong of *cake* or *blossoms*. She wailed for the boiling pot and the herbicide. Put her down in the centre of a room and she'd crawl straight for the closest power point. Threats went unheeded. Bribery was futile. Before she'd started to walk Alice was back at the hospital for burns and coins that she scoffed straight out of my purse.

After we settled her down each night we would just stand there, holding one another, aghast. Why had we done it? This was a terrible mistake. We'd put life into what didn't want it. Our baby ghoul.

It is true that I had unmotherly thoughts. And I may have done some unmotherly things. A few times I tied her into her highchair. Thinking *once bitten*, I watched her scoot right up to the oven and put her hands on the door. After a furious tantrum I gave her three dollars to suck on. Tom was at work, so he had nothing to say about it.

This part has only come back to me recently, because it was a stage Alice passed through and eventually grew out of. I'd stopped thinking of her as a child with a death wish by the time she was four. As a girl she was lively and exasperating. Tom changed jobs and we took the opportunity to move up to the country. There I envisaged our daughter developing the kind of hardy resourcefulness and the love of nature that I recalled from my own childhood. I hoped that we'd all reset.

What I can't decide now is whether I was right in the beginning, or if it was what I did afterwards that made me right in the end.

*

All the food served in the Cirrus Club is made flat so that guests are not reminded of their altitude. We're over two hundred metres up in the air here, floating above a chambered abyss. The menu is written in lower case. Today's specials are mushrooms, steak carpaccio with capers, and a lemon tart as thin as cardboard.

Eat enough, though, and you can still get fat on flat food.

Paul has ordered an entrée but I stick to bread and butter. And the wine. He holds his glass at the top of the stem without drinking and asks how I'm finding the hotel. Surely, he suggests, I'm bored of eating the same meals day in, day out? He has mistaken my decision not to order for a lack of appetite. In fact I already ate two entrées before Paul arrived. I tell him that the specials change daily, about the in-room delivery service and the ordering-out guide. Although he's right about one thing. Up here, nothing tastes very good.

What I want to know about, but do not ask, is my garden. Paul isn't the kind of man who'd be interested in plants – he's a teacher, social studies and geography (an indoor subject now) – so I doubt he'd recognise which species have regenerated and which have died. I am wondering if Alice has thought to put in cuttings. The soil will be too alkaline for most things, but there's an acacia I'm hoping has seeded. The risk is that the top-soil will blow off otherwise. Succulents would be best to start off with. False agave, houseleek, baby toes, pigface: felonious names. Sticks-of-fire and mother-in-law's tongue; a bad joke. But the weeds will have pushed through before anything else. By now the weeds will be hip-deep.

A waiter brings Paul's entrée, a green soup, and lays our linen napkins in our laps. More bread is set out too, sourdough and grain. They are attentive here. They anticipate my endless craving for side dishes and carbonated drinks. If no one else is with me, I don't even bother with the bread. I just eat the butter, square by square, listening to it evaporate into a greasy gas at the base of my tongue. There is a flickering around my tonsils.

It's a pea soup, with a sprig of mint, and it smells like turned earth.

A vision rushes up at me from below then, of vegetables burned on their plots. Marrows like skulls. The past hot and sudden. Or am I confused? Is it possible *they were skulls I thought were marrows*? No. No, it's a memory from before the fires, in the dry, of someone's shrivelled gourds brought to the gardening centre for advice. People often stopped by with blighted leaves or fruit, because we were a kind of hospital, too, for plants.

The misplacement of the image shakes me, though. Could that be the first connection burning through? Something tensile snapping open? What early warning is this?

I pour from the bottle and concentrate on Paul's rodent vowels. Something about people pulling together. He talks too fast. About people joining hands to rebuild a bowling club, a classroom and a swimming pool. But how does a swimming pool burn down?

'Cheers,' says Paul, who has raised his glass expectantly, 'To?'

'Oh. Marriage, naturally.' This is the very smallest part of what he wants me to toast, to permit. 'To union, then. To wedlock, to nuptials, to the happy day,'

'To Alice,' he drinks. 'To love,' and now he is going too far, 'To family.'

'Family.' Yes. To goddamn family. *To being in it, together.*

As he begins the soup I look down at my hand under the brim of the table. Whose thumb are you, there? I nudge it, but it stays fat and strange. When I push my fork in under the nail, it doesn't hurt at all.

*

My girlhood was also spent in the country, but in the west. Until our early teens my family lived in Quairading, a wheatbelt town, although we had relocated to Perth by the time my sister and I reached high-school age. Those wheatbelt summers were vicious, I remember. Forty-degree heat waves that went on for weeks. Days stuck back to back with stupefying nights. The breathlessness. As if the air were laced with something granular. Split lips, mouthfuls of iron. Power lines that crepitated with the dust overhead. That kind of weather will taper you down, first to temper, then to superstition and deep paranoia.

Midday is still vivid in my mind: so clean, dazzling and still. No wheat hissing in the fields, no stock bleating. You could hear every separate wing-beat of a crow as it flew low between the houses. It was as if an atomic bomb had rinsed through the sky and killed the wind. Which was entirely feasible back then – the end of the world could happen someplace else (the Pacific Ocean, a Soviet state) and arrive days *before* the radio announced it. My sister and I would sprawl, like victims of unseen radiation, on the cool linoleum in the kitchen. When our mother tired of stepping over our bodies and ordered us up, we left behind sweat-angels – the slithery calligraphy of fallen girls.

The phrase *pole-top fire* rings out from that time, and yet I also remember that the blackouts meant we all slept with fire-starting items stored beside our beds. Boxes of Redheads, candles, kerosene for the lamp. Readied for electrical outages. Children didn't play with matches then. Small domestic fires were ordinary, and even on the hottest summer night the Metters stove was stoked for cooking. There was no illicit appeal there. We didn't play much of anything in that weather, anyhow. Listless, limp, limbo: in the summer, the speaking tongue unsticks from the roof of the mouth and drops into the lower jaw. We were too lethargic to use our imagination.

In the year I turned ten, families in our street started receiving

visits from two door-to-door preachers. Dusk gossip on the
verandas called them 'the Fire Evangelists.' Fraudsters for God,
wearing trade suits. One afternoon they appeared at our flyscreen – a well-dressed man, affable, carrying a briefcase and
accompanied by his young son – offering a forty-point fire-safety
check on the house. Courtesy, no cost. The man claimed to be
tasked by the power company and, not knowing otherwise, my
mother let him in. My sister and I learnt the boy's name, Jacob,
while his father inspected the ceiling insulation.

'Can you stop, drop and roll?' Jacob asked us, adding in hand
gestures, in case we didn't follow. 'Stop. *Dropp.* Androll?

We were sceptical, but on Jacob's lead my sister was soon practising it down the front path as I kneeled on the steps.

'Stop your sinning! Drop your idols! Roll to Jesus!'

'STOP your sinning. DROP your idols. And *ROLL* to JESUS!'

Crumbed in gravel, Jacob rolled up onto my sister, and then
there was a moment that had very little to do with Jesus.

Meanwhile, our mother's voice had grown to a shout inside
the house.

*Don't give me brimstone, mister, I know brimstone. I'll show you
brimstone!*

The Fire Evangelist swung through the screen-door as if he'd
been shoved, clutching his briefcase to his chest. He took up his
son's hand and marched him through the front gate, shouting
over his shoulder.

'Your home, missus! You have not built your home against the
fires of Hell!' He pointed at us, 'You need to send your girls *to
church.*'

Because that's what they did, these door-to-door preachers. In
between pointing out the hazards of a heater sat near the curtains, and night-candles in the children's rooms, they began to
talk of the consuming fires *underneath* the house. That briefcase
was heavy with bibles.

When I was a girl, it was expected that the end of the world
would happen in the Christian way. Yes, there would be fallout,
and there would be brimstone – but then, someone would always
be around to warn you. You would be given enough time to
repent.

*

There are sirens in the streets below the hotel. I notice that sound more specifically, and even though it's as faint as cutlery pulled down the glass, it still gets under my skin. Across the table Paul has ordered veal scaloppini with infant vegetables for main course, and I have squab paupiette, a pigeon chick killed before its maiden flight. Everything is wrong with the food here today.

A week ago, I came across a bird trapped inside one of the highest hallways of the hotel. I don't know how a bird ended up on the fortieth floor in a building where the windows are sealed by design. It flew from cornice to cornice, this ordinary small brown bird, hooking through the air. I watched it for nearly an hour, collecting carpet threads to furnish an eggless nest. For some reason, that bird made me want to cry.

Clearly Alice has dressed Paul for our meeting. The tight, olive knit-shirt and the zippered jacket hung over the back of the chair; these are not the kind of clothes that a man Paul's age feels comfortable in. A three-day beard the colour of wet salt blooms on his face and his hair is cropped short to offset baldness. It passes for grooming now – perhaps even for style – but if he keeps this up, in a few years it will be seen as vanity and, with a young wife, taken as a sign of insecurity. You don't have to be a genius to imagine what they're saying in the staff room. Tom never paid that much attention to his appearance in his life.

Tom died five years ago now. He had been swimming in the lake, something he did every morning. It was a heart attack. He wasn't exactly young for it, but his death still came as a shock. In fact, this is why Alice was taking the CPR course. In the years since her father's death, she's done all the refreshers and passed every level in first-aid certificates. One thing I regret is that she was there when they pulled him from the water. Alice has a fear of abandonment which I am sure can be tracked back to the moment she saw Tom lying dead on the mud.

All the same, this relationship is something you don't ever want for your daughter. To be *other*. Other woman, second wife. I'm OK with the so-called 'modern family.' I am not priggish. Those are hang-ups we could all do without. Some things, however, do not change, and one of those things is: men who have been married before are unsteady. Needless to say, Alice knows it.

Paul has moved the conversation on to details of the wedding. He's testing the perimeter of a demand, equivocating outside the point. At the moment, it's the vows and the readings. Nothing biblical, naturally, but then what could they have? *Yea, though I walk through the valley of the shadow of death.* Not a single guest would believe it. Not now.

'We've decided on bowl food,' he says. 'Instead of a buffet. Bowl food with a fusion theme.'

Alice sent me the menu in the mail last week, but I pretend I haven't seen it when he slides it across the tablecloth. She sends me other letters too, and I put them away in the drawer where the King James Bible hides. *Forgive us our sins, as we forgive those.*

'And there'll be those sweet candy nuts' Paul says. 'In little bags to take home. It doesn't say that there.'

He is hoping for my approval, but bowls and bags? Will the guests play pin the tail on the donkey after the ceremony? It is a children's party they have planned, not a wedding. Alice, the infanta in her white gown.

'You know, Paul,' I put the menu down. 'If you're getting cold feet on this, everyone would understand. I, for one, would understand.'

'*What?*' he whispers, and glances over his shoulder. 'I know it's soon but it's devotion, completely. No question.' He sits back. 'The wedding's going ahead, whether you're there or not. I won't call it off.'

An image comes to me then, of Paul pumping on my daughter's breastbone with his arms held straight. *Breath, breath, pump, pump, breath, breath.* Depress the solar plexus, that sun under the skin. Do it as punctual as a heartbeat.

The kiss of life. That's what it used to be called.

'And your wife?' I ask.

'We're divorced. *I'm* divorced.'

I don't need to remind him there are doubts.

'Look,' he raises his voice, shaky. 'A lot got clarified recently. For everyone. We're not the same as we were *before*.' In my peripheral vision I see the maître d' take a few steps towards us but I stop him with an open hand. Paul cuts a bite-sized carrot in two, eats it, and squeezes his fists on the table.

'I know what I want.' He takes a drink. 'I'm committed to Alice.

Any prevarication, that's in the past. We've put it behind us. If it's the age difference you're worried about, that I can understand. You're her mother, of course. Wanting what's best.'

'You are making a mistake, Paul,' I say, without colour.

'Have you asked Alice? Because actually, she doesn't care what age I am. Perhaps *what's best for Alice*, and I mean no disrespect, but perhaps what's best for Alice is that she gets to make her own decisions. She's old enough to know.' His face is screwed into the centre of his head.

But the mistake I was referring to has nothing to do with Paul's age, or his habit in the past of returning to his wife. The mistake is to think that there is a *before* or an *after* the fires. Time is snagged on that day, and things are still burning down around it, here and elsewhere. Just because Paul can't see it, doesn't mean it isn't happening.

Paul pushes his chair out and considers his plate, streaky with sauce. Perhaps he is going to leave. I pick at crusts in the breadbasket. After a minute he taps his thighs and shuffles back.

'The green is coming back,' he says. 'Nature popping up again. Your place looks good.'

'Not your wife's place, though.'

'My *ex*-wife's house, for which she has insurance. You were lucky, though, I'm sure you know. There's no reason you couldn't move back in. Only the garden needs work, but the fires missed your house. Miraculous. Other people lost everything. Shit, other people lost every*one*.'

He means that the emptiness inside me has nothing to say to the unthinkable emptiness that other people have had grow outside of them. I knew those people, of course, and their wives and husbands, their families. Some of those people were regular customers at the gardening centre. One was a neighbour. I watched the memorials on television, but in the stark glow of it all it was difficult to connect their names to the idea of their bodies. Their bodies in gardens, bodies working hard to shovel and smooth, to turn soil and lop wood. Because for a while there weren't any bodies – there were only 'remains.' Ash, in ash, in ash. Before the sifting and the identification, the dental records and DNA, the television kept referring to these 'remains.' For me, that snipped the strings between the names and the people.

The maître d' brings over a water jug, and I motion to the finished wine bottle for another. Paul's glass is still full but this conversation needs more than that. The water is poured; the maître d' says nothing out loud.

'I can understand the funerals,' Paul retracts, grasping for my hand but falling short on the table. 'That must have been unthinkably hard. But this is a *wedding*. It's a fresh start. And this right here is *the day before the wedding*. Can't we find a way to be happy today? To put the past behind us?'

But those are Alice's words in his mouth. And the past Alice made up refuses to stay behind us.

*

The day before. The fires race backwards and ignite anything I have left inside that day. The fires race forwards to reduce the future to charcoal. What I remember now is edgeless and spreading. It's like trying to stick those ashes together to make a new tree, trying to find a name in the remains. Come back with me, towards the disarray of memories around this 'day before.' See what things blow into it and blow out of it. How the day falls apart under our touch.

I woke up suddenly, falling through myself onto the mattress. Kiln heat. Past midnight. My tongue was skinny and dry. There was no dream in my head. After dark the temperature had continued to climb. From the garden came a noise like hot oil in a pan. *Snap, snap, snap.* My first thought was of a kangaroo caught in the fence. I got out of bed. Outside, the garden was lit by a low-wattage moon. The eucalypts were motionless, leaves glinting like scissors. I was afraid of what was out there. Momentarily, I felt the absence of Tom and put a hand out into the air where he might otherwise have been standing. Then I looked closer.

Clouds of earth were puffing up from the bare flowerbeds. Bubbles bursting in the ground, spitting *pf, pf, pf.* I bent for a closer look. Was the soil literally boiling? Then it hit me: how it must be the bulbs, dormant at this time of year. Crocus and hyacinth, far down. They'd died, of course, in the heat – become desiccated and hollow. But it had got so hot that the bulbs were exploding underground. Like buried light globes. *Pf, pf, pf.* A minute, maybe longer, and then everything fell silent. I climbed back into bed, feet dirtying the sheets. But I could still feel the moon through the wall.

Later. In the morning I was driving. A shallow vapour spooled out across the road like a fine sea-sand. I couldn't see any smoke plumes or flames, although a gritty taste filtered in through the vents. A dust front, rolling over from where the fire was. The radio had been broadcasting the 'stay or go' message for the hour prior but the main blaze was kilometres away and I was prepared. I was returning from the gardening centre having set the sprinklers to a timer just in case, but at that point it didn't look likely that the danger would push any nearer. Thinking I must bring in the load strung on the line, I put on one of Alice's CDs – what she calls *battle arias* – and the music made me feel powerful and baroque, like a murderess in the air-conditioning. The sky turned from daisy to jaundice.

But the CD was scratched, and I turned it off after a few tracks. Then I heard a terrible sound. At first I thought it was the engine, but I stopped the car and the noise continued, coming from outside. I opened the door, parked next to a paddock. A sound of ripping, like sheet metal being torn. The air was glowing and through the haze I made out the shapes of cattle. The cows were coming fast over a ridge, running under yellow curtains of smoke. I couldn't tell it at first, standing there by the side of the road, but then I saw it. The legs of the cows were on fire. Their legs were on fire and they were making that noise, it came from their throats, that metal tearing. You wouldn't know that cows could make that sound. But they can, they did. The cows came running, shrieking to me, and I could do nothing but watch.

*

The day before. A day more like a night, like a dark that won't lift. Alice walked in from the gloom. Shaking, staggering, horrified. Holding out her hands like someone who wants to show they are unarmed at a checkpoint. Here, my daughter's hands said, I am without weapons. And I held her there, because I knew she was lying. I knew what she'd done.

But then I let her go.

*

I push the skin around on the plate, like a soothsayer reading omens in the entrails. The maître d' and the other waiters are watching. I have lived through one thing and so they expect me to be able to see the next. Soon, they hope, I will turn to forecasting their simple endings: their stair-falls at eighty, their last breaths drawn in sleep. This is the quid pro quo for how they feed me. 'Indecently' is the word. But all I can do here is glut. I bury myself deeper into myself, until I can see nothing of the future. Tags of fat hang over my eyes and those feet are still mouldering under the table.

*

Many lifeless vegetables were brought into the gardening centre in the weeks leading up to the fires. Plants turned directly to powder under the sun without ever catching alight, and whole orchards of fruit went black. The ground was as loose and as pale as bottle formula. Some customers came in with jars of soil scooped from their land, to show me. In disbelief we pored over it on the counter, let it fall through our fingertips in search of missing humus. Nothing would grow in this. One customer said something I can't get out of my mind: she said, *It's like we've slept through the worst bushfire in Australian history.* That's exactly what the ground looked like. As if it had fallen backward from the aftermath, thin and sterilised by extreme heat.

It was around that time, a fortnight or so before the fires, that the pharmacist came by the gardening centre because she wanted to kill a tree. A white box eucalypt suffering in the heat, the tree had shrunk back to its wet, green wick inside the woody coffin of its trunk. Several large branches had been dropped near her house – the tree giving up deadwood, as is its way in a drought – and she wanted to know how to cut it down. But that was only the ruse, her cover story. Really, she had come to gloat because after some indecision, after loud arguments and threatening phone calls, Paul had returned to their marital bed, while Alice – grief-stricken and inconsolable – had moved back into her old bedroom at my place.

'Don't they call those trees "widow-makers"?' the pharmacist said, gripping the counter with her nails. 'I won't have it anywhere near my home anymore. It disgusts me, this tree.' I refused to serve her and then someone else sent her away.

The days burned long. In snatched naps I dreamt I was digging with a shovel and instead of water pooling in the pit, a fire started there. There were no birds in the garden. Alice wailed, as pained and low as a wounded animal in her bedroom, refusing to eat, showing no sign of getting over the affair. She wouldn't be reasoned with, bribed or cajoled; it was Paul that she wanted. Sometimes I could hear her hyperventilating behind the locked door, spilling into panic, but she refused to let me in. I went on long walks. In the forest dozens of brightly feathered bodies studded the leaf-litter. Entire flocks of parrots had dropped dead of thirst.

Late on that last evening, drawn narrow in the heat, I came home and caught Alice cutting herself. Not with suicidal intent but with the desperate, sawing motions of a creature caught in barbed wire. Trying to free herself from herself. The bread knife flashed fast against the gristle of her forearm, her teeth were clenched. It felt as if I was falling, the rushing in my ears, all the air taken out from under me. I seized her and sent the knife skittling across the kitchen tiles. There was blood in the crockery drawer, and in the sink, and in my hands. My baby. She slumped to the floor, exhausted.

After that there finally came a calm. We sat together on the tiles, sticky and beaten. I sopped her in Betadine and bandaged the arm. She found the last of Tom's best whiskey and poured it into two eggcups. Everything moved slowly, night beating back the daylight. As the shadows lengthened Alice began to talk of the pharmacist, how Paul truckled to his wife, and how she manipulated him in all the ways a wife is able. Their house was the pharmacist's trump card. Paul had built it with her, brick by brick, and it was newly completed when he met Alice at the aquatic complex. An elegant homestead, it featured in design quarterlies; wide porches and wood restored from a ship. High ceilings with fans that peeled off a breeze and let it settle in loops like orange-skin over the occupants. Paul had considerable debt sunk into it.

Alice's breath was flammable and close as she explained what she thought about doing. Exacting revenge on the pharmacist, acts of fevered and hateful retaliation, terrible things that made her want to cut off her own hands. How every morning she wrote *Stop It* in texta on both of her palms. I held her close and remembered the time I stuffed coins into her mouth until she went quiet. Alice would tear herself up in this house, trying not to want what she wanted. The thought of her being involved with Paul left a bad taste in my mouth, but now that she was, if she gave in there would be nothing left of my daughter to take care of. She would hurt herself more seriously – accidentally or deliberately – and I would be powerless to stop it. What would my hands say about that? So I made up a smaller deed of vengeance, a retribution with symbolic logic. Not because I believed Paul would leave his wife, but to show Alice she wasn't defeated. I confess: I pushed the seed of the terrible idea into her mind.

I told Alice how we sometimes killed trees, when we had to do it. Poison at the roots. Pool salt will work, I said, if you can get it. And I told her, hypothetically, how to drill the holes in one side, so that any strong gust would cause it to come down on top of a house. Alice sat thinking as I emphasised that she should make it so the tree hit the carport or the laundry, a room no one was likely to be in. *That's the lesson you want to teach her,* I said. *That's the threat to make.*

Alice plucked at her bandages, and stared into the skylight. 'Pool salt's a bit obvious, don't you think?' she said. 'Given where I met Paul.'

*

'Dessert menu, sir?' asks the maître d', but Paul doesn't answer. He's ready to take his jacket and leave, inwardly seething. I can see that in him – swearing impotently at the steering wheel, in the tunnel, slamming doors. All Paul's anger is subterranean, without fruiting body. He's wondering how Alice will take it, now that he's failed to convince me to return for the wedding. What he'll find surprising, I imagine, is that Alice won't be surprised.

'Wonderful,' I say, and open the menu. Paul thought we'd finished, but this thirst is not quenched and my insides stay empty.

'Coffee, Paul?' I ask, 'or will you indulge? Sugared almonds aren't enough, if we're celebrating.'

He allows a sallow grin and yields to the ceasefire – ordering chocolate slice and an espresso. It's the day before, and he deserves it. He doesn't have to watch his weight like I do. For Paul there is no danger that he will collapse in on himself at ground level, as I would, if I were to descend from the elevated regions of the hotel. There is a kind of pressure system at the Broadbeach that keeps me from combusting. Flames need oxygen, and up here there is very little of that. We drift in the smothered atmosphere of the Cirrus Club.

The special, Bombe Alaska, sounds delicious. Whisked oil and syrup, honey and cream; who wouldn't be pacified? I order. After Paul leaves, I will probably get a second and a third dessert, and choke myself blue on sugar.

What I can't do is go back and tell him the truth. The way in which he's been misled into marrying my daughter. How when the distant fires started burning, Alice saw a chance to drive over to the pharmacist's house and fell the tree. No one was home. As she'd expected, Paul and the pharmacist had decided to leave early. The doors were locked, a hose dripped over the eaves and the paths were raked clear. Alice took my drill and some poison, but then she couldn't bring herself to kill the white box eucalypt. The tree was strong and ominous, and in the heat it rippled. She lent against its thick muscles and listened to the water tweaking inside it. Those trees drink to fill themselves up when the lightest shred of smoke is in the air. All her life I'd taught her to watch for the life around her, for plants and birds. But here is the backfire: thinking about the single tree, Alice lost her sense of scale. She did something so out of proportion to anything Paul or the pharmacist was guilty of that it would later be called 'unimaginable,' a thing so awful it can barely be thought about or written down.

She went back to the house. Some of the windows were open so that the heat wouldn't shatter them. And Alice, my ghoul, my daughter, found a box of matches on a ledge.

You strike one match. And maybe you think the wet roof and the cleared paths will hold it, but when you strike one match in that weather, with other fires raging all around, you burn back through every kind of boundary. Through time, through birth. You burn back into yourself, like a terminal star. In the end, your edges become its edges. Heavy and lit. Alice's burning house joined to the other fire fronts and swept through the town.

*

The maître d' is bringing our desserts and his compliments. Paul is magnanimous, the old groom, taking admiration and a pat on the back. I open up my face and smile, trying not to show the glimmering behind my teeth. I say something about bowl-food eaten in a garden of ash. And here is my Bombe Alaska, a little glacier leaking sugar-water onto the plate. The lights are dimmed. The maître d' has a small pitcher of rum and before I realise what is about to happen he is tipping the liquor over my plate. The waiters applaud. There is a flick, and a spark. Again, the whole world is ablaze.

Overland

Istanbul

Sarah Holland-Batt

Toby said Istanbul, though not even he really knew where the Maynards had gone. In the end it didn't matter. The point was they were gone, Jamie was gone. He had taken his scrawny hand-rolled greyhounds and his careless, wolfish mouth with him, and Toby and I were at a loose end all summer. January in Newstead stretched out, dangerous and glittering as the lapis at the lip of an artesian well, deceptively far off. So far off, you felt you could drown before you reached the end of it.

Toby and I played squash that month. We were hardly even friends; he barely spoke to me back at Knox. But there was nothing to do with the hours except waste them, so we met Monday and Thursday afternoons at Ascot and hammered a rubber ball as hard as we could at a black smudge on the wall. Sometimes Toby would feign an injury when he was out of breath.

'Christ,' he would say, bending over. 'My ankle.' He would rub his shin, wincing, then fiddle with his racquet head.

'For Christ's sake,' I would say, exasperated. 'Get on with it.'

We would turn back to the wall. Squash must be the most draining sport on earth. The rhythm of it made everything recede. Toby cut across me, a clean white blur. After a while, I could feel something in me hurtling off and breaking up. A dangerous feeling, a falling away.

*

It was after one of those sweltering games that Toby suggested we go to the Maynards' place. We were in the change room, a dank space where the closed-in smell of men – sweat, Right Guard, menthol salve, Lux – was both arousing and vaguely sickening.

'February,' he said.

I looked up. Toby was eating an egg sandwich. He must have packed it in his bag.

'They're not back until February. Jamie said.' His face was bland, freckly. I knew that expression from school.

'So?'

'They've got a swimming pool.' He angled the sandwich into his mouth artfully, so as not to lose any of the egg.

I tried to imagine it: Jamie's pool. My stomach turned. 'Porter, *you've* got a bloody swimming pool.'

'Not like that. It's half-Olympic.' He paused. 'You've never even been, have you?'

'Why would I want to?'

'I don't know.' He looked at me shrewdly. 'Why would you?'

Toby must have known it even then. There wasn't an instant that summer I wasn't excruciatingly aware that Jamie wasn't here, was out there somewhere, with his parents, with the witch Cecelia. It was a kind of fever: my mind kept reaching out airy feelers, sweeping its corners for some scrap and returning with dust.

'Fine.'

'I thought so,' Toby said smugly, pulling his shirt off. 'Jamie told me you like swimming.'

I felt a slow burn creep across my face. I thought, quite disconnectedly, that I could kill him, that it would be easy to do it.

'Shut up.'

'God, calm down.' He sounded pleased with himself. 'Look, you don't have to.'

'Piss off. I'm coming.'

I felt for the key in my pocket. No one would be home. My mother would still be at work; my sister would be at her pottery class, making another one of the lumpy vases that were converging in an unruly line on the kitchen windowsill.

Coming home for the holidays had become an awkward,

uneasy affair. I had grown inexorably apart from the both of them, from my mother's solicitous attempts to read my essay on Whiteley's *Summer at Carcoar*, from Katie's pitiable infatuation with David Bowie, her tatty photos cut from magazines and sticky-taped to her school books. I felt further than ever from our house on Kingsholme Street, its chipping gunmetal-green stairs, the tired orange trumpet creeper shrinking against the fence.

Even Brisbane itself had begun to feel limp, burnt out, sun-blasted. As Toby and I left the building, the air was smothering.

Toby swore. 'That bastard.'

'What?'

'That bastard'll be lazing about, being fanned by palm leaves. Jesus Christ.' He grinned. 'They're probably feeding him horses' bollocks.'

'What the hell are you talking about?' I unlocked my bike chain.

'Jamie, idiot. In Istanbul.'

'They don't eat horse, you dunce.' I felt victorious. 'They eat dates and chickpeas. Apricots. It's not China.'

'Whatever,' Toby said casually. 'Anyway, we're going to Greece again for mid-year. To Milos.'

I didn't have anything to say to that. In July I would be killing time back in Brisbane, holed up in the State Library reading Caulaincourt or Horace, or cycling along the river to prolong going home to *Countdown* with Katie and my mother.

'What about you?' Toby said.

'What about me.'

We pulled up at the bottom of the hill. Hamilton rose up in front of us, block by block, sandy brick and cream. There was a patch of green up the top, and an enormous gothic revival house, its roof gleaming in the sun.

Toby was breathing hard. 'What're you doing for break?'

'Nothing,' I said. It was true.

'You're on scholarship, aren't you?'

'None of your business.'

We pushed our bicycles up the hill in silence. The houses on the road were large and shaded by trees, their fences tall and uninviting. A dog was barking steadily somewhere. I tried to imagine Jamie walking up this hill when he was young, before Knox, but I could only conjure an image of the Jamie I knew, his shirtsleeves rolled to the elbow, his waist slim and firm, his back coolly turned away.

*

The Maynards' place was just below the hill's crest, a white and brown mock-Tudor monstrosity behind a patterned brick wall. Through the gate, the garden looked mannered and spare; the footpath was lined with mock oranges and there was a row of savagely pruned rose bushes beneath the front windows. I kicked my bike stand and let Toby go ahead.

Inside the gate, a little path of stepping stones led along the side of the house to a lattice gazebo. There was a set of white wicker chairs in there, and an empty glass ashtray on the table. Perhaps Jamie smoked here at night once his parents had gone to bed. I traced the edge of the ashtray. I was in Jamie's garden. I was going to swim in Jamie's pool.

Toby yelled something from around the back.

'Porter?' He didn't answer. I slung my shirt and shorts over a chair and followed his voice to the pool.

Jamie hadn't been lying: it was half-Olympic. I could see the sky cut up in its surface, splinters of sun peaking and breaking. In the shallow end, Toby was floating on his back in his boxers, which ballooned like parachute silk around his thighs.

'Not bad,' Toby said. He kicked a few times, then cupped his hands behind his head. 'That prick. Not bad.'

As I dived in, the water shattered over my head, cold and clear. Veins of light rippled over the tiles. I swam along the bottom until I could feel my lungs burn, then I pushed up. Hold your breath: it was an old game Katie and I used to play at the Spring Hill baths. In those seconds before breaking through to air, I imagined I was a corpse, drifting dumbly towards the surface. I dived down again and again, sinking and rising until my heart was hammering and I couldn't swim anymore.

*

I had probably only been going down to the Knox pool a few weeks before Jamie caught me, although those hours feel endless now, inviolate; nothing can or will ever touch them. The mornings he trained I left the dorm early, in the half-light, and took my books down to the pool. I would crouch in the stands with my scarf wrapping my mouth and nose; then when I picked out Jamie making his way across the grounds, I would pore over my book with a pencil. I never lifted my head until he was in the pool.

The day it happened was clear and cold. It must have been close to six-thirty; I could hear the thin pipe of a whistle intermittently from the oval. My book was open at a colour plate of Zurbaran's Saint Agatha, who was holding her severed breasts on a tray like, the caption said, *two heavenly pink scoops of gelato.* Her face was pale and soft, and the rich red cloth was spilling off her shoulder like a ribbon of blood. The image was strange, savage; it seemed to me to signify neither revelation nor transcendence.

It was September, so the water would have still been freezing. Lines of flags snapped overhead in the wind. Jamie dived from the blocks and struck out at a sprint. The water churned white behind him, then stilled. I felt a thrill rush through me. Watching him swim was my first apprehension of something approaching beauty: the dark lines of his back, his hands dragging and reaching in the water.

By the time Jamie was finished training there were a few other swimmers, and he lingered with them at one end, his arms folded on a plastic barrier. As always, he was at the centre of it all, laughing with someone I didn't recognise in a blue swimming cap.

At any rate, it was far too late when I realised I was being watched. Two of the boys had seen and one of them elbowed Jamie. I ducked my head.

'Wentworth,' Jamie yelled.

I stared at the page. The words winnowed and slid.

'Wentworth.'

I could see his chest beaded with water, the sliver of his smile. I lifted an arm.

'You fucking fag.' He was grinning. Behind him, the boy in the blue cap laughed and said something I couldn't hear.

'What's your problem, Maynard?'

'You're a fucking fag.' He was drying his back with a towel. 'What the fuck are you doing down here, anyway?'

'Reading.'

'What?'

'I was reading, in case you hadn't noticed.' My voice sounded reedy, weak. I felt as if I was seeing myself from a great distance – from the future, even – as a wretched, faltering thing, an insect trying to make itself invisible.

'What, *Arsefuckers*? *Cocks and Frocks*?' Jamie laughed. 'Fuck off.'

'Yeah, fuck off,' one of the others yelled. Anders, from Sinclair. 'Jamie's already got a girlfriend.'

Everyone was watching now, from the shallow end. The one in the blue cap smiled mockingly at me.

'Get stuffed.' My heart was beating dizzyingly fast. I scrabbled for my things.

'You wish,' Jamie said. Someone whistled. 'Now fuck off out of here.'

*

From the Maynards' pool, the city was faint as a backdrop in a play. Blocks and bands of light glinted coolly in the sun: windows. And behind them, people working; behind one of them, my mother. Beyond the city, suburbs stretched out in an endless expanse. Hidden somewhere in the cubist mosaic of roofs was our house, but it was impossible to make anything out from this distance.

'Istanbul.' I said it more to myself than to Toby.

'What?' Toby asked suspiciously, propping himself up on one elbow.

'Why would you go to Istanbul?'

'What do you mean?'

'Nothing.'

Toby sighed, then laid back down. His skin was mottling pink in the sun.

'Would you stop that?' he said abruptly.

'Stop what?'

'You're staring at me. I can feel it. Just stop.'

'I wasn't.'

'Why are you always staring at everyone?'

'I'm not. Don't be ridiculous.' I felt a sudden swerve of hatred for him. 'You're going red, you idiot.'

'Don't call me an idiot,' Toby said sharply.

'I'll call you an idiot if I want to,' I said. 'I'll call you one if you're acting like one.'

I could feel the rage roaring up in me. This perilous sliver of time might be the only afternoon I would ever be here, at the Maynards', and Toby, thick, fatuous Toby, was ruining it.

'Porter.' My pulse was thrumming.

Toby shifted his leg slightly and said nothing.

'Porter, you stupid arse. You're burning.'

Up close, there was nothing to like in his face: the disturbing translucence of his cheeks, his fleshy lips, the bulbous flare of his nose. Before Jamie came to tolerate Toby, he used to call him Pufferfish, and even once the nickname died, the image remained, lodged in my mind for good.

'What the hell are you doing?' he said. He was the one who was staring now, dispassionately, at me.

'What do you mean, what am I doing?' I said irritably.

'I mean here. What the hell are you doing here?'

'What's your problem?'

'Jamie doesn't even like you. He said he wouldn't piss on you if you were on fire.'

'You suggested this, you imbecile.' I was shaking all over.

'You wanted to come.'

'Of course I did,' I said. 'I wanted a fucking swim! You wanted one too, remember?'

Toby just looked at me. There was nothing to read in the glaze of his eyes, his slack, slightly opened mouth.

'Everybody knows, you know,' he said.

'What?'

'About the pool.' Toby said. 'Everybody knows.'

I let it sink in once, quickly, then I turned and dropped down into the water. I sank to the bottom and held my breath, then pushed back up to the surface for air. I sank back down again and again and when I finally turned around, Toby was gone.

*

It was late by the time I realised Toby had taken my clothes with him. The houses next door were quiet and dark and the sky was pale and washed out. I could see the lights across the river beginning to flicker in the water's surface. There was nobody anywhere.

I walked around the house a few times, looking for a sign. Nothing. The Maynards' pool was a faint silver and I could see the lines of the roof cut up in it. The city looked cold and sepulchral over the water, a dark echo of its daytime self.

I thought about going around and smashing in the Maynards' windows, but I didn't do anything. I just sat there.

My mother and Katie would be standing, now, in front of the sink, listening to the radio and clearing the dinner plates, probing my absence like a bad tooth.

I picked the ashtray up. Behind me, the lights in the house clicked on; the Maynards must have set a timer. I let my hand sag with the weight of the glass. I could throw it, now, through one of the second-floor windows, Jamie's perhaps, so that when the family came home, they would find it. They would stand around the bed for a long minute like a nativity, trying to divine some message in the pattern of splinters and shards fanned over the sheets, then someone would gather the glass away.

The Adelaide Review

The Men Outside My Room

Michael Sala

When my brother used to beat me, a part of me wanted to encourage him. It felt like he was getting something out of his system. He'd be focused on the task, like when he was juggling a soccer ball with his feet or threading a worm onto a hook. I'd usually curl up and play dead, but there were times where my outrage became too much, and I'd scream. He'd keep going, although a bitterness would kink his closed mouth – he saw this as a betrayal – and through my screaming, I'd hear the creaking stairs carry our stepfather's heavy breathing and guttural curses to the room we shared: *God Verdomme! God Verdomme!*

Dutch is an awkward language. It sounds humorous to me even now, except when used in anger. When my stepfather cursed, I imagined dirt in his lungs, old black farming earth from the north of Holland, clotted with blood and bone.

The door swings open; Harry enters the room and my brother backs away. My brother is particularly handsome at times like this, upright, very alert. He doesn't show fear, not like I do.

My stepfather's head swings from him to me, and back again. 'What did I tell you? Idiyote! *God Verdomme!*'

From where I sit on the floor, I can see the crack of his arse, huge and pale, with a swirl of black hair plunging into his corduroy pants. He wrenches off a paint-stained work boot and lifts it over his head. My brother throws a hateful glance my way before Harry's back obscures him.

I wish that I could take satisfaction in what happens next, but I'm not at all well. I am sick – I should be in hospital – I have a watery core of illness and my spine is disintegrating. I am not going to hospital; I am waiting for my turn with my stepfather. I am always second in line when we are due for a beating. With each lift of that boot, I glimpse my future. Whenever I hear the word 'anticipation,' or try to imagine what will happen next in my life, that feeling laps up against me, even now, thirty years on, with my stepfather nowhere in sight.

*

Metal chains squeal in protest with each thrust of my arms. May is two, and she has learned how to say 'more' and 'push' and 'harder.' With these three words, she keeps me busy. I push her on the swing and she keeps returning to me, hair floating on the air like an afterthought, a determined line in her jaw when she throws me a quick glance to make sure I won't give up.

This is one of the things we do together. Half of every week I take care of my daughter by myself and we wander around the city looking for things to do. The other half of my daughter's week belongs to my wife. We are not divorced, we live in the same house, but our lives are neatly separated all the same. There are times when we do things together as a family, visits to the beach or the park or some other outing, and my wife always says, 'This is good, isn't it?' and I agree although my eyes don't. My eyes have always betrayed me. But I have learned to look away at the crucial moments. I have learned that it is possible to do this with an entire life.

The time that my wife and I spend alone together happens after May is asleep, when we sit in front of the television. We massage each other's shoulders with oil for lovers and exchange conversation in the advertising spaces that dismember the usual television programs about crime and death. I don't mind talking then, because we are staring in the same direction. I have come to see television as one of the sacrifices you make for love.

*

After the park, I take May to the library. We walk in through the large, open doors, just as a young woman walks out. She is wearing those pants that look like a cross between jeans and tights. My gaze snags on her and I glance over my shoulder as she walks off. I experience regret, and an erection that withers with the next few steps.

Whenever such longing comes, I think of my real father. One of the ghosts of my childhood left behind when my mother moved us to the opposite side of the world with a different man. My father, I am told, was famous for his wandering eye, though he was generally forgiven for it because of his charming nature. I know more of my father through what my mother has given me than through my own interactions with him. He still lives in another country and is caring for his other ex-wife, who is dying of cancer. We haven't spoken in twenty years but information trickles through.

'It's strange,' my mother will tell me, 'how you hardly saw him, but then you laugh or move your hand, just like that and I can see him there, just like when I fell in love with him.'

May is singing a song. I lift a finger to my mouth and catch her eye, and she smiles, then frowns and falls silent and runs ahead into the open spaces of the library. I imagine sometimes that I am moving through life like some kind of blundering surgeon, pinching off possibilities as if they are arteries.

*

This is the story I have of how my parents fell in love: my father was dating my mother's best friend, but he was always close and talking to my mother whenever her friend was out of the room, a brush of his hand, a smile, playful and light, as if they were brother and sister. One day, he hugged his girlfriend, stared lingeringly at my mother and winked, like they were sharing a joke.

It was the kind of joke that never gets old.

A year later, my brother was born, and three years after that, I came along, a home birth on the thirteenth floor of an apartment block in a town near the southern border of Holland. My first words were Dutch, but I can't remember them.

I arrived early by kicking a hole in my mother's stomach; so I believed as a boy. I was always accused of a terrible clumsiness when I was young, and this version of events made sense to me.

The midwife coughed and smoked through the whole labour and had to wipe the ash from my face before she announced in a voice dry as paper that I was the handsomest baby she'd ever laid eyes on. When my father returned from whatever errands had been absorbing him, he borrowed money from my grandfather for a bunch of flowers, came into the bedroom with the flowers in one fist, his other hand in his pocket, and stared at me long and hard, with a look equal parts disappointment and doubt.

'Are you sure that I'm the father?' he asked.

We moved on from Holland to England and rented an apartment where everything was coin operated: the heating; the stove; the shower; the phone. We didn't have a lot of coins. My father was struggling to find work. He had borrowed five thousand guilders from my grandparents, but most of that money had vanished. There was a mystery to this money that I would hear of years later, but what I grew up knowing is that we didn't have anything; that it caused the inevitable conflicts; that I would often turn blue with cold of a night-time; that the walls ran with condensation; that my father was not often around; that I was not a good sleeper. My mother would walk the streets of London by herself, driven by loneliness and the crying that leaked out of me as if I were connected to some limitless reservoir beneath the city. 'The moment that I saw you,' my mother said, 'I knew that you'd been here before.'

I think that my mother confuses unhappiness with experience.

*

In the library, May wanders into the wide-open spaces of the children's section and fondles the spines of books. She pulls the books out and leaves them splayed open in her wake. Someone ought to pull her into line. I take a book about the decline of the Roman Empire from a shelf and sink into a chair. My daughter comes up to me and touches my knee.

'Done poo poo,' she tells me.

We collect our things and go to the toilet. I use up half a packet of wipes to clean her and her underwear goes into the bin. My daughter stands on the counter next to the sink, catches sight of herself in the mirror and starts swaying her hips from side to side and humming under her breath. I tell her to stop, and she puts more sideways thrust into her hips.

'Just cut it *out*,' I tell her in a sharper tone and her body tenses and stops.

I regret my tone immediately. My daughter is not afraid of my wife, only of me. I get irritable when I am tired, and these days I am tired all the time. I have lost control of what I had always assumed would be mine: sleep. I knew that it was coming – plenty of people warned me – I just didn't know how *bad* that lack would be. My daughter wakes sometimes in the middle of the night crying so fiercely that her face develops a rash, and in that hysteria, she is impossible to communicate with. She looks enraged, as if she does not recognise a thing in this world. My wife, who gets up exactly half the time with her, holds her and rocks her and pleads and eventually starts crying herself. Please go back to sleep, she tells my daughter. Please, please, please go back to sleep. This can go on for hours. I can't help but listen. The muscles in my arse are like the workings of a clock that mark the passage of this time by winding more tightly into themselves.

When it is my turn, I pick my daughter up and I too tell her to stop. If this doesn't work, I take her to the shower and hold her head near a stream of cold water and threaten to put her under. Twice I have put her head under. When I make this threat, she bites at her own sobs until they retreat back into her chest. Sometimes I imagine my daughter, twenty years from now, shrugging when someone asks about her overwhelming fear of water. I hold her after she has calmed down until she goes to sleep and feel tender at her peacefulness, her vulnerability, but I am ashamed rather than satisfied and my wife treats me with a wounded contempt that transmits itself in the angle of her body as it turns away from me in the bed.

With my daughter asleep, I lie down beside my wife, separated from the mattress by my own knotted muscles. I lie there, listening to my wife breathe, and wait to fall asleep myself. Something clicks in the back of my wife's throat when she sleeps. I imagine it is the last sound someone might make before they die. I know that my daughter could start up again at any moment. Her distress stays with me like the pain of a burn long after she has drifted off. Falling asleep is like putting my head between the jaws of a lion.

Keep it open, I think to myself, keep it open, but I am no longer talking about a lion and instead thinking of a door that connected me to the outside world when I lay in bed at night as a boy.

I was terrified of the dark. My stepfather, who did not share my father's doubts about paternity, would open the door and look in at me over his thick black beard.

'You'll never learn,' he would say, 'if I don't teach you.'

Then the door shuts.

*

May and I have left the toilet and returned to the library. I sink into a chair with my book. I start flicking through the pages, reading summaries about the late Roman emperors and how they spent their lives going mad or patching up ruptured borders, chasing barbarians out of the slowly disintegrating limbs of the empire, quelling the mutinies of their own armies. The decline of civilisation, onset of the dark ages, all of that. It must have been daunting for an emperor to wake up every morning knowing that there was just one problem after another, making decisions that could wipe out cities or nations, just to keep something going for a few decades more. It fascinates me how all the intricate struggles of countless human beings over several decades can be shoe-horned into a couple of paragraphs on a piece of paper. So many people can disappear between those words.

A familiar-looking mother walks past, glances at my daughter and then at me.

'Gosh, she's grown,' the woman says. 'It goes so fast, doesn't it?'

'Yes,' I reply. 'It does.'

'Best make the most of it,' she tells me.

'OK,' I say, fighting the urge to salute. 'I will.'

I don't say anything else and the woman walks off. My daughter has come to sit in the chair beside me. She has collected a pile of books and is making a show of reading one. We read together for a little while in silence. She lifts one sandalled foot onto the chair cushion and hums softly as she pushes it back and forth in a dreamy way. I note this from the corner of my eye and then turn to look at her more directly. She is pushing something with that foot, and when I look at it closely, I realise that it is shit. It's vital stuff, shit, a sure sign of life, as compelling as any book. I pick her up and put her on the floor.

'Don't move.'

The shit is all over the chair. I glance from this to her legs and see streaks of it along her thighs, a clump hanging like a pendulum on the inside of her shorts. It is all over the floor, too. She's just been to the toilet. Where did this all *come* from? I feel like I have just woken up, like I'm still groggy, trying to disentangle myself from my own thoughts.

'Don't you *dare* move!'

I take out a wipe and run it across the chair. I succeed in spreading the shit over the cushion, turning it into the kind of economical but expressive flourish you might see in a Japanese symbol. I back away, feel myself flush with despair, pick up several clumps from the carpet, fold them in a wipe, drop them into my pocket, and look towards the service desk, where a young woman runs a stack of books under the scanner.

'Look, Daddy,' my daughter exclaims behind me in a voice that rings through the quiet. 'More poo, there on the carpet! And there!'

I have some on my fingers. Everyone will turn around soon to see me and my poo-stained hands standing guiltily in the middle of all this. My daughter will be happy to point out the sights. She is giggling with delight. I grab her hand and pull her small, light body along.

As we pass the woman at the service desk I almost yell at her, 'We don't have any books!' I imagine myself smuggling drugs through customs.

In the toilet, I clean my daughter up the best I can. I am infuriated at her betrayal. 'Why didn't you tell me sooner? Why?'

I throw her pants in a plastic bag, put another bag against her bare arse – it sticks there without a problem and waves sadly as I put her in the pram. She's finally realised how upset I am and doesn't even attempt to sing. We begin walking home at a brisk pace. She quietly asks for her wrap. She likes to put the corner in her mouth and suck on it for comfort.

'No,' I snarl at her. 'Not your wrap. You're not getting your damn wrap! Don't you dare even *ask* for it again!'

There's shit everywhere, in the pram, on her belly, on the plastic bag flapping up between her legs, tar-like and sticky. I don't want it getting into her mouth, but I can't deny it; I also want to make her suffer a little. It's not as bad as I think, I tell myself. I suppose that there are other libraries I can go to around the city. Maybe there's a witness protection program for people who leave shit in chairs for other people to sit in.

My daughter begins sobbing.

'Not a sound out of you!' I snarl loud enough for people across the road to look at me. This makes me more ashamed and angry at May all at once. I know that I'm being an arsehole, but I know it only from a distance. 'All you have to do is tell me when you need to do a poo, or afterwards. You don't *sit* in it and play with it! Not at the library! Daddy's not happy at all. When we get home, you're getting a bath and going to bed. I don't even want to *talk* to you anymore.'

We walk on in silence. My daughter chokes back her tears. When we get home, I put her under the shower. I wash her without any tenderness and even stick her head under the water, which makes her finally break into sobs. Then I put her pyjamas on and put her into her bed. Finally I stop moving and I look down at her. My daughter has put her wrap in her mouth. She feeds the corner between her lips and works it with a slight, repetitive motion of her jaw. Her sad blue eyes are turned up at me.

'All you have to do is tell me,' I say softly but I feel the conviction, the rage, draining out of me.

She nods. I stand over her and think suddenly of how small she is – her nose the size of my thumbnail – and how tall I must seem, the fury written on my face, my hands hanging by my sides. My hands are very different from how I remember my stepfather's, but suddenly they feel just as heavy. I walk out of the room and stand in the middle of the living room, staring out the window at the cliffs overlooking the ocean in the distance.

*

When I return to her bedroom, my daughter doesn't notice at first, or pretends not to. She lies on her side, staring at the ceiling, her small jaw still working away. Then her gaze slides towards me.

I stare down at her. 'You want a hug?'

She nods and I pick her up, hold her body against mine, and I shudder with love and self-loathing. My daughter frees an arm from my embrace and points down at the floor.

'No poo,' she declares with a solemn sweep of her arm. 'No poo anywhere.'

'Yes,' I concede softly. 'Wonderful. You want some lunch?'

My daughter wants rice bubbles and eats two bowls that I feed her, although she knows very well how to do it herself. After that she goes to sleep without a sound. I lie on my bed and doze and snap out of it when the door to the apartment opens and shuts. I walk into the living room and my wife throws me a smile. We are always throwing each other smiles and expressions. They are barely caught, as if we are keeping something up in the air that is doomed to give in to gravity sooner or later.

'How was your morning?'

I tell her that it was OK. I look away. I get my stuff together, kiss her on the cheek, and leave the house. I tell her that I'll be back soon, but as I close the front door, I imagine myself leaving her for good.

*

When my brother and I get together for a drink, he talks some-times about the past and the way he used to beat me. He doesn't get it. He doesn't know why he did it; he feels like it wasn't him.

Who was it, then?

I tell him that it's OK, that I understand. He still doesn't know where his anger comes from, when he gets drunk for example and something happens and it boils up. Then his pleasant man-ner evaporates and he acts in ways that are hazy in his memory, though the fragments he recalls are enough to fill him with a shame that takes a little longer to dispel.

You could say that my brother is an old soul.

*

'Do you know what your father did with our money?' my mother asked me one day. 'He spent it on boys, when we were living in

London. Prostitutes. That's where your father spent his nights. That's where he was when you were born. That's why we were so poor.'

I wish that this were the most unpleasant thing that I knew of him.

*

And my stepfather – who emigrated to Australia with us, and brought with him his language of heavy curses – has become no more than stories and memories too; the sort that unwrap inside your head even when you don't want them to. I have an image of him tamping his pipe, lifting it to his mouth hidden in the dense mass of his beard, bringing the lighter close with his other hand and making the knot of tobacco at the centre flare into life. That sense I have of his heavy calmness and how quickly it could change.

I have never hit my own daughter. I never would. But when you have such a past, there is an awareness of the possibilities, a question that stays with you, that aches whenever you stray near.

*

After my divorce, which came soon enough and then felt as if it had been there forever, when I was alone and my daughter spent the nights with me, she slept more soundly. I would stand sometimes at the doorway of her room, and think of the men that stood at the threshold of mine, that stand there still, and what they had left in me.

No further than this, I warn them. No further. I watch her sleeping, the peacefulness of her expression, and feel better about the world. She sleeps through the night, although sometimes she still wakes when she is sick or restless. I don't make her go back to sleep but let her sit beside me on the couch while I read a book. She is happy to be there, to eat a sandwich, to watch a cartoon and glance over occasionally with a knowing smile, like we are both visiting someone else.

Matter

Miriam Sved

On the morning of the first fitness test, Ranga saw a bloke on a bike get hit by a car.

They'd only just moved to the neighbourhood – moving in the wrong direction, from a suburb with trees and private schools into this inner-city place, a warehouse Lisa called funky, the streets a blur of colour and sound. Ranga heard the cyclist go down before he saw anything. A flat-bodied thud. On a footy field you get to know the sound of bodies colliding and before long you can predict how serious from the noise they make – not in medical but in seasonal terms. A three-week injury, a six-week one. Ranga heard the cyclist go down and thought, *season ender.*

It was on the main road near their new place, a road with tram tracks. There'd been a tram going by just before it happened – probably had something to do with it, the hulking metal caterpillar blocking everyone's vision. Ranga heard the thud and when he looked up the bike was still in motion, skidding towards the curb a good ten metres from the man on the ground, the front wheel bent at a ridiculous angle. The man wasn't wearing a helmet. He had brown corduroys, one leg rolled above the knee.

Ranga was too close. Even though there were other people around – the guy in the car already out, creeping towards the cyclist with a weird bent-back posture, pedestrians half-running from further down the road and people coming out of the post office, mobile phones ready – even though they didn't need him there, he couldn't risk walking away. He wasn't a top-echelon player, but he'd been playing for eleven years so it was inevitable he got recognised, especially with the hair. It wouldn't look good – *Ranga McPhee, he was right there when it happened, never even stopped to help* – so he hovered through the fractured bursts of movement (the guy who'd been in the car was running now, then skidding down on his knees by the cyclist; other people running from the shops; a frantic little glut on the arterial road). Ranga hovered, buggered if he knew what to do. There'd been a St John Ambulance course a few years ago where they'd been taught CPR and the recovery position and all that, but what was the point when the doc was on hand at every game and training session, and all you had to know for yourself were the overnight signs of concussion. Ranga doubted whether the guy on the ground wanted to know the signs of concussion. But even though there was nothing to be done and the bloke from the car was already there doing it, down on all fours beside the man (*Hello? Mate? Can you hear me? Didn't see you, you all right, mate?*), Ranga found he couldn't move if he'd wanted to. He stared at the cyclist's body, which wasn't quite still anymore. One of the legs, the one with the pants rolled up, twitched on the slick concrete; the head made little juddering movements. Weak and meaningless like the last protests of a grounded fish. Ranga watched it and the kit bag over his shoulder felt heavy.

The ambulance came and he forced himself to move off.

*

It was January. The worst of the sting of last season's last game had dulled and the necessity and leeway to party were fading. They'd all had to sign off-season contracts, committing to what Cob called the bare minimum – basically that they wouldn't kill themselves or anyone else or turn into fat bastards. That was a month ago, and a contract could only stand up so well against the drawn-out summer days, massage sessions that left you wilting in a tingling new skin, the euphoria of that first dehydrated pull of beer.

In the old leafy suburb, Ranga and Lisa were just down the road from Kev, the team's warhorse ruckman, famous on the field for the length of his reach and the stretches he could go without speaking, and off it for the amount he could drink without falling over. The four of them – Ranga, Lisa, Kev and his wife Linda – sitting out after Linda put Rochelle to bed, sweating it up on the patio, summer all around them like a warm bath making it easy to forget about the last game and the pre-season to come. Kev chugged down one beer after another, Ranga tried to look like he wasn't trying to keep up, and Linda brought fruity alcoholic concoctions from the blender for Lisa and herself. Ranga remembers his first summer as a player. The smug feeling of time on the clock – two months that were basically your own, bankrolled by the club, sprinkled with a few media appearances. It was fun. The whole game, the whole thing was fun, but summer was like the childhood dream of grown-up freedom.

Now Ranga gets to the grounds with ten minutes to spare and heads to the walloping room – a little antechamber tacked onto the massive gym – where almost all the boys are already sitting in neat primary-school formation. They're waiting for Cob to arrive. Kev's already there, with his freakishly long arms crossed at his chest. He gives a twitch of his head towards the seat beside him – Ranga's seat, the one he's sat in for pre- and post-session wallopings the last nine years, and for a moment Ranga thinks the whole day – the cyclist, the heavy gym bag and the betrayal of summer – the whole thing is just an upsetting dream, one of those dreams where your past and present selves become confused. The kid sitting in Ranga's seat is skinny and ginger and can't be more than eighteen, the same age as Ranga when he started with the club. Then someone up the back of the room laughs and Ranga notices how quiet it is. They've all been waiting for him to get here and find the ginger mutt in his seat.

With everyone watching on, Ranga can't let the kid get away with it, even though he's thrown back to his own first training session – a different, smaller gym, but they always seem to keep the ratio of chairs to guys a humiliating constant: forty men, thirty chairs and a terrible decision to make. All the boys are waiting to see what he'll do, and the sense of expectation puts Ranga in mind of that moment when the ball's trajectory gets you in its sights, and for that second before action the spectrum of possibilities is endless. Physical possibility is what he thinks about as he moves towards the kid in his chair – the possibility of, say, himself standing in the back line during a game and watching the ball float by like some graceful unpredictable insect, relative to the possibility of a cyclist dodging safely out of the path of a moving car. And at the same time he's taking a closer look at the kid – skinny and unfortunate-looking, freckles to blot out the sun (at least Ranga escaped *that* red-headed genetic betrayal) – and, with his head back on straight, Ranga knows exactly who the kid is. The draft pick (Mike? Mick?), the one they scored partly because of Ranga's screw-up in the last game. There's been a lot of fuss about him in the footy press – supposedly the second coming of Ablett or something. You'd not think him a big shot to look at him – the matchstick arms and legs, and something in his face that's too eager for a number-two pick (you can generally tell a high draft pick from a rookie just by the way they carry themselves, a slight glow of entitlement around the older blokes). But the realisation still adds force to Ranga's advancing buttocks. He sits down in his regular place, first row second seat from the wall, on top of a pair of skinny freckled thighs.

The guys behind him laugh – Steve and Buta the loudest as usual – and he hears the boy laugh beneath him, a dry sliver of a laugh. Ranga shifts his weight to give the kid a chance; there's a lot of mulchy flesh noise and he oozes out one leg at a time. With nowhere else to sit he hovers beside Ranga for a few seconds, then backs up slowly till he's against the wall and leans back all casual like he's waiting for a bus. His face is flaming. His posture puts Ranga in mind of a man he once saw waiting for an actual bus – a man who leant back against what he thought was the solid wall of a bus shelter and kept going, shooting through the vacancy where there should have been glass. What struck Ranga as funny was the deliberate, devil-may-care casualness of the man falling through space – he'd looped one ankle over the other and folded his arms like some kind of case study: Man Waiting for Bus. The ginger kid's stance is exactly the same, which is all Ranga needs; he didn't mean to be cruel, but the stress of the morning, the cyclist's twitching body on the road and the knowledge of what his own body's about to be put through, all of it builds up inside him – tinder that the kid accidentally strikes a match to. He gets the laughing up-chucks, and

by the time Cob walks in to punish them all with the fierce glow
of his belief and disappointment, by that time Steve and Buta,
and Kev beside him, and most of the guys behind him and most
of all Ranga himself – all of them are in different poses of out-
of-control. Ranga is bent double, his body shaking, and there's
the new kid blaring red while a sallow little smile maintains the
fiction – for himself or the rest of them or the dour coach who
just walked in – that he's in on the joke. Ranga catches Cob's eye
mid laugh-spew and the coach raises one eyebrow in that way
only he can – might almost be seductive on anyone else, but on
Cob it's pure distilled threat – and Ranga stops laughing, sits up
straight and looks down at his big hands. The other guys stop
laughing too.

Now that it's over, the kid by the wall looks suddenly pissed
off, his crossed arms defensive and hurt.

'Let's get on with it then, shall we,' says Cob, and nobody
makes eye contact with anybody.

*

The kid's a midfielder. Michael Reece. Cob said his name casually, along with two other new players, not like an introduction
so much as a reminder to the more slow-witted guys who might
have forgotten their own teammates. He said it towards the end
of a longish speech about moving on from last season, about how
the mark of a great team, an enduring team, is how they come
back after defeat. The kid is put in the same training group as
Ranga, who plays fullback, and Kev – ruck and rover.

This is Ranga's fifth season in defence. He knows roughly what
the fitness testing will involve and as they warm up in the gym
he reminds himself that he's done it all before and that his body
always comes through the pain of the first day. He remembers
last year – the same stiffness and soreness carried over from the
year before, with the new-skinned feeling of a month in the sun,
too much beer, the gentle forgiving pain of a recent massage. All
these sensations were just as present, just as urgent then. And
he's been running, of course, he reminds himself that he's never
stopped running (knowing though that what he does on his own
could barely be called running in the context of the game –
really he's just a jogger, chasing down the zone, huffing through

the first few minutes for the sake of an hour's calm water, his breathing dropping into a regular pattern and his muscles expanding and contracting with a regularity that feels like rest).

He and Kev team up for the first circuit – mostly agility. Right and left dodging around the poles, knees up through the ladder then a series of sprints across an expanding pitch. They're timed as a duo, the theory being that they'll push their own limits for the sake of their mate, but maybe Ranga and Kev trust each other too much, maybe they know each other too well to care about a little betrayal on the fitness circuit, because Ranga huffs through the last sprint with he and Kev a good thirty seconds short of the pack. O'Brien, the fitness coach, who has none of the cruel finesse of Cob, shouts at them that they're a couple of burnt-out fatties and they'd better get their bloody acts together before the skin-folds test or they'll be out on their arses. Then he splits them up and they each get paired with one of the duo who came in first. Ranga is paired with the new kid. Mick? Mike?

'Michaela!' Ranga says, but it comes out less hearty than he'd like because the pain in his lungs is only beginning to fade. The kid looks like he's barely broken a sweat; what's worse, he's making an elaborate show of relacing his boots, clearly giving Ranga a chance to pull himself together.

'Don't gimme any of your newbie shit,' Ranga says, breathing evenly with a drastic effort. 'Just do like the man says and we'll both get out of this alive.'

The kid laughs feebly. Ranga remembers '05, the preliminary final when he took a high contested mark dead centre in front of goal – commentators called it the mark of the year although it didn't win mark of the year. That was pressure. That was making the play when it mattered. Not many players could have taken that ball, whereas anyone could be eighteen with an infinite supply of oxygen. They start the first leg of the agility course.

'Three around,' O'Brien shouts, and Ranga tries to forget about the kid, to concentrate on willing his body forward.

At the end of three circuits Ranga has given up every semblance of composure – bent double, huffing and spitting with his hands on his knees. The kid walks a little way off, breathing heavily, but Ranga can tell from the straightness of his posture that he's pretending to be more puffed than he is. Ranga's played in four finals series and doesn't need some new kid's charity, so he jogs up level with him, spits to the side, traps a bubble of oxygen deep in his chest and commits to breathing evenly as they make their way across the ground towards the rooms and towards O'Brien.

'Where you from?' he says out the corner of his mouth.

'Up north, little place just outside Mt Cobb.' The kid speaks in a rush. 'You probably wouldn't know it.'

Ranga grunts.

'You must have been all over.' He's forgotten to keep up the heavy breathing. 'With the team, lots of away games last year, yeah?'

Another grunt.

'I've been to Sydney for the carnival last year, and the AIS week in Canberra. My mate went to Perth for the under-eighteen cup but I had an exam and my bloody mum made me stay home for it.' He blushes at the mention of his mum. Jesus, Ranga thinks, this one's for real.

The others are spread out around the oval, going through various circuits. He sees Kev doing a hand passing exercise and thinks longingly of silence – Kev's comfortable silence on the field.

'You must have been all over, yeah?' the kid says again, and Ranga shrugs. They jog up to where O'Brien is standing outside the rooms and Ranga's fantasy of being allowed past, down the ramp and into the cool sanctuary beneath with the drinks table already laid out – this beautiful vision collapses with a wave of O'Brien's hand. He sends them off to the sprint course. An upsurge of pain and Ranga completely loses the recovering rhythm of his breathing – he hasn't been concentrating hard enough on his breathing, he's been concentrating on looking like he's not concentrating on his breathing.

They jog towards the witches' hats around the goal square and the kid says, 'That finals series, what was it, '05? *Man.*'

He's talking about the last time they played Ranga up front. Six years into his career, body hardened and ready for the fight. He'd been able to relax into the game in a way that had eluded him in previous finals series. In '05 he was confident. His body knew what it was there to do.

'Man,' the kid says again. 'That mark you took, right in front of goal ...'

Ranga says nothing. They're approaching the first set of witches' hats and the kid breaks into an easy canter. It doesn't look easy – he has an awkward running style, arms too far out from his body, no rhythm to his stride – but Ranga can tell it's easy because, unthinkably, when they reach the first witch's hat and double back on themselves the kid is still speaking fluidly.

'I was watching that game with my dad, you know, and he hated you guys.' He laughs. 'I was s'posed to as well but I never did, and then when you took that mark I forgot all about Dad and I'm jumpin' around shouting at the telly along with whatshisname, that bloody commentator who always used to do the finals – you must have watched it, right? When you took the grab and whatshisname yells, *"Ranga McPhee saves the season!"* That was ... man! You must have partied that night.'

Huffing along beside the kid, Ranga detects a note of self-consciousness creeping into his voice but still no sign of fatigue. It's unreal. They're in the last leg of the sprint course, which is a descending series of distances – first a long run to the furthest of the witches' hats, maybe forty metres away, then two to the one in front of that, three to the next and so on, so that in the end you're running back and forth, back and forth over the ten metres between the goal post and the closest hat. It's this ten metres that'll break your spirit, not because of the sprinting but the turning – every few seconds the quivering flesh of your thighs forced to stop ninety-five kilos of momentum and swivel the machine, start it off in a new, juddering direction.

Ranga looks up and realises he and the kid are alone on the circuits; the rest of the guys are jogging a cool-down lap up the other end of the oval. It looks heavenly, that jogging – the steady, comforting rhythm of a stable heartbeat. At least the kid's finally stopped talking, but he's still keeping pace with Ranga, shadowing him back and forth around the hats. Infuriating, humiliating. O'Brien wanders over and draws a line under the humiliation, loud enough for the guys up the other end of the field to hear.

'C'mon, Reece,' he shouts. 'Stop holding yourself back to that limp dick's pace. You wanna be a fat bastard when you grow up too, is that it?' And the kid, with a slippery sidelong glance at

Ranga, takes off with the cruellest, easiest spring around the witches' hat.

Ranga's breathing is all over the place now and his thighs aren't even the biggest problem anymore – it's that he can feel the lactic acid building, poison leaking from his overstretched muscles and rising in his gut. Everyone gets it at some stage during the season; there are players who'll go down to the rooms and have a chuck like some clockwork part of their quarter-time ritual, but Ranga's never been one of them, he's never been an easy chucker and besides, this isn't the adrenalin-pumped intensity of a game. The first training session. He swallows hard and tries to empty his mind. The kid laps him; four more to go. Jesus, the pain in his legs, his chest.

He manages to get to the end of the circuit without losing his breakfast, but by then the rest of the guys are done with the cool-down and O'Brien is bossing them into groups for a game of bash and grab. A tackling exercise no more sophisticated than the old primary school game of bullrush – famous for more broken bones than the asphalt around the monkey bars. Two on one with a lone man shepherding – more like a rugby exercise than footy since the goal is to get the ball past the tacklers without a mark to kick to. Whatever the coaching staff say about this game – about strength and agility, the quick-thinking reflexes of dodge and shimmy – bash and grab is really about one thing: fear. Ranga's still heaving when he is lined up with three others, eyes blurred with sweat so he doesn't even register who they are at first. Only when they're broken into twos he sees that the kid, Mick, is still with him. A surge of something that could be lactic acid – scalding heat bubbling up his torso. That fucking kid will be the end of him today.

'Mate, you right?'

Ranga turns and finds Kev at his shoulder – O'Brien has given them another chance training together. The acidic tide recedes a bit.

'Thought you were gonna have an eppi on that sprint circuit,' Kev says.

'Yeah, well, I saw the colour of your face on the jog, so don't gimme any shit.' This is easier – much, much easier than the kid's humiliating solidarity.

They're at the fifty-metre line and they line up for the tackle. The kid's got the ball and Case, one of the small forwards, is shepherding for him. O'Brien is there, watching them warm up, and it occurs to Ranga that the fitness coach has badly mismatched their group – usually he sets up players against others roughly their own size. Maybe during the season, if a small guy's gonna get a heavy tag, O'Brien might match him with some talls to feel what he's in for. But this, in the first session – Ranga and Kev, two of the biggest bodies on the team, both of them there to impede the flimsy kid. O'Brien catches Ranga looking at him and raises his eyebrows.

'Thought you might like a chance to show the newbie one area where you can kick his skinny arse in,' he says.

Ranga pulls the sides of his mouth into a smile and looks back at the kid, who's bouncing from side to side with the ball tucked under one arm. Maybe seventy kilos of him, seventy-five, tops; his torso must be the width of one of Ranga's thighs. Ranga's still sweating from the sprints but he feels suddenly cold. He tries to jog himself loose, kicking his bum with his heels.

O'Brien blows his whistle and the kid stops his bouncing and begins to run. The world slows down. Out the corner of his vision Ranga sees another team down the ground. He looks back at the kid running towards him and instead of bracing for the tackle he can't stop noticing things – the flap of the kid's left hand as though it's churning through air; the expression on his face, which reminds Ranga somehow of Kev's kid Rochelle, when she digs in behind some demand (*Don't wanna go to bed!*); and then suddenly the kid's whole body becomes a suggestion of childhood: the way his chest has developed beyond the scope of his limbs, the extra billowing fabric of his guernsey. And the self-belief of childhood. The kid's speed and determination as he runs towards Ranga and Kev, towards a wall of grown-up muscle – Ranga sees this for what it is: a stupid decision. In footy there are decisions you make which in life would get you committed to the loony bin. Step backwards into the stampede of bodies, thinking only about the fall of a lifeless knot of synthesis and pig-skin (the ball tucked beneath the kid's arm, dangerous goitre, close enough now for Ranga to see the familiar stitching along its edge). Anywhere else a decision like that would be called reckless, irresponsible. With Cob or O'Brien watching it's called *putting your body on the line*. The kid is maybe twenty metres away now, putting his body on the line, the line beyond which there could be, what? Ranga sees the man on the road, the twitching blackness. A punctured spleen is one common tackling-related injury; Ranga knows two men it's happened to, the organ's poison flooding out into the body's delicate mechanisms.

Or maybe it'll be nothing like that – probably this tackle is no more menacing, no more significant than any of the thousands, literally thousands of tackles he's laid before. What's wrong with him? He must be going soft, which is the worst way for a professional footballer – a hard man – to go. And not even soft for himself but on behalf of some snotty kid – number-two draft pick, probably got footy scholarships to the best schools and now going into the league on a good salary, maybe not that much less than Ranga himself makes.

Ranga hunkers down and for a moment the world speeds up again and he's back in the flow of it, the automatic momentum of the game. But the kid's maybe ten metres away and now he ducks his head down. In a game it could be playing for the free, but the thought of tackling the kid head-first closes Ranga's window of calm and makes everything a decision again – the decision to send a fire-bolt of ripples down the fragile stalk of a neck. Cob and O'Brien are both watching from the outskirts of the field. Ranga's sweating badly; he can't stop thinking about how young the kid is, and how he probably hasn't even got his end away yet, let alone all the other stuff. Then it all starts tramping through his brain – stuff you're only supposed to think about when you're about to snuff it – the first time with Lisa, then the hospital after the prelim final that second season, Lisa and his mum standing over him (good boy, Steve, his mum said, you done well), and then the four of them – him and Kev and Lisa and Linda. The long December nights, the colours of the sky.

Thinking of Kev makes him aware of the ruckman's body crouched beside him, and he realises for the first time that the decision, the terrible decision running towards him is not only his to make. It's Kev's too. The ruckman's big body will rob the kid of everything. Cob and O'Brien are watching on, and Ranga's a man who needs his contract extended, but it's no use.

It's no use because suddenly he understands with an awful clarity the message of the man on the road, of his twitching flesh. The message is matter. Contracts don't matter as much as cells, and it's not really Ranga's decision so much as the decision of survival itself that makes him shift his tackling position away from the kid and towards Kev, towards his best mate's menacing bulk. Now he has both the hard man and the running kid in his sights, and he braces for impact.

Meanjin

Space Under the Sun

Liam Davison

It's light now when she's coming off the wards. The windows are like milk and she feels she's surfacing, or waking from a long sleep. The foyer is already starting to fill with women. Some are veiled. Some carry bags of food. They come prepared to wait, the same as they do at home.

As always, she is thinking of Udai, and the thought of him now is linked to the smells and cries of birthing and the soft hiss of the rain that has been falling all through the night. Udai. Her beautiful boy. Her space under the sun.

He would be waking now to the same morning light with no mother to smooth his hair or warm his breakfast. There would be no sweet cake or spiced chapati for his midday meal; no one to hear his prayers. They are apart together now, and it pains her that they have travelled so far only to be alone.

The floors are wet where people have brought the rain in. She signs her discharge summaries and ticks the boxes in her log: two assists and an unassisted rotational. All girls, poor things. She can still smell their mothers on her, despite the gloves and scrub. There had been no complications and the midwives had let her know she was in the way. *Excuse me, doctor. Doctor, if you wouldn't mind.* Their polite dismissal made it clear she wasn't needed.

They were big women, and capable. *Thank you, doctor.*

She has delivered more children than they could dream of: boy babies and girls; wanted and unwanted; damaged and perfect as hope. But as Dr McNee says, there are many different ways to skin the cat.

She's back on in six hours. There's a daybed in outpatients, but she wants for the comfort of her own space and the knowledge that the small bag of Udai's clothes is safe beneath her as she sleeps.

If she's lucky, she'll be out for four hours then back for clinic before her talk with Dr McNee: his little chat. She's rehearsed what she wants to say but when the time comes, she won't say it. She'll listen to him and nod. *Yes, doctor. Thank you, doctor. I will try harder.*

Her assessment is after rounds, with Mrs Al-Garni.

*

Outside, the forecourt is wet and shining and a small queue of yellow taxis is already waiting in the rain.

'Good morning,' she says

'Good morning, madam.' The driver looks at her in the mirror. 'Namaste.'

The windows are fogged from the heater, and the hospital dissolves to a soft blur of light and shade as he slides the big car out of the service lane.

'Do you work here,' he asks, 'in this hospital?'

'Yes,' she says.

'And you are a doctor?'

'Yes.' She squints across the top of her glasses to the card on the dash that gives him a number but no name. Her own name, she realises, is clearly displayed on the staff card swinging from her neck. Dr Sanghmitra Jethani. Her husband's name.

'Your father must be very proud,' he says. 'A daughter who is a doctor must be a great relief.'

Pride is not a thing she associates with her father. Her success may have provided some consolation for her absence in the years before he died, but she doubts she offered him relief.

'I have two daughters,' he continues. 'Perhaps there is hope.'

'Hope?' she says.

'That they will be happy. That they will water their father's ground. Do you have daughters, doctor?'

She clears a patch of glass with the back of her hand and makes out the smudged remains of the old gasworks and the vast expanse of containers waiting to be shipped. Beyond them, beyond the scope of her failing vision, the city towers would be shrouded in low cloud like distant peaks. His question is well meant.

'No,' she says. 'I have a son.'

'Ah. Your father is doubly blessed.'

*

When her father died, her husband had already made his plans for her.

'You have a brother,' he said. 'It is his responsibility now. Your mother is fortunate to have a son.'

But fortune had nothing to do with Kaamil. For all the privilege he'd been afforded – his education, the debts of gratitude owed to his father in business and bestowed in kind on the son – he'd done nothing but gamble and dream.

'Kaamil can't help,' she'd said. 'He owes more than he owns; you know that, Rajit. He is a liability.'

'He is your mother's son,' Rajit had replied. 'And I am your husband.'

She'd thought about defying him and staying with her mother after the funeral. She could practise in Kota. Her mother could sell the store, though there was little value in it. The department stores had stolen their custom long ago. They sold lights cheaper than her father could buy them. Any fool could plug them in.

'Light used to be like magic,' he said before he'd died. 'It could kill you like that.' He touched two fingers together like electric wires. 'Now ... phhht.'

He took to stocking batteries for mobile phones, butane, plastic watchbands. The radio whispered all day at the back of the shop, its valves glowing softly as they delivered the world to him in barely audible waves.

When she'd married Rajit, her parents had given his family the last of the great chandeliers that had hung like a jewel from the ceiling of the shop. They'd also given two washing machines, a television and a sum of money that neither family revealed to her.

'They have these things already,' she'd said. 'Mother still washes by hand.'

'We are very fortunate, Sanghmitra,' her father had said. 'The Jethanis are a good family. They are well connected. His father once dined with Jinnah, do you know?'

She knew the cost of staying with her mother against Rajit's wishes. She may have been Udai's mother, but he was Rajit Jethani's son.

'You will go to Australia,' Rajit had said. 'It is all arranged. Udai will go too.'

It was her one consolation.

'You will have an Australian qualification. Udai will have an education.'

His own qualification had come from England, like his father's. His parents had paid the fees and he'd spent two years in London perfecting his accent and learning the intricacies of tax minimisation.

'Business is what you learn on the streets of Karol Bagh,' he'd said. 'A qualification is something else. Believe me, Sanghmitra, it is for the best.'

'I have a qualification, Rajit,' she said. 'There are women here who will not be seeing a doctor if I go.'

'Then think of our son, Sanghmitra. Think of my father's grandson.'

*

The week after she left, Kaamil sold the freehold on his father's shop to settle his debts. He would hold the lease and carry on as his father had done, buying cheap and selling at a small profit. But by the time Udai was enrolled in his Australian school and Sanghmitra had finished her first rotation five hours drive away from him, he had missed three payments and Sun Lighting & Electrical was gone.

Sanghmitra's salary paid Udai's fees. A small remittance went to her mother each month. Rajit directed most of what was left to his business ventures. He owned three clinics in Jammu and a string of private rooms that Sanghmitra no longer discussed with him.

'They are opportunities,' he'd said.

His father had told him that a successful man didn't work for money. The clinics served women whose families transferred funds to a company in Delhi that made no reference to the Jethani name.

'It's a service, Sanghmitra, like any other,' he'd said. 'If they wish, they can go to the Sacred Heart. They can go to the midwives in Market Lane. They can go to you.'

'You know they can't, Rajit. We are bound.'

'You say it yourself. It is a service. We offer them information. They should not be denied what can be offered.'

'You know as well as I, Rajit, it's not the information but what they do with it.'

'We are not responsible for their actions,' he'd said. 'They will do the same if it comes from the market women or the temples or the interpreters of dreams. What right do we have to withhold this knowledge?'

'There are times, Rajit, when it's better they didn't know.'

*

Mrs Al-Garni was waiting in outpatients for more than an hour before they found her. She'd arrived early and had sat like a shadow in the end row, waiting to be called.

'It's a routine procedure, Sanghmitra,' Dr McNee had said. 'Mrs Al-Garni will be anxious. It's her first. But you. There's no advantage.'

'Yes, doctor,' she'd said.

'In fact, you have a responsibility to be calm. It's not about you, Sanghmitra. Forget you are even being assessed.'

How could she forget she was being assessed? It was not possible. When she'd left Udai in Perth and travelled to Melbourne, she'd assumed her assessment would be over on the same day.

'When I come back,' she'd told him, 'we'll take a flat by the river and watch the boats. We'll imagine it is the Jumna. Is that possible, Udai, that the Jumna should be so clean? What a beautiful misfortune to be so far from home.' She'd held him and felt his thickening shoulders soft beneath her hands. 'And you will study hard and we'll return home together, to your father.'

But two years later, she was still not finished with her assessment and Udai was barely a boy anymore. Rajit had visited once. She carried her book of failings with her from one hospital appointment to the next while Udai stayed where he was in school. And each time she left him, something tore inside her. She couldn't credit the physicality of it. His absence was a hollow ache.

'So, you are signed off on surgical skills,' Dr McNee said.

'Yes, doctor.'

'And communications.'

'Yes, communications also.'

'And the ultrasound. How many previous attempts?'

He knew the answer. How could he not know? It was there in front of him in the book, with the dates and the notes written in his own hand, and the assessment scheduled for later today with Mrs Al-Garni.

'Two, doctor. Two previous attempts.' She had already cleared the exams. There was nothing else but this.

'And at home, in your own country, did you have exposure to ultrasound?'

How could she answer such a question? He assumed they had nothing. Knew nothing. She had told him over and over.

'A little,' she said. 'It's not routine as it is here, doctor.'

'Quite,' he said.

Her own first trimester scan had occurred in Rajit's mobile clinic the same year she'd passed her exams. He had invested in three machines and three Toyotas from the government auctions. 'It's like a gift, Sanghmitra,' Rajit had said. 'This will change our lives. It can change the whole of India.' Despite his fastidious attention to detail – the white curtains, the sterilised plastic sheets, the methylated swabs – the van still smelt of diesel and dust.

There were no restrictions then. Anyone with money or a line of credit could purchase a machine and practise. He covered the whole of Uttar Pradesh, bringing the magic of sound and light to women whose husbands and fathers were desperate to know their futures. The machines were cheap and well used. They had articulated arms and screens that were so small she could barely see the shadowed images they displayed.

'There,' the sonographer had said. 'Just there, do you see?'

It was like peering through scratched glass into an ocean. Things moved as clouds or schools of fish move. Dark shapes loomed like shallows then faded into light.

This was his magic, then. This was what Rajit meant: her own

self, echoing like something already lost. And there, for the brief-
est of moments, all arms and legs like a Hindu god surfacing
from the deep. She gasped at the sight of it.

'Shhh!' the sonographer said. 'Your babies are developing
well, Mrs Jethani. There, you can see. Just there, just there.' She
isolated a detail that Sanghmitra could barely see. 'You will be
having a daughter.'

She held her breath. Rajit let go of her hand and turned his
attention to the machine. He scanned the dial across the fre-
quencies. The screen flared and dimmed. The arm rattled as it
swung across her.

'Still,' he told her. 'Lie still.'

'It is for no purpose, sir,' the sonographer said. 'The second is
in the other's shadow. Both your children are well, sir. That is all
that can be determined today.'

All Sanghmitra could see was shadow and noise. She tried to
decipher something – anything – from the screen, but her eyes
continued to fail her. And each time after that, each day until
Rajit could rest assured, it was the same: like the scratched flick-
erings of a magic lantern show withholding the thing she most
longed to see.

*

After the Act, Rajit serviced Jammu and the parts of Kashmir
where his mobile clinics broke no law. His vans gradually gave
way to leased premises, then to two-roomed freeholds with street
addresses and basic furnishings. When Sanghmitra gained her
qualification, he registered her with the Central Supervisory
Board and ordered new machines from Russia.

'Leave it,' he'd said to her. 'You are doing nothing wrong,
Sanghmitra. You are registered for diagnostic purposes.'

'But Rajit.'

'You must appreciate this, of all people. How can you not? You
are a doctor now, and soon to be a mother. How can this be
wrong, Sanghy?'

It wasn't her place to argue. She saw the results passed to the
mothers on blue or pink sheets, the relief or resignation that
accompanied them.

'Please, Rajit. I am not a fool.'

'Then you will see that what I say is right.'

When Udai was born the Jethanis regarded her with new respect. A doctor was one thing but the mother of a son was something of a different order altogether. It was as though she had been reborn herself. Even her father, who had regarded her studies as a clever interest that would pass, viewed her now with respectful admiration, as though what she had done might somehow compensate for the failures of his own son.

'You have brought the light, Sanghmitra,' he said. 'And it shines on you. This is your calling.'

Nobody mentioned her loss.

The birth was difficult. And when her ordeal was over, the Jethanis made their arrangements and showered her with gifts. Her first responsibility was to her son.

'You are a mother now,' Rajit had said, and he'd stroked Udai's cheek with such gentle affection she felt she might be complete after all, despite the emptiness she felt. 'We must look to our blessing.'

But Sanghmitra felt her loss as keenly as her gain. The nurses consoled her with talk of viability and things being for the best, but nothing could dislodge the shadowed image of her absent daughter.

'I can feel her,' she told them. 'When I watch him, I can feel her.'

And as Udai grew, she was always there: mirroring his milestones and achievements with unspoken regret, and pulling against her happiness like a phantom limb. And whatever joy she drew from Udai was tempered by the fear of losing him too. How swiftly sunshine cast its shadow.

*

Daliya Al-Garni's husband worked in the mines five weeks out of six. He was entitled to flights home, but if he worked six straight there were bonuses. In Tunisia, a lifetime ago now, he was an engineer.

Daliya had seen him three times in the past six months. Each visit was like his first, when he'd come timidly to her family's home in Tunis. He was still a boy, even now. And each time he left, she longed for his return.

'It's her first,' Dr McNee said. 'She will be anxious. The husband is fly-in, fly-out. She'll be on her own today.'

'She isn't here,' Sanghmitra said. 'There are two waiting but there's no sign.'

Dr McNee checked his watch and put the blank assessment sheets aside. 'You'll be assessed as an independent operator,' he said. 'Patient interactions. Technical competence. I'm here to observe.'

'Yes Doctor, it's the same as ...'

'Last time. Yes. Ten minutes.'

He stepped out and left her alone in the darkened room with the soft glow of the machine.

*

She'd seen Daliya Al-Garni once before for a routine antenatal. She was like a young bird blown from its nest. Each time Sanghmitra had tried to engage her she had withdrawn further into herself. There was a wide-eyed vulnerability to her that invited sympathy, but Sanghmitra had sensed a quiet resilience too behind her startled features. Daliya reminded her of women she'd helped birth at home, women who had delivered their children with stoic diligence as though they were fulfilling a duty.

At the end of her consultation, Daliya had asked whether she would know her baby's gender.

'That will be possible,' she'd said. 'Though not always certain. Some families wish to know this.'

Daliya held her gaze.

'Is this something you would like to know?' Sanghmitra asked.

'I have only brothers,' she said. 'My sister has only sons. But my husband doesn't wish to know before the birth. He will love a son or daughter as is God's wish.'

'And you?' Sanghmitra asked. 'Do you want this information?'

Daliya dropped her gaze.

'I will respect my husband's wish. A daughter will choose her own time.' And she'd smiled for the first time as though they now shared some secret between them.

*

There was the possibility that Daliya Al-Garni had decided not to come. The screening was not compulsory. Her husband may have ruled against it. Her absence was palpable in the half-dark of the suite and Sanghmitra willed her to appear, as though she could be conjured from the shadows by simply turning on the machine. There were two appointments waiting. Dr McNee had not returned.

Her own assessment seemed less important now than the missed appointment. She thought of Daliya Al-Garni at home alone, nursing her ill-formed secret. There were tests and screenings that should be done, apart from the information that her husband wished withheld. So, when Daliya was ushered into the room like a recalcitrant child by the orderly who'd found her waiting quietly in outpatients, Sanghmitra felt a mixture of relief and satisfaction that she was there before her.

'Hello,' she said. 'It's good to see you.'

'Your hospital is very large, doctor.'

Sanghmitra smoothed the sheet on the bed and guided Daliya to it.

'Dr McNee will be attending also,' Sanghmitra said. 'But I will be your consulting doctor.'

'Two doctors for a simple visit?'

'I am your doctor today,' she said. 'Dr McNee will be observing me.'

She stepped Daliya through the procedure and entered her details into the machine, calibrating the settings and depth of field while Dr McNee retrieved the assessment sheets from the counter and introduced himself.

The equipment was nothing like that at home, even the machines Rajit had purchased for his clinics in the cities. The images were clear and sharp. She could adjust the scope and contrast, make it brighter if she wished. But even so, her eyes could fail her as they'd done before. Light could meld into shadow. Shapes could shift. Dr McNee said nothing but scratched his notes as she worked her way methodically through the screening.

Daliya Al-Garni's child displayed no abnormalities. She measured the sac and pole, recorded the heart rate and amniotic volume. Everything was as expected: clear and unambiguously miraculous as she slid the probe smoothly across Daliya's distended abdomen. She made her records and explained what the images revealed.

'There,' she said. 'You can see your baby's hand and shoulder. There.'

She zoomed the focus and as she did, the baby turned to reveal its unmistakeable female features. Even to the untrained eye it must be clear. She said nothing as the image filled the screen. It was a luminous echo that transfixed her to the moment. And when she moved the probe, she felt the soft touch of Daliya's hand against her own holding it still against her skin.

*

Later, she would explain the findings and write her report. Dr McNee would sign the forms. Tomorrow, she would submit them for approval. There had been no complications. She knew this. She would inform Rajit that she was done and he would make his plans for her. Already he was looking at investment opportunities in fertility labs and selective engineering.

'It is a service, Sanghmitra,' he'd said. 'We have a responsibility. One can do no harm to something not conceived.'

She ticks the boxes in her log and walks through the foyer to the line of taxis. She's back on in six hours. As always, she is thinking of Udai, her beautiful boy. At home, she slides the small bag of clothes from beneath the bed and lays them out: trousers, shirt, a knitted cap her mother made. She assembles them before her on the bed, tracing the contours of a shape he has outgrown already. And she lays beside him and shuts her eyes, alert to the weight of the empty bag beside her.

Where There's Smoke

Chris Womersley

Once, when I was about nine years old, I was kicking a football around in the back garden late in the afternoon. I was alone, as usual – or thought I was – and the day was nearly over. It was late autumn. The air was still blue and smoky from the piles of burning leaves in the neighbourhood gutters. Shooting for goal from an impossible angle, my football bounced into a tangle of bushes beside the high wooden fence that bordered our neighbour's house and when I crawled in to retrieve it, I discovered a woman crouching there, damp leaves stuck to her hair like a crown. She clutched her knees, which were bare and knobbly where her dress had ridden up. I was too stunned to say a word.

'You must be Nick,' she said.

I nodded. My scuffed football was just behind her.

'How did you know?' I said when at last I found my voice.

She glanced up at the old house, at the lighted lounge-room window warm as a lozenge in the failing light. Soon one of my sisters would draw the curtains and the house would be absorbed into the falling night, safe and sound against the cold and dark. Realising I was clearly not the sort of child to run screaming upon finding a stranger in his backyard, she took a few seconds to adjust her position, which must have been quite uncomfortable.

'Oh, I know *lots* of interesting things about you.'

I heard Mrs Thomson singing to herself in her kitchen next door, the *chink* of cutlery being taken from a drawer. Having stopped running around, I was getting cold and a graze on my elbow where I had fallen over on the bricks began to sting.

'I know that you love football,' the woman went on, looking around as if assembling the information from the nearby air. 'Aaaaand that you love *Star Wars*, that you've got lots of *Star Wars* toys and things. Little figurines, I guess you'd call them.'

This was true. I'd seen *Star Wars* four times, once with my dad and then with my friend Shaun and then twice at other kids' birthday parties. In addition, I had a book of *Star Wars*, a model of an X-Wing Fighter, comics and several posters on my wall. The distant planet of Tattooine – with its twin suns, where Luke Skywalker had grown up – was more real to me than Darwin or the Amazon.

I inspected the stranger more closely in the fading light. She was pretty, with long hair and freckles across her nose. She wasn't as old as my mum, but maybe a bit older than my teacher at school, Miss Dillinger.

It didn't seem right that this woman was sneaking about in our garden and I was mentally preparing to say something to that effect when she leaned forward, whispering, her red mouth suddenly so close I felt her breath on my ear.

'I *also* know that it was you who broke Mr Miller's window last month.'

A chill seeped through me. Several weeks ago, Shaun and I were hitting a tennis ball around in his grassy garden when we discovered a much more interesting game; by employing the tennis rackets we could launch unripe lemons vast distances. Green lemons the size of golf balls were the best and, if struck correctly, would travel across several houses – maybe even as far as a kilometre, or so we imagined. With no one around – who knew where Shaun's parents were? – we amused ourselves in this fashion until the predictable happened and we heard the smash of a distant window, followed by furious shouting that went on for several minutes. Terrified, we stashed the tennis rackets back in the shed, cleaned up the lemons and scurried inside to watch television and listen out for sirens or the blunt knock of a policeman at the front door. We heard later that the police were indeed summoned, but no one thought to question us about the damage because it happened so far from our houses and who would have dreamed we could throw lemons so far? Nothing was ever proved and he vehemently denied any involvement, but blame was sheeted home to an older kid called Glen Taylor, who lived closer to the Millers and was known to be a troublemaker. Our apparent escape didn't stop me from dwelling on our crime most days and even now, weeks later, the sight of a police car filled me with dread, with terrifying visions of handcuffs and juvenile detention.

The stranger sat back on her haunches, evidently satisfied. I felt the shameful heat of incipient tears. 'Are you the police?'

'Hardly.'

'Then who are you?'

She coughed once into her fist and looked around again, as if she were unsure herself. 'Don't cry,' she said at last. 'It's all right, I won't hurt you. My name is … Anne.'

I wiped my nose. 'But what are you doing hiding in our garden?'

A fresh pause, another glance towards my house. 'I'm not *hiding*, thank you very much. I'm always here.'

'What do you mean?'

'I'm waiting for my turn on the throne.' The woman looked at me again, and it seemed to me her mouth had tightened. 'Princess Anne, waiting to enter the castle as queen at last.'

By now it was almost dark. The woman's dress was indistinguishable from the foliage surrounding us, so that only her pale face was visible, the deep pools of her eyes. She jumped when my mother called out for me to come inside for dinner – looked set to run off, in fact – before relaxing again at the sound of retreating footsteps and the screen door slapping shut.

'Yell out you're coming,' she whispered.

Succumbing to the innate authority adults wield over children, I did as I was told.

'Smells delicious,' she said a few seconds later. 'Like lamb.'

I nodded.

'I hear your mother is a *good little cook*.'

I was suffused with filial pride. 'She is. She makes a beautiful apple crumble, too.'

'Keeps a nice house. Tucks you in, reads you stories, makes *biscuits*.'

My mum didn't make biscuits. The curious woman didn't even seem to be addressing me but, rather, talking out loud to herself.

'That's very nice,' she continued, as if I had agreed with her summation of my mother's housekeeping capabilities. 'Why don't you bring me back some of that lamb later. Wrap a few slices in some wax paper or something. Let me try this famous lamb.'

'I don't know—'

'Go on, be a sport. And one of your father's cigarettes.'

'He gave up.'

The woman sniggered. 'Like hell he did. Look in his study. There's a green volume of Dickens on the top shelf of his bookcase. *Great Expectations*, naturally. It's hollowed out and there's a packet of Marlboros hidden in there. Bring me a couple. Don't forget the matches.'

I didn't ask how she knew this. I had become unaccountably afraid in the past minute or so and stood up as best I could beneath the low branches to leave. At school they advised us not to talk to strangers in the street or at the park, but no one said anything about finding one in your own garden.

'I suppose you want your ball.'

'Yes, please.'

She slung me the football. 'Nice manners. Don't forget to bring me those cigarettes after dinner. I'll be right here.'

'OK.'

'Don't smoke them all yourself, will you, now you know where they're hidden? They're for grown-ups.'

'I don't smoke.'

'Good boy. It was nice meeting you at last. You can't tell anyone you saw me, though. Remember what I know about you and those lemons. A certain broken *window*. Don't want your mum to find out, do you? Or the police. Tell anyone you saw me here and I'll blow your whole house down. Just like whatshername, Princess Leia.'

I didn't bother to correct her version of who Princess Leia was or what she might be capable of and went inside for dinner. Afterwards, when everyone was watching TV, I went into my dad's study and found the cigarettes exactly where she said they were. I stood there a long time staring at them before lifting the packet out of the miniature grave carved into the book. The smell of dry tobacco was both familiar and exotic, full of dark promise. On the calendar stuck on our kitchen wall were marked the months since my father had smoked his last cigarette and the money his hard-won abstinence was saving our family. The ways of adults were as mysterious to me as a forest; they spoke often in their own unintelligible tongue. In the other room my family laughed at *M*A*S*H*, even though they were all repeats.

Without really knowing what I was doing – much less why – I withdrew a cigarette from the packet, put it between my lips and lit it. The flavour was strong and terrible. Smoke wafted into my eyes. My immediate coughing fit brought my two older sisters running to the study doorway, where they stood giggling with disbelief after calling out for our mum.

When she arrived, my mother slapped the cigarette away and demanded to know what the hell I was doing. My father was the last to arrive on the scene and he weathered my mother's tirade with his gaze fixed not on the book with its cigarette packet-shaped hole that my mother brandished at him as evidence of his flagrant dishonesty, but on the curtained window, as if expecting to see something unwelcome step in from outside.

The Big Issue

The Sleepers in That Quiet Earth

Debra Adelaide

'Having formed these beings, she did not know what she had done.'
—CHARLOTTE BRONTË, preface to *Wuthering Heights*, 1850

She had planned the story and already written something that could be an opening chapter. From time to time when ideas came she would write them down in a book her mother had given her. It was not the sort of notebook she would have chosen to write in, not stories anyway, but it happened to be there when she needed it. A spiral-bound notebook, the paper rough and absorbent. The cover was the wrong colour, a fake kind of purple, a purple trying too hard, a purple that didn't even fool small children. She wondered if it was meant to be a children's notebook, if her mother, in her frail condition, had bought it not thinking about it as much as she normally would. The cardboard cover felt like plastic. Her fountain pen would not work on the paper. She would write the story on her laptop computer.

But the purple notebook contained a list of recent contact details, and Dove had brought it into bed with her one evening along with the phone. She reached for the notebook early the next morning. She had had a restless night and had woken several times, then again before five. For ten minutes or so she lay there, seeing the story in her head, the story she would write, she could write, when she had emptied her mind: that day's work, then the bills and emails that needed attending to, calls she would have to make before the end of the day. Her mother's case-worker had left three messages, of increasing frustration and, she suspected, hostility.

Yet her mind seemed unusually focused on the story already. She wrote down the ideas that had awoken her, then showered and dressed, but she continued to see it unfolding. Unlike in a dream, she could see details of the clothes upon her character, the colours of the houses and the lawns that she was passing, then the bus that she was riding and where she sat on it, three seats behind two women with rose-tinted hair and string shopping bags. The bus was almost empty.

As Dove made her breakfast and put a load in the washing machine, she continued to see her character and hear her voice. The cat butted at her ankles, wailing. She bent down to the floor with its bowl. 'Here you go, puss cat.' She rarely used its name. The cat pushed its face into the biscuits and Dove ran her hand along its back. It could eat and purr at the same time, or maybe that was growl. Dove had little affection for it, and even less knowledge of cats, but it had had nowhere else to go. The mewling wail barely abated as it chewed its food then sat to lick its chest. But even the cat could not block out the sound of her own story in her ears as she tidied her breakfast things and went to the bathroom.

'See you, puss.' By the time she grabbed her bag and keys and shut the front door, the whole story was clear already, again, clearer than a dream. She even knew the weather that day, could see the sky with its shredded-tissue clouds, on that warm day in the suburbs. It was mid-morning, a Tuesday. Her character's name, Ellis, was unusual for a woman.

*

Ellis was visiting her father, in his home in Ashfield. Riding the bus, Ellis thought about the names of these suburbs, on this summer's day when men like her father were busy in their gardens. Ashfield, Haberfield, Strathfield. She thought, as she pushed open the window of the bus to let in more air, how odd a name like Ashfield was, how the negative connotation of the first syllable contrasted with the romantic one of the last. How the place was, in its orderly suburban way, filled with houses and parks, cabbage tree palms and eucalypts and camphor laurels – so unlike that of an ashy field – but that once it must have been something like a wasteland, to gain the name. On this particular day the air smelled like a field, a great one, of hay perhaps, or wheat, recently mown. As if all its men had conspired to cut their front lawns that morning, infusing the warm air with the smell of freshly sliced grass, which Ellis breathed in as she pushed her face up to the window of the bus. She wondered if the inhabitants of Ashfield, so comfortable and untroubled, ever thought the name, Ashfield, was odd, discordant.

It was a slow journey, but once they had turned off Parramatta Road, she didn't mind. At this time it was a pleasant way to travel, if one were not in a hurry, though at other times the buses could be frustrating. Into town, for instance, where the journey past Railway Square and down George Street was always slow. She had not yet learned to drive, although she thought she would. Vince had urged it, especially now, but she had not been keen for her husband to teach her. She suspected that his amiable nature would change once she slid behind the wheel of his Valiant. Her father, who rarely went out these days but who held strong opinions, thought Annandale where she and Vince lived a lowly, seedy suburb with too many migrants and not enough footpaths, and that if she at least drove she could get away more. But Ellis's father had never gone all the way down to the waterside and seen the gardens, the massive homes on the escarpment, and experienced the grandeur of the place. He equated Annandale with the grimy strip of shops on Parramatta Road, the crowded terraces closer to Glebe, the motor workshop on the main road where Vince worked. Ellis suspected he had never dwelt on the name, Annandale.

*

Dove did not know why her character's name was Ellis, but as she saw her alight that bus, at the stop before the gate of her father's house, she knew without any doubt that this was her name. Lately she had been reading *Wuthering Heights*. It was possible that the name Ellis Bell had stuck in her mind, although every way she examined it, she could find no connection between her character, a young woman in suburban Sydney some time in the late 1960s, and that of the novel or its author or the author's pseudonym. She was only aware that she liked names commencing with E and with the El sound especially. They seemed natural, mellifluous (a mellifluous word, itself) and rolled pleasingly across the tongue and out the lips. Eliza, Ellis, Ellen, Elizabeth, Eleanor. If she were going to have a character in a novel – and it seemed that this might be the case – she would want to utter that character's name over and over, at least in her mind, and roll it around, easy and smooth, a sweet lozenge.

At what point she knew that Ellis had a baby she could not say. But the baby must have been there all along. Reviewing the scenes she had already visualised – it was like pausing and replaying a film in her head – Dove now saw Ellis well before she reached the bus stop where she would alight. She saw her shifting the baby on her lap. The rose-tinted elderly women had cooed at him as Ellis had boarded and made her way past them to her seat. But after she had passed them, what Ellis did not see, preoccupied with propping the collapsible pram against her seat so it would not roll away, and settling the baby in her lap, was these two women whispering something disapproving about babies needing to wear more than singlets even if the weather was warm. One of them remarked on the absence of his sunhat, but Ellis had removed this and placed it in her shoulder bag before boarding the bus, since he was prone to flinging it off. Her father had given her the hat, and she would place it on the baby's head again before she walked through her father's front gate. It would make him glad to see his grandson wearing it. He was so very happy to have a grandson.

*

During her lunch break, Dove phoned her mother's caseworker, then the hospital ward manager, and finally the care facility ten minutes' drive from her home. She had been ringing every day lately.

'Good news,' said the Grange's residential services officer. 'We can take your mother soon. Possibly even next Monday.'

If there are no further hitches, Dove thought. Instead she said, 'Wonderful. I've been waiting for ages. We've been waiting.' Then, in case this was construed as a complaint of sorts, 'It's such a relief. Mum will be so much better off with you.'

She tried not to think about why the room, which last week was only a possibility, was now available.

'And,' he said, with finality, 'we won't be able to … accommodate any other changes. Again.'

'I realise that,' Dove said. She would try and discuss it tonight, though her mother could only speak with great effort, rationing her words out one or two at a time. Her lucid periods were mainly in the early evenings. A month or so ago she had breathed the words, 'Nursing home, Dove. Less trouble,' into her daughter's ear and reached for her hand and pressed it. Dove had spent considerable time at work on the phone, and later at home in the evenings sending emails. Except on the designated day of the move, having taken the morning off work, she had arrived at the hospital to find her mother sitting up in bed, preternaturally alert.

'I'm going back home,' she had declared with unusual clarity.

'Mum, you can't …'

'Viv will be missing me.'

'But the Grange, they're expecting you. It's all arranged.'

Her mother had stared as if she'd never heard of such a place.

'He needs me,' she said.

Dove had folded her lips together then and not reminded her mother that the cat had not lived there for two months, that her flat was on the second floor, and that managing stairs had long been out of the question. Instead she had sat down and rearranged the reading glasses and tube of hand cream on the bedside table, until her mother lay back on her pillows and closed her eyes. Her mother had spoken three languages and played principal violin with a symphony orchestra. She had given music lessons and translated documents to put her daughter through university. Dove placed her hand on her mother's cheek, kissed her on the nose and returned to work.

Now as she put down the phone she hoped the arrangements would not be undone again. Perhaps she should visit straight from work. It would mean not getting home until after seven and by then the cat would be hysterical. It was slight and fussy and had cost her mother a small fortune over the years in vet's fees. How long did Burmese cats live? She had thought about smuggling it into the hospital but had visions of it leaping out of its basket and running through the wards, the kitchens, snarling in some corner of a closet, or worse, an operating theatre, bright and sterile, ready for surgery.

But then, it was possible the cat would snuggle into her mother's neck, as it had every night of its life, and sleep. And her mother might relax, without her medication, sleep more deeply, or for longer. Or forever. Dove wondered if the prospect she had had in her mind from time to time, of the two sleepers together, slipping quietly into death, was such a bad thing. The cat was stricken enough as it was. When she had first grabbed it at her mother's place, the day she had arrived, it had wailed and scratched her. Her mother had been lying on the kitchen floor since the night before, unable to move. Dove didn't want to think of the cat leaping across her mother's legs and kneading her chest in its anguish. Her mother had still been playing the violin when she bought the cat. She would remark on the cat's peculiar attentiveness. 'If cats could play a musical instrument,' she once said, 'it would be the violin.'

Tonight, they might have a conversation of sorts. Her mother might ask about her writing. But probably Dove would just read to her again. At first she wasn't sure if her mother was necessarily paying attention, or even enjoying being read to, but she never complained and was always quiet. Sometimes she lay there awake, saying nothing at all, and Dove would put the book down, say goodbye and leave as her mother stared into a distance no one else could see. And sometimes she simply closed her eyes and drifted into sleep.

*

Dove was surprised to discover her character was so stable and dependable. Ellis had developed into a good wife, a fond mother, a devoted daughter. There was no evidence of the sadness of her early years, of the great hole in her life. At sixteen, she had returned to Ashfield from boarding school and gone to secretarial college. It was when she commenced working in the garage on Parramatta Road, typing invoices and managing orders, that she had met Vince. She took another stenography course at night school and had just completed it when she became pregnant. Dove suspected Ellis was a little too dependable, and wondered if she was even boring or unexciting. But then she knew about Ellis's deep and terrible fears. Sometimes these fears manifested themselves in dreams so strong they woke Ellis, and she would sit up in bed sweating and clutching her chest. Or worse, so strong that she did not wake even though she struggled violently to do so. Many of these dreams were about entrapment. Ellis would cry with all the might of her chest to be let out of some dark and stifling place but her cries were mute, her struggles impotent. Though if Vince had woken and watched her as she slept beside him dreaming these terrifying dreams, he would have thought her sleep was benign, as peaceful as the slumbers of the dead in the quiet earth.

One of these recurring dreams involved Ellis on a hospital bed in an operating theatre. She was anaesthetised to the point where she was incapable of making a sound or a movement and yet her mind was awake and alert and she knew that the operation about to be performed was all wrong, that her organs were perfectly healthy, and that the doctors had to stop. Stop, stop, stop. She always tried to yell this, tried to claw her way through the fog of the anaesthetic, but there were no exclamation marks in her speech. She mouthed the words and there was no noise. She tried to lift her arms and form fists but could only look at her hands lying useless and heavy like sandbags on either side of her body. Although she was surrounded by lights and covered in sheets she felt as if she had been nailed into a coffin and lowered into the ground. She wept dry, unformed tears as she realised how she was only going to sink back into the fate of being sliced open and violated, and how no one would hear her, and no one would ever know. The unfairness of it. And they would never know how hard she had fought to stay alive.

*

Dove sat upright in bed as she held her hands out to Ellis and lifted her free of the dream, just in time. She herself was sweating, almost gasping with the effort. The cat was pinning down the bed covers. She nudged it aside and got out of bed. It was the early morning, when dreams were at their most powerful. She had never felt more connected to someone, more concerned on their behalf, and yet Ellis was only a character, in a story that had barely begun to be written. The cat followed her as she went down to the kitchen for a glass of water. Standing at the sink, she felt a strange urge to get dressed and drive to the hospital. At four a.m. no one would notice or care if she slipped in. She could perhaps take the cat. If her mother was asleep she could just sit there and read.

They had chosen *Wuthering Heights* because it was shorter than *Jane Eyre*. She had read the novel, several times, but as Dove sat beside her mother's hospital bed in the evenings or on a Sunday afternoon, she had begun to entertain doubts about this. The story was far more complex and surprising than she had imagined. She was not sure if her mother had taken any of it in, but she had lain there for a half or an entire hour, day after day, as Dove read, neither objecting nor expressing interest in the story. Sometimes she fell asleep and Dove would keep reading aloud until the end of a chapter. On the following visit, her mother would murmur assent if Dove offered to read, and if she suggested something else would just shake her head and almost smile.

*

As she thought about it more, she became aware that she had not so much dreamed this character with the curious name Ellis, as rescued her from the soil of her imagination. Ellis Bell – the name ringing, alive with possibilities – was on the 1847 facsimile title page of the novel, reproduced in her Penguin English Library edition. It was there in the biographical notice by the author's sister Charlotte, also included in her paperback edition and marked in her own hand, proof that she had indeed read it, and read it attentively, even though she seemed to remember a different novel altogether. And the more she considered it, the more she felt she had read the name Ellis often enough so that it lodged in her mind like a speck of grit, eventually turning into something hard and polished.

Except her character was nothing like a pearl, waiting to be plucked from its shell. Ellis was unformed, limp. She was more like an abandoned creature that Dove had found somewhere, beside a remote road, leading nowhere. Sometimes, she would lie half awake in the early mornings, feeling the cold autumn air, listening to the clock's gentle pip pip pipping, the alarm set for six-thirty, and think of this character whom she may have dreamed up, or who may have been someone she knew, from her past, but had forgotten, or had met once, on a bus or in a shop somewhere, or was somehow connected with a novel written over a hundred and fifty years ago.

She dragged this mute creature back into being, and it was a physical effort, as hard as pulling oneself awake when one knows one is not yet there at the crack of wakefulness. It was like dragging her out of the ground itself, the soil clinging to her, damp and cold. She sat her there, in a ditch, and watched the rise and fall of her chest, and knew she would live. It was half light, barely dawn. Why had she been beside the road? Had she fallen, or been pushed from a vehicle? There was nothing else about, no cars, no people, no buildings. There was not even a sound, nor any trees. The road emerged from a scrubby background and curved to the same drab vanishing point. Ellis was clad in ordinary clothes, pedal pushers and a boat-neck knit sweater, striped orange and cream. Her hair was half across her face, tangled and dirty, but recognisable as a pageboy style. It was reddish brown. But her body was half coated in black soil and her legs were oddly straight from being dragged into the light, her bare feet – her shoes were lost – pointing back towards the ditch, and rolling beyond it the landscape disappearing in a black-green cloud.

But even as Dove dragged her from the oblivion of total unconsciousness, as she heaved and struggled and swore for those last crucial metres in order to get the limp form away from where the cold earth and the dark scrub conspired to hold Ellis back, she was also seeing Ellis, in the story in her mind, in another place altogether. In the suburbs, in fact, in Ashfield, juggling her baby and stroller on that bus. It was rerunning in her mind but it was not the same scene replayed, rather the same scene viewed from a different angle, and she noted new things: Ellis holding out a coin, the driver jerking the bus away from the stop, Ellis careful not to fall, sliding into the red seat halfway along, on the left, the baby on her lap. He was called Charlie. The women three seats in front, having discussed the absence of his sunhat with muted disapproval, were now holding their heads up high, gazing this way and that in the anxious manner of old people, looking out for their stop at the corner store.

Then Ellis was walking down that street in Ashfield. It was wide, lined with cabbage-tree palms. She was walking along the warm concrete footpath, smelling again the scent of grass and of dust, of boiled onion and meat dinners, from the houses that she passed. Brick homes, most of them, neat, silent and unwelcoming, their front gardens fenced, with hydrangeas, lassiandra and plumbago – why were the flowers all blue and purple? – her father's place no exception.

She had reached the front gate, she was through it, and had then turned to push it shut, listening for the latch's oiled snick on the green wire gate, before walking up the path when Dove realised Ellis had forgotten to replace Charlie's sunhat as she had meant to before she met her father, and there was nothing she could do about it.

*

The images in her head refused to emerge from the pages. Cathy racing barefoot across the moors. Heathcliff beside her, both yelling with delight. *Wuthering Heights* was not about wild free childhood at all. It was barely even Cathy's story. Instead it was the story of a servant, the housekeeper, the only one of her generation to survive. It was orderly, controlled, quiet. The novel had been swept and folded and locked. All the interesting, passionate characters were dead and buried before their time.

How had this happened? How had its author, Emily Jane Brontë – Ellis Bell – so independent and stubborn, let this maddening, self-righteous housekeeper, this character who pretended to be much older than she was, steal the narrative like that? Dove recalled wisps of stories about the author of *Wuthering Heights*. Her potent imaginary world. How she refused social obligations. The visions she saw on the moors behind the parsonage at Haworth. How she once took a poker from the fire and scorched the bite of a rabid dog on her forearm. Her refusal to accept medical attention until the hour before her death. *You can send for a doctor if you like.* How she then turned her face to the wall and closed her eyes forever.

As Dove read the final chapter, where a woman sat in the kitchen sewing while her young charges played with words in books, she marvelled at its author. Emily Brontë had been braver than anything. She had permitted her story to be rewritten. She had abandoned it to the control of its readers. Although she conceived it, wrote it, published it – with a dodgy publisher, against the advice of her sister Charlotte – she had then let it go, entirely. It was no longer her story. She had created a magnificent illusion. Dove thought about why she had never realised this before, and why her reading of the novel was now so different.

'"… and wondered,"' Dove read, '"how anyone could ever imagine unquiet slumbers, for the sleepers in that quiet earth."'

She closed the book and stared at her mother, whose eyes were shut. It was so simple, but it did not occur to her until she was placing the book in her bag to take home. It was not just that she had read the novel at the bedside of her dying mother. She had, for the first time, spoken the words aloud.

*

When she abandoned the purple notebook and began to steal a half hour in the morning before work, or ate instant noodles at the computer in the evening, she wrote with a sense of compulsion, almost peril. She dreaded interruption. The phone would ring. Someone might knock on the door. She feared the story would slither off and disappear like a snake into the bush. Or that she might just grab it by its tail and pick it up only to see it transform into something quite unlike the story that had brought her awake those weeks back, awake with such clarity and urgency that she had reached for the notebook and scribbled pages of draft scenes before getting out of bed.

As her mother began to be less agitated, more compliant, the phone calls, the meetings, the arrangements, began to dwindle. Dove rang the Grange for the last time.

'I'm sorry,' and even as she said it she wondered why she was apologising. 'But my mother won't be leaving the neurological ward.'

The residential services officer cancelled the booking with cool efficiency.

'We can refund your interim deposit,' he said, making it seem like a very special favour when Dove knew the waiting list was long. 'But you'll need to invoice us.'

Back in the hospital, the staff began answering her questions with increasing vagueness. The evening nurse smiled and said, 'Your mother isn't suffering. Don't worry, we're monitoring her every day.'

Dove asked the resident outright, 'Will she die soon?'

The resident cocked her head and shifted her folder to another arm. 'The important thing is that she's remaining stable. And we're doing all we can to keep her comfortable.'

And Dove had to concur. Her mother was at peace, lying back on clean linen, her white hair, her white skin, smoothed and thin, exposing the bones of her face. Sometimes she would accept a few mouthfuls of soup or ice cream, a cup of tea. Other times she wanted nothing, waved her daughter away, her hand stiff like a dry leaf.

Dove had by then written enough of her story to begin revising it, and so she sat beside her mother's bed with her laptop. A structure emerged. As she worked she learned to block out the noises of the hospital. And she began to understand how to suspend work, quickly if necessary, hitting the save key and closing the computer if her mother called out, or if one of the nurses came by. She began to trust that the story would stay with her, and that her character, if she were strong enough, would remain in her imagination. And it was true that just as Ellis had lain on the earth choking for air, her breathing becoming less ragged, more regular, and as she had surmounted the ordeal of the nightmare operation, she would survive being tucked into a corner of Dove's life as she waited at the bedside of her dying mother.

Now that Ellis continued to live in the story that was still being written Dove wondered at her fluidity, how she could be there in the ditch in the growing dawn, gasping and leaning on her elbows, struggling to sit up, crushed and exhausted yet clearly, undeniably, alive, and yet at the same time be walking to her father's house. Her mother coughed softly beside her.

As she saw Ellis at that gate, Dove wondered why she was even making this visit at all but, having watched her place Charlie on the path where he would take his first unassisted baby steps and then hold her hand out and take him further up to the front door, which was now being opened by her father – who was saying 'Hi-dee-hi' as he had for as long as Ellis could remember – she knew why Ellis was here, on the same day each week that she always visited. She knew that knowing this could be painful, and that she would have to be brave with her story just as Emily Brontë had been brave, and follow it where it had to go and then let it run ahead of her, alone. Ellis was here because her own mother was not and had not been for a long time, not since she was a baby. Dove finally understood this, and she typed this in between paragraphs, just a note in case she forgot, as her mother began to cough slightly again, a noise more like a groan. And now that Ellis was a parent, she came to prepare meals and clean the house for her father, with his only grandson. Charlie was beaming, arms out, tightrope walking, wobbling as he stepped forward, once, twice, three times, as Ellis laughed, reached out and grabbed him just in time before he fell and swung him up to her delighted father on the front step. Dove's mother coughed once more. She wished she had brought the cat in after all.

Everybody Wins on Kid Planet

Nick Smith

When Dad asks my nine-year-old cousin, Scott, how he's going to reimburse him for the seven-dollar-fifty entry fee to Kid Planet, I know things are getting out of hand. A mother behind us, waiting to pay for three blond kids, laughs. When Dad doesn't laugh, she keeps laughing, but nervously. And then Dad does laugh because he knows how he sometimes appears to other people. And then they laugh together.

Ha ha ha.

I join in and then the kids join in too. All except for Scott, who is wondering where he is going to find seven bucks fifty because this is no joke.

Scott is a stoic boy who knows he should be above the juvenile pleasures of Kid Planet, the gaudy plastic jungle gyms with tube slides entwined DNA-style, the jumping castles, the crash mats and the endless white nets, enough to trap a hundred baby animals. But he isn't. I can see the ticking muscles under his skin, the eagerness to walk quickly across the mopped lino floor and be lost in childhood again.

Later I will lend him the money. I like things to be sweet.

*

Kid Planet takes its commitment to international peace and harmony very seriously. In the Kid Planet brochure – which I once found under an empty lunch box on the footpath – it says that

Kid Planet is 'serious about creating a positive learning environment which promotes a respect for the earth and all the peoples who live on it, regardless of their colour or beliefs.'

I guess it's intended as some kind of a pitch to middle-class parents who take their kids there so they – the parents, not the kids – can tune out over a magazine and a muggacino. They're encouraged to believe this place is educational. Better than TV, at any rate, which it certainly is.

On the walls are words like 'Happiness,' 'Joy' and 'Peace' in a variety of languages.

Szép napot!

Which is Hungarian for 'Have a nice day!' That's the benefit of a half-finished university education for you.

There are a few thin brown sticks that make a rough fence, which is supposed to be an African village. And there's a section of castle wall in giant primary-colour bricks that hints at the Great Wall of China.

Inside one of the jungle gyms there are six 'people of the world' as life-size plush cushions. You can stand them up or lie them down. Or run into them and knock them down. I did this once.

One is Chinese. Or maybe Japanese. One is German with lederhosen. Another is Mexican with a wide sombrero, even wider than its outstretched arms, always looking for a hug. One is African. The other two are random Southern Europeans. Maybe Italian, maybe Spanish or Greek. It's unclear whether they're men or women, all so much sexless velour.

Dad is annoyed that none of them is 'Australian' or 'even white, really, except for the Kraut.' I don't think Dad has much of a commitment to respecting the earth and the peoples that live on it. I could go on but I don't like to make a fuss.

*

I'm smooth. I'm so smooth I don't need to wear socks on the big slide.

To go on the big slide you need to either be a kid or have a kid on your lap. Or maybe be demonstrating to a kid that he or she won't break any limbs. Anyway, you need to have a kid nearby otherwise you're being a *bad grown-up* or worse, in my view, a sneering teenager who is ruining the fun for everyone. So if I use the slide without good reason – say, being able to show Scott that he has nothing to fear – I'm kind of midway between both kinds of undesirable.

Dad, I think, could be a *very* bad grown-up if he were at all inclined to use the equipment, but he's not.

Scott is too old to feel physical fear in Kid Planet and too old even to use the slide except as a nostalgic gesture at the end of any visit. So I almost never get the excuse to use it and show off my smoothness.

But sometimes, just sometimes, I've seen my chance and dashed up there to beat Scott to a place at the top of the slide.

'Look, Scott, there's nothing to worry about,' I've said to him patiently. 'It can't hurt you. Just keep your legs straight and your arms tucked at your sides, like this.' And then I've slipped down, so smooth, demonstrating beautifully.

Sometimes Scott has ignored me and gone down a different slide and sometimes he has stalked away in disgust, walking back down the stairs, going past all the little kids climbing in the opposite direction. But this is OK, preferable even.

Hey, I've shrugged, to anyone watching me at the bottom of the slide. *Hey, I tried, but the kid was just too scared. Even though he's nearly ten!*

This is what he has sometimes hissed at me at the top of the slide. *Cut it out! I'm nearly ten!*

Well, hell, I'm twenty and what's more I'm paying your entry fee. This is what I will say to him if I get a chance on the slide today. Or maybe I'll just think it as I slip on down.

So smooth.

*

You can tell that Scott never learns anything because he begs my father for two bucks to play Everybody Wins.

One, my Dad is thinking, *you already owe me seven bucks fifty. Why would I give you another two dollars? And two, Everybody Wins is the worst rip-off ever.* Everybody loses but the house, as my Dad calls it.

It's a large glass box with two claws manipulated by a single joystick. One side is soft toys, the other side is sweets. It's called

Everybody Wins because if your claw comes up empty from the crawling heap of velour creatures, then you get a chance (or six chances!) with the other claw in the sweets. You're pretty well guaranteed to get some lollies but they're cheap no-names from some Asian sweatshop with more sweat than sugar.

Dad tried once to get a purple gorilla for me. He had two tries but each time the steel hooks just slipped out from under the gorilla's toy bulk. Dad banged the glass with an open palm. *What the fuck!*

He's been contemptuous of Everybody Wins ever since. If he walks past it, he can't help but sneer at it and maybe give it a discreet kick on his way through.

'Let me give you a lesson for free,' he says to me and Scott. 'Nobody wins. Ever. Full stop. And that's the most you'll ever get in life for nothing.'

Scott and I nod when he says this. It sounds like the kind of world-weary adult wisdom that should be nodded at, about the only thing the next generation can learn from an adult like my father.

*

Scott is not a big kid, short for his age but wiry. He can't quite reach the flying fox that passes over the little valley where the six plush people of the world reside.

It's sad and funny to see him trying to jump up to catch the handle. Dad encourages him to tip over the plush Chinese person and stand on its face to give him a bit of extra height.

'Go on, stand on chinky, you won't hurt him.'

There's a young Asian mother searching for two small children temporarily lost in a sea of coloured balls. I think she's Korean because she's wearing a T-shirt that says 'Korea!!' like it's a swear word. She stares hard at my father until she is distracted by a hand that suddenly thrusts up out of the spheres.

The Korean mother pulls her child gasping from the plastic ocean as Scott careens off the supine Chinaman and through the valley, knocking down the plush Spaniard on the way.

'Huh,' my dad says with satisfaction. Job well done. Uncle duties accomplished, he turns away and heads back to his cooling flat white. In a moment of madness, he elected to have skim milk and is still paying the price. I see him grimace when he sips.

*

Dad is still grimacing later when he comes back from the toilet. The two Korean kids, now on dry land again, are staring at the mound of toys in Everybody Wins, their noses pressed against the glass, nostrils vast and cavernous.

Eventually their mother is prevailed upon to feed coins into its steel belly and wrestle with the joystick. Twice she tries and twice she fails. My dad is lounging against a pillar with his arms crossed, taking in the action. His face has transformed from a scowl to a knowing smirk.

He shakes his head in mock disgust as the mother hauls her kids away, one of whom, the youngest, has begun to cry. They've set their little hearts on a seven-legged green octopus wearing a white sailor's cap.

Dad looks at me as if to say: *You see?*

*

When Dad is down the other end of Kid Planet with his newspaper and a fresh coffee – and he says he is not an optimist – I take my chance at glory. The twenty dollars I was going to make last the whole weekend I convert into tiny golden two-dollar coins. It seems a generous exchange, a piece of paper for all that weight and solidity.

I walk over to the machine and begin. One dollar for one go. Two dollars for two goes. Value!

Coins come and coins go. Again and again, the steel claws grasp at the velour mollusc only to slip away at the last moment. It would be easier, I think, to catch a real green octopus from the real green ocean.

A small crowd forms around me, kids and parents admiring my pluck, groaning in disappointment at each fresh failure or grinning discreetly as another coin is lost. My father is happily still engaged in his paper but I am worried to see, between claw manipulations, that the Korean family is packing up.

I'm doing this for you, I think, *and you won't even be here!* But luckily they're taking their sweet time and the kids are diving back into the equipment, requiring a new recovery mission every few minutes.

And then I'm down to my last two dollars. I knew it would come to this. Winning the prize at the last minute, as all hope seems lost. I wipe my brow and blink my eyes to clear them.

'OK,' I say out loud. 'OK, this time.' I have learnt much in my previous attempts. The joystick is like an old friend's hand in mine and I guide the claw sweetly to the octopus's garden. It drops sharply on the toy's body in just the spot I was aiming for, its three prongs arranged neatly on key pressure points. I press the button and it draws in, locking on the green abdomen and raising the octopus into the air.

The octopus rises, further and higher than ever before, up out of the sea of its mates and towards the steel bin and freedom. I am holding my breath. The crowd is holding its breath.

And then it slips. The creature slips back to the mound. There is a collective gasp of horror. Or it could have been just me. I can't tell.

I have my final turn but my hands are shaking now and the joystick is laughing at me. This time, the drop is not even close. I am finished.

My father is still reading the paper and I am so glad he is not here to see this, his spectacular vindication. The little crowd is beginning to drift away and I can see the Korean family finally making progress towards this end of the hall. My father looks up from his newspaper, sensing some kind of electrical charge around him. He sniffs the air like a wild animal.

The dream, the beautiful dream, is over. But then there is a voice in my ear.

'Here you go, son, try again.' A strange man, older than my father, grey and thin, wearing a black tracksuit, is at my side and pressing a two-dollar coin into my hand. Before he can change his mind, I have slipped it into the machine and I flash him a quick smile of 'Thank you' before again taking the joystick.

This time, everything is different. It's like I'm not even running things, simply that something has changed inside the machine and it now wants to divulge its treasures. The octopus practically leaps into the claw, gluing itself there with nothing but hope and static electricity.

The creature drops into the steel bin and I whip it out just as the Korean family is passing.

'Wait!' I say, loudly so that they stop, so that my father looks up again. 'Wait. You might want *this*.' The parents look at me strangely but the youngest child lights up and grabs the octopus from me, squirming with joy.

I nod at the parents. No need to thank me. They don't and walk away but the child stares back at me the whole time.

And then my father is by my side, looking at me weirdly, taking in the Korean kid, the octopus, my cocky stance next to the machine, taking it all in. Scott is there too, grinning madly. In your face, Uncle.

'So, Scott,' my Dad says, 'how are you going to pay me the seven-fifty you owe me to get in here?'

'I – I, um. He was going to lend me the money,' Scott says, pointing at me.

Dad turns to me, holds out one palm.

'Seven-fifty.'

I put my hand in my pocket before realising that I have nothing left. 'You see, son, even when you win, you lose. Now,' he says, turning back to Scott and placing one hand on his shoulder, 'now, let's talk about interest.'

fourW

The Road to Nowhere

Russell King

Pat and Ray were arguing about their names.

'It stands to reason,' said Ray, his hands firmly at ten to two, high up in the cab of the Willebago Esperance, 'we'll be meeting a lot of folk on the road and it's confusing.'

He was imagining the introductions around the evening barbeque with retired real-estate developers and superannuated stock traders, and the ambiguity of their genderless first names.

'All I'm asking,' he said, 'is that for the next three months you become Trisha.'

Ray decided he liked looking down on the other vehicles from the comfort of his padded throne. As they edged north out of Sydney a youth in the rear of the Nissan Skyline in front was removing his socks. Ray looked away.

'I knew a Trisha once,' said Pat, 'in my aqua aerobics class at Arncliffe Aquatic Centre. Couldn't stand her. I'd swear she did botox. Lips were what kept her afloat.'

'You don't "do" botox,' said Ray. 'It's not illegal.'

'She was so into herself,' said Pat, one foot on the dashboard as she touched up her nail polish. Not an easy task given the stop–start motion of the Willebago. Vixen was her new colour: a pink-purple compromise.

'Careful where you put that stuff.' Ray eyed the pristine interior, leather seats, twelve-stacker sound system with iPod accessories and the bottle of Vixen.

He checked the mirror, saw the sumptuous living space behind and ran a hand through his still-abundant salt and pepper hair. More pepper than salt these days, thanks to his new hairdresser. The tag of 'grey nomads' seriously rankled. He wore his new short-sleeved Nautilus shirt, cream knee-length shorts by Blazer and deck shoes by Colorado. Sockless, of course. Felt good.

'Why can't I stay as Pat and you become Raymondo?' she giggled, replacing the lid. The cab now stank of sickly acetate so Ray increased the fan speed on the light-touch climate control. Diesel fumes from the semitrailer two metres in front belched into the vehicle.

*

Ray had stuck the Australian Geographic 'Map for Explorers and Adventurers' on the kitchen wall six months ago. Two years' worth of issues still in their plastic jackets were stowed under a seat in the rear. Dick Smith was his hero. Not that his knowledge of Mr Smith extended past a face on the peanut-butter jar and a vague notion about ballooning, but he felt fellow explorers and adventurers would share his admiration.

Pat was busying herself trying to find the music folder on the iPod. They'd met a year ago when she arrived as a temporary receptionist at McLeod and McLeod, Distributors of Distinction. Plump and fifty, her husband had left her for his personal trainer, as men of that age seemed to do. She was the worst temp they'd ever employed and on her first day Ray showed her how to use the fax. Eight months later she'd moved in. Needs must.

'How'd you fancy the Bee Gees?' she said. 'Stayin' Alive' was her favourite track of all time.

They'd meticulously packed the motorhome ('Motorhome, Pat. Not van.') over many weeks and affixed stickers to the rear.

'Home is where you take it!' was hers. 'Spending the kids' inheritance!' was his. The fact that Pat had no children ('women's problems') and his only daughter was a corporate lawyer earning three times his salary didn't seem to spoil the joke.

Pat settled on Fleetwood Mac and sang along to 'Don't Stop Thinkin' 'bout Tomorrow' while Ray worked the clutch brake cycle in the traffic morass.

'Thing is,' said Pat, 'you don't really think about tomorrow until something really bad happens, like when they told me about the warning cells on my pap smear.'

'Too much information, Pat,' said Ray.

His last visit to the doctor had been to have the papers signed so he could access his superannuation early. And now here he was driving it around Australia!

He'd found Dr Vitenko in a 24-hour medical centre at Bondi Junction. A certificate from the University of Kiev hung on the wall. Ray had purposely worn jeans and sneakers but kept his Rolex on. He wanted to create the impression of a senior exec who had succumbed to ill health. Not that it was a real Rolex, of course, but who was going to take it off his wrist to check?

Ray explained about his debilitating reflux, his intolerance to rich foods and how it had impacted on his ability to function as a top-level middle manager.

Dr Vitenko ticked the box 'Unable to work in gainful employment now or in the foreseeable future.' Underneath he wrote, 'Severe ulcerating reflux oesophagitis.' No fools, these Bulgarian doctors.

'Nice watch,' Dr Vitenko had said. 'I buy three the same last year in the market at Sevastopol.'

*

At six p.m. they finally turned off the Pacific Highway at Nambucca Heads. Not as far as planned, true, but hey, they were free agents.

It was a humid late November evening and a banner in the main street welcomed schoolies week with the puzzling message, 'Have fun! Don't become a statistic!'

They eventually found a park without an illuminated 'No Vacancy' sign and turned into the Bali-Hi Van Park and Resort.

'Jesus. Enough tents here to house the Russian army,' said Ray.

'I just think it's lovely to see so many young people having a good time,' said Pat.

The owner, with a complexion of weathered hardwood, directed them through a maze of tents to a piece of worn turf at the back of the ground.

Perhaps it was a blessing he hadn't been able to run to the eight-metre Esperance, settling instead for the slightly inferior

7.2-metre. Still, it featured the toothbrush and toilet-roll holders Ray envisaged showing fellow travellers at a more salubrious location.

Pat unfolded two chairs and a table.

'Bickies, dip and wine time. Best part of the day!' she said like the seasoned camper she wasn't.

Ray headed off to find the barbeque. He had just finished scraping some unidentifiable goo from the hotplate when a man of similar age ambled over carrying sausages. This was more like it.

'Been far today?' said Ray. 'Mine's the Willebago Esperance up the back.'

'No, mate. Shirl and I live 'ere. In the donga, down the front.'

Ray didn't stop to talk about Dick Smith. He carried the steaks and lamb-with-thyme gourmet sausages back to the site, noting with irritation the grease marks on his shorts.

Pat was inside tossing a salad – out of a packet into a Tupperware container. Pages of her *Hello!* magazine flapped in the breeze that had suddenly come up.

'Trisha!' he called too loudly. '*Bon appétit!*'

*

Ray awoke at one a.m., his body bombarded with a cacophony of sound. Rain was drumming on the metal roof of the cab about eight inches from his pillow. The motorhome chassis was vibrating to the sounds of dance music.

'What the hell?' he thought, climbing down from the bunk to find his clothes. Pat lay on her back, fast asleep, snoring gently.

When he opened the door, rain was coming down in oversized sheets. Nobody else in the whole campsite apart from Pat appeared to be asleep. Music thudded; there were lecherous screams; torch beams scanned across the night sky. Somewhere a glass broke, followed by laughter, and from a nearby tent the unmentionable sounds of two young people getting to know each other.

'It's like bloody Woodstock,' he muttered as he trudged off, mud caking his Colorados, to find the owner.

At nine a.m. two pimply youths helped tow the Willebago from where it had become stuck in the mud using their P-plated bomb and the towrope he had been keeping for the croc-infested waters of Far North Queensland.

'I could drive,' said Pat.

More chance of her being allowed to cook steak on the barbie than sitting behind the wheel. Ray said nothing and swung out of the campground at a pace some may have considered reckless.

And as he did the corner of a tile overhanging the roof of reception caught the side of the Willebago, ripping along its length like an old-fashioned can opener.

*

The owner said he'd seen it happen before.

'Young couple from South Australia. Same thing exactly. Apparently insurance wouldn't pay as it happened off-road.'

Pat and Ray didn't speak until they were back in Rockdale. Ray seethed in apoplectic rage while Pat stared out the window. He dropped the Willebago off at the panel beaters and they took a cab home. He'd be damned if he was going to let the neighbours gloat. He'd tell them they'd returned early because his mother had been taken ill and hope they wouldn't remember she'd died in her sleep three years ago.

The map was stuck back on the kitchen wall and new lines in red-tip marker were drawn.

'We'll head south,' said Ray. 'Maybe meet some Melburnians in Merimbula. But, Pat, this time let me choose the campground.'

Pat stopped stirring her Tony Ferguson milkshake and looked up.

'I've been thinking,' she said. 'I wouldn't mind "Patsy". You know, like that singer Patsy Cline.'

The Gills of Fish

Karen Manton

Sand burns underfoot. The sun is high, merciless. No clouds dare share the sky with it. It seems a long way to the Point today and Nina wonders if she's going to make it. Each of her footsteps sinks deep into hot sand under the weight of the unseen boy child in her belly. She feels as if she's moving in slow motion. Unlike her one-year-old, Samuel, who is dancing his way across the white glare, weaving a path between rocks. He inspects them all for tiny shells or foot holes he might use to climb.

She squints her eyes against the brightness to see him. The heat on her shoulders burns. He sees her approaching and flings aside his hat to run a giddy caper away from her. His hair flares out white blonde in the salty breeze.

'Samuel!' she pants. Her voice scatters in the wind, unheard by him.

Ahead of her marches Luke. She watches his legs thudding to the ground, feet out to the side like a ballet dancer or a merman. The muscles in his calves bulge with the strain of carrying such a walk. His cap is jammed down on his head. He is pacing ahead in some kind of impatient funk. Why can't he be calm, even if only for her, this day when she needs him to be steady? Instead: chaos, exasperation, tension. He is annoyed with the hour of the day, the height of the sun, the fact they are an hour later than planned. The shade around the corner, that he had predicted to be there for all of them, may be gone by now.

She tries to walk near the waterline for firmer sand, but her footsteps sink lower, craters in the smooth surface. She looks out to the great expanse of water, warm as soup and no comfort with its stingers and crocodiles. She has not thought carefully enough about the shade and how little she will like this whole expedition if she can't sit down soon. If turning back was on offer, she would. But Luke is out of earshot.

*

It had been his idea to go for a beach walk. It seemed a good idea at the time. The day before a planned caesarian has a strangeness to it, like being in a waiting room to catch a spaceship to another planet. Neither of them wanted to hang around the house. We'll have to go early, they'd agreed. Before the sun gets too high. Luke had in mind a possibly shady place around the Point – if they could get there in time.

But the lateness of things delayed them. The more Nina tried to get everyone ready, the more things seemed to unravel. Luke was getting wound up. Nina's mother didn't want to trek across a hot beach looking for shade and thought her daughter should stay home and rest. Fraught discussions followed. At the last minute no one could find the camera. Samuel was wailing for a missing toy. A glass fell off the bench and broke.

*

It is almost noon. The beach is deserted. Hardly anyone braves the heat at this hour. They walk quite a way before coming across a fisherman wilting by his line. Fish are laid out on the sand nearby, air popping from heaving gills. Another in a red bucket listlessly wanders its circle out of life.

'Oh!' the little boy is fascinated by this one.

'Just leave it,' Nina tries to say calmly, with a jaded smile to the fisherman.

Her breath is fading with the effort of walking. This is how it must be to be old. To just stop. To have the will but not the power to keep going.

*

They round the Point at last. There it is – the shade, and with it an expanse of shallow water, trapped between sand and rocks after the tide has gone out and free of any dangerous creatures. The water is dark in the shadow of the sandstone cliff, its surface rippling softly in the breeze. An oasis.

'See,' Luke says, 'Just as I said. Plenty of shade.' He sighs. 'So it's a pity your mother isn't here …'

He looks behind him to a spot way up the beach where Nina's mother is lying prostrate under a tree in a real and definite piece of shade not far from the car park.

'She could've held the camera,' Luke is muttering. 'You know, to take footage of the three of us. On the last day. It's symbolic.'

Nina has never heard him mention the symbolic before. Not long ago she had to explain what a metaphor was. For a moment she feels a glimmer of hope. Perhaps, after all, they do have a connection. These are the kinds of thin threads that hold people together in a family. But then, she thinks, the thread is as thin as a spider's web. She feels herself flailing at the end of one such tenuous, silvery rope, about to drop.

Sam scampers into the water. Fish flee his stomping legs. His white skin looks greenish in the water, magnified. Puffs of sand curl slowly from under his feet. His little hands splash with mad delight, stopping now and then to lift up in the air so he can watch drops of water bejewelled with sunlight flick from his fingers.

'Stay still,' says Luke, 'and the fish will come back.'

They wait, father and son, for the return of underwater travellers. Here come the brave ones, fins waving to and fro.

'Give me the camera,' she says. 'I'll film you.'

'Yes, but I wanted the three of us.' He hesitates, looking back up the beach to a distant place where his mother-in-law has gone.

'Well, we'll have to make the best of it.' She takes the camera from him.

'Look at all the fish,' Luke is saying to Sam, trying to get the boy to be still enough for the fish to gather close and nibble at their toes. But Sam will not pause in his exuberance. It is all about splashing.

'Look at the fish,' Luke insists.

She is about to ask Luke to film her and the child, but decides against it and presses 'pause' on the camera. Never mind, she thinks, and starts the walk around the water in all her heaviness. She doesn't want to be on camera anyway. It's not just the current bulk of her, but the demise in general that mortifies her. Something has happened between thirty-one and forty-one – the fall, the decline, the decay. She feels keenly that she is not beautiful. She lowers herself onto the rock she has chosen as a throne for this her great weight. She hopes the stone doesn't dent the unborn child's head.

Luke comes to retrieve the camera.

'I want to film the fish,' he says and then remembers himself. 'Do you want me to film you two now?'

'Oh, no,' she lies, at the same time trying to stop the truth from drowning. 'Later maybe … when there's the right moment … you take it,' and she holds out the camera to him.

Despite the shade cast by the cliff, the glare of the sun is all around. She shields her face, looking up the sandstone wall to a single tree growing out of the rock face, its roots reaching down the cliff into the shadows while a narrow, twisting trunk edged in a halo of sunlight reaches for blue sky. Along the cliff top grass wavers.

Sand bugs crawl over her feet, bringing her gaze back to her toes. In the shadows Luke is intent on his project of fish in the dark.

How can he see them, she wonders. How can he not see us?

She wants someone to be with, to ponder the stillness of this secret lagoon behind the shadow of the sandstone wall, absorbing the quiet hum of sand and stone the day before a second child is born.

A peal of laughter from Sam interrupts her thoughts. She wishes she could hold him in a moment of recognition of what is about to pass from them and what is about to arrive to become part of them. He splashes with increasing vigour until he stumbles, crying out as he falls into the water.

'Watch him,' she calls to Luke.

'I am,' he says, eye to the viewfinder.

'Watch him,' she calls again more urgently.

Exasperated with the interruption, distracted by the underwater opportunities, Luke hauls the one-year-old out of the water. Sam is crying now.

'I'm just trying to film the fish,' Luke protests.

Sam is too sad to care about fish.

'Come here,' she calls and the little boy runs, wailing at first and then laughing at his own speed. He hurtles towards her between rocks sticking up out of the sand that bear razor-sharp shells. She tries to see the lethal peaks of jutting rock as little stepping stones and keeps the smile of welcome on her face as his feet haphazardly approach each point, missing every one. He runs at her, full pelt, laughing his head off and she calls out to Luke because this is the moment she has waited to capture, the sheer love of everything that comes running into her and holds her in a hug, the last hug of a kind.

But Luke with his eye to the viewfinder will not hear.

The world spins around mother and child – rocks, the tree and its halo of light, the luminous band of grass, the shady water, the sand and beyond, the sea with its wavelets tumbling in. As the world rights itself Sam is looking up, breathless, into her face, and the sky, around. Suddenly he is off again, whooping free, his footsteps the only echo of his track to her.

'I'm just getting these insects on the wall,' announces Luke, eye still to viewfinder, camera pointed at the rock face made dark in the shade.

She gets up and starts to follow the little boy's footprints.

Luke pauses as she walks by. 'Did you want the camera?'

'Don't worry, the moment's passed.'

Salty water drops fall down her legs. She marches resolutely back, eyes smarting. It is as if great rocks are set down between them – stones made of things like predicted shade and symbolic moments. They become boulders with time and cannot be shifted.

Familiar tentacles of doubt creep in to sting. Perhaps the silver thread is tearing. Perhaps it is already torn and she is just free-falling. Too late to be thinking like this now. Nothing to do but lumber on.

She calls to her mother, so far away, a cheery wave mustering the much-needed disguise.

*

Three a.m. Nina wakes suddenly, gasping for air. Her fingers are swollen and aching. She shifts herself higher up on the pillows to breathe more easily, and tries to flex her fingers. If it's not her dreams it's her body that prevents her from sleeping these days. Strange nightmares creep in as she rests, like the one from which she's just escaped. She goes over it again in her mind, searching for a happy ending.

She is walking along the beach. The rocks that in the day had just protruded through the sand have grown. They are enormous boulders, pillars of rock, immoveable. She is lumbering across the sand, Samuel on her hip, the great weight of the unborn child making a boulder of her body. Luke is leading the way. They get to a ridge of sandstone. It is smooth, unable to be climbed without ropes and pegs. It stretches across the sand in both directions, even into the water. They must get over it for some reason. Perhaps the hospital is on the other side. Perhaps her time has come. It is the rock Luke must move. But he is just standing there, quoting Samuel's favourite book – *We're Going on a Bear Hunt* – 'We can't go over it, we can't go under it, we'll have to go *through* it!'

Meanwhile the tide is coming in. Soon they will all be under water – husband, toddler, mother – weightless corpses. And the unseen child? The sound of bubbles fills her ears. The large shadow of a fish glides by, weightless, elegant, at ease, weaving between the rocks on a warm current, every now and then passing so close its silver scales caress a stone.

*

The dream will not alter its storyline, and Nina lies awake. On the bedside table her alarm clock ticks. Three hours to go. The lamp is not working so she can't turn it on to read. She lies in the dark, a woman in waiting.

Beside her Luke does not stir. He sleeps in a kind of deep, undreaming way, uninterrupted at last. On the other side of her lies Samuel, breath whistling through his nose. His face is so trusting in repose. She wonders how it will change, this little face of the child on the outside, soon to be joined by the child on the inside. In the next room her mother the matriarch is asleep with thoughts of a new grandchild coming and the challenge of minding the grandson for a few days on her own. She will get up early tomorrow when she hears her daughter stir, stumble out and say

'Good luck,' and wave them off.

The unborn child rolls. The night Nina first felt him move he was like a sea creature brushing behind the skin of her belly. Now he is a creature of weight, a ball with feet and toes and hands and fingers that leave an imprint. She will miss this sensation. The inner kicks and stretches. The quiet humour between them. The link, the talking, the language of it. The friend within. She wonders what are the hidden thoughts swimming through his mind; does he absorb her private musing through the secret water they share? Do they traverse together, her thoughts and his, in shoals of fin and silver eye?

He pauses again. A different kind of silence, the silence of his stillness returns.

She thinks of the gills of a resting fish, opening and closing. Her underwater boy breathes in a similar way, lungs submerged. In three hours it will all change. Valves in the heart will shut. Others will open. The whole system will alter to disable his talent for breathing in fluid and enable him to inhale air. The way of a fish is a state to which he will never return.

What must it feel like, she wonders, to breathe through gills?

*

'I'm here,' says a voice.

A hand squeezes hers tight. It is the obstetrician, swathed in white gown and mask. Luke is by her on the other side, warm hand on her shoulder. She keeps her head bowed as the needle sears into her spine.

'Don't move,' instructs the anaesthetist.

It is a quiet and chilling order. The hand in hers holds tight, the hand on the shoulder is firm. She is glad of them both.

'That's it,' says the anaesthetist and they lay her down, a great bulk on a narrow table. Suddenly everything is happening. They are stringing up the pale-blue curtain in front of her – although they tie it so low she can almost see over the top.

'Incision now.'

She feels nothing and breathes easier. For some reason she's had nightmares about the spinal block not working.

'I'm going to vomit,' she says.

A silver bowl waits by her mouth.

'What is it with vomiting and childbirth?' the obstetrician laughs. 'Everyone seems to vomit.'

Nina looks at the mask and cap hovering behind the curtain, thinking that vomit could hardly be a surprise considering the tugging and pulling at her insides. She watches the mask and cap, the focused eyes of the obstetrician. She could be a baker kneading bread.

'Not long now,' the assistant surgeon says.

'Good,' murmurs Nina, with another heave into the bowl.

'Oh,' exclaims the obstetrician suddenly, 'Don't go!'

There's a sudden flurry of gloves and masks.

'He's diving back in!' she laughs.

The assistant is holding onto a long white tape, which Nina imagines is lassoed around an errant ankle. Is that how they bring them in, a fish on the end of a line? She has visions of her newborn slithering to the floor and flapping around. But now she hears a cry. Someone has got hold of him and demanded he be human. They lower the blue drape.

He is a large creature, with enormous hands turning blue and red and blue and red.

'Is he all right?' she wonders out loud.

'He's fine,' says the goodly doctor, 'just the oxygen swapping over.'

Luke has the camera, though his eyes are not on the view-finder. He's peering over the cloth to a point she can't see, where the squally newborn wrangles and the fat, twisting cord between mother and child is severed. They will leave a good length of it for him to cut later. For now she watches a wave pass through him – of fear, of pride, of responsibility forever theirs. It transposes him from the father of one to the father of two, and is connected somehow to his worries about shade and the symbolic, and his determined footsteps across sand. It's the kind of love they don't sing about – this standing side by side to receive oncoming water and live amongst the tides. Perhaps the thread still holds.

Her child's cry is strong and wild. The blue curtain has dropped further so she can see him better. She watches the great hands clenching and opening, stretching and curling, calling in the red across the blue.

There are exclamations of approval and congratulations. He is a big boy. Healthy, with a good set of lungs. Listen to that cry, you'll know about him. Look at those hands. He's a rugby player.

But Nina knows otherwise. She watches his great hands and listens to his voice and hears from her emptied body a whisper,

'When he is a man, he will move rocks.'

Street Sweeper

Leah Swann

You'll remember this day your dog Winston dies, this day and this night, but right now the afternoon is fresh and untouched by future events. Here you are on the concrete steps, in front of a shabby weatherboard: Mathew Greene at fourteen, with a skateboard under one arm, the other filled with the shaggy warmth of Winston.

Listless, you feel in need of something. But it won't be found in the kitchen – where your mother, Molly, makes jam with Bridget like it's an hilarious science experiment – nor downstairs in the mad slurry of Monopoly money and scone crumbs left by the children. You're too old to play.

Greene senior, the father who gave you Winston on your third birthday, is not here. He married someone else and lives in America with new children. It's no one's fault; it's just the way things are. Last time he visited, you played footy on the street. You told me it was the best hour of your life.

*

You hear the women's conversation through the open front door. You're dimly aware that this jam-making business is somehow attached to your mother's need to be accepted by the brigade of Other Mothers. You can't stand her ostentatious efforts. If she cut off her dreadlocks and removed a few earrings, she might get further. But you can't say such things. You don't want to.

'My goodness, if my mother could see me now,' Molly says. Knives slash and chop on the cutting boards.

'My mother didn't make jam either,' says Bridget. 'But it's a good antidote to the madness of modern life.'

'These mandarins are appalling.'

'Not enough rain.'

'Satisfying to make them into jam, though,' says Molly.

There are cigarette butts in the geranium pot by the steps, Marlboro Lights, Molly's brand. Citrus infuses the air like a pungent teabag. Hearing a cork pop, you know Molly's opened a bottle of wine and your chest kinks with anger. The one bright spot of your day is the evening walk, when you and Molly and your little brother and sister walk the dog. It will be awful if she's drunk – and she could well be drunk by then.

You're hungry but you can't bear to return to the kitchen. You don't want to enter that warm, womanly fug of jam and alcohol and Bridget's cleavage. Now they're testing the jam on a cold saucer; you can hear your mother worrying that it's too runny.

You're itching for something. You don't know what, though later you wonder if you were waiting for the car that screamed around the corner, the car that killed Winston, and the girl in velvet hipsters who tumbled out of the driver's seat, weeping.

You set out to skate from the letterbox to the fire hydrant and back. Winston follows, arthritic and shambling. You've already skated two lengths before the dog's made it to the nature strip to relieve himself. He's wandered out on the road when you hear the car's engine too close and too fast.

'Winston!'

The great bushy head lifts to attention, his eyes obscured by a long fringe of grey and white hair. He doesn't move.

'Winston, come here!'

Ponderous, as if moving through water, the dog raises a paw like a Clydesdale hoof and puts it down again. The red Astra hurtles around the bend. Brakes squealing, the car smashes into Winston and sends him soaring along the road. The Astra screeches to a stop and the driver climbs out. She's already crying.

Winston must be dead. You run to him and pick up his front and back paws. You're dragging him to the kerb when you see that he's split open – his guts are rolling out. Behind you, the girl gives a short scream.

'Don't worry,' you hear yourself say. 'Don't worry about it. I'll get a spade. I'll clean it up.'

The girl's shoulders are shaking. 'Oh my god, oh my god! I'm so sorry.'

'You can go home if you want,' you say. *Please go home. Please go. I can't stand it.*

The girl's eyes are dripping black over her lovely face: she's the kind of girl you'd be in awe of in other circumstances. A navel diamanté winks up at you from her flat belly, making you hot and uncomfortable.

'No, let me help,' she pleads.

'*I* want to do it,' you say. 'Please.'

'Do you want me to go?'

'Yes.'

*

Running down the driveway, through the noisy kitchen to the back door, you find the spade and walk back through the kitchen. The wine bottle is almost empty. A foaming pot of gold on the stove threatens to boil over, guarded by a giggling Molly with her wine glass and wooden spoon; Bridget's ladling the first batch into washed jars. A row of finished jars sits on the window-sill, backlit by sunshine, each one full of a dense and radiant orange.

'What the hell's Matt doing with a spade?' you hear Bridget say.

'God knows. Spot of gardening, perhaps?' says Molly. A gale of laughter follows you up the driveway and you think to yourself, *bitch*; but only minutes later she's out there beside you, helping you, proving you wrong.

*

When you tell me of the evening walks your voice is tender. How the littlies hold hands and walk in front, hauling Winston on the leash, while your mother's beside you, deftly winding the conversation this way and that way and listening intently to whatever you say about school, dreams, football, skateboards

– even girls. You only notice this skilfulness in retrospect. But you bask in her attention; these walks are when you love her best.

She knows how to handle you. When she arrives on the street that unforgettable spring day, Winston spread over the bitumen like the Pro Hart carpet advertisement, she says in a low voice, 'What we need here, Mathew, is a box. Run across to the Stuarts' and see if they have one, as big as you can find.'

Bridget is standing nearby. Molly leans over and says something to her you can't hear. Glad to leave the scene for a moment, you hand Molly the spade and dash over to the neighbours' house.

Molly must have worked like lightning, because by the time you get back most of the dog is in an oversized pillowslip and another, smaller slip. The small one has a faded Thomas the Tank Engine print on it, the one you insisted on having until you were ten. You set the box onto the nature strip and lift the sacks into the box. Each is knotted, so no furry vestiges of poor Winston protrude. Blood's staining the cotton, fast.

'I think it's best if Georgia and Stefan don't see this,' says Molly, wiping sweat from her forehead.

'I'll take them for tea at my house,' says Bridget.

Once you've carried the box to the backyard, you go inside to clean up. In the bathroom, you wash your hands and face. There are voices outside, followed by Bridget's car driving away. In the mirror you see a whisker poking from your chin and yank it out with your thumb and forefinger. You walk into the bedroom. Sinking into the bed, your hand stretches by habit to feel Winston's head and swishes through empty air. You lean forward all the way and press your eye sockets into your kneecaps and cry. Tears soak your jeans.

Eventually you go back to the garden, where Molly is busily digging under the old mandarin tree. She looks small and skinny with the apron – donned for jam-making – still hanging off her unmotherly form, dust-blonde dreadlocks tucked behind earlobes bristling with silver. There's a tattoo of a sun on her right bicep. The arm that stirred the pot. The arm that dug the grave. It's shaking with effort.

'Let me do that, Mum,' you say.

She hands you the spade gratefully, and wipes at the muck and tears smearing her face.

Later, there will be a memorial service. Georgia and Stefan will toss flowers onto the grave and say poems in Winston's memory. Right now, their absence lets the two of you cry freely. All is quiet, save for the sound of tears and dirt falling over blood-stained pillowslips.

'He was a good dog,' chokes Molly, when it's almost done.

'The best,' you say, and put your arm around her and again you notice the slightness of her, this woman so big in your life.

*

During the night you can't stop thinking about Winston's body coming apart. You want to stop but your mind keeps going back to it, probing it like a finger on a scab.

You try to think of the mandarins and the hands of the women, their chopping blades, sectioning, stripping, peeling. Dozens of mandarins slashed in half, their dry gold bellies face-up. Pips and pith and shells of orange skin sitting in heaps between the blue packets of sugar. The driver's face comes to mind and you wonder if she's awake too, disturbed by killing a dog. Despite your efforts, you keep seeing red guts and other stuff, brown and shiny and sausage-like, on the hard road.

Finally you fall into a hot, fitful sleep, only to be woken by the harsh noise of a street sweeper. The vast mechanical brooms whirr through the quiet, breaking it up into so many shards.

*

When you put on your runners, you slip through the bedroom window and out onto the street. It's late. You pad along, jogging lightly. Cold moonlight spilling over a blossom tree makes it so sharply beautiful, so unearthly – it takes you by surprise. You will always remember its fragrance, its stillness, its lambent white blossoms.

Up the road comes the street sweeper. You avert your eyes from the glaring gold lights, sitting on the truck like upturned jam jars, but nothing can block the noise. It passes you slowly, a moving edifice of brutal efficiency, its raucous vacuum strong enough to suck up a house brick or a dead possum. Even bits of Winston. But Molly did such a good job, there's barely a trace of Winston left; every piece has been wrapped and buried. At least he was saved from that.

As you hurry back along the street to your house, you see a light on in Molly's room. Leaping through your window and sliding into bed, your heart thumps. She's talking to someone on the phone. At this time of night it could only be America. Molly's voice is too muffled to hear what she's saying. Maybe the bad school report. Maybe Winston.

When the conversation ends, you creep into your mother's bedroom. She's in her singlet top and pyjama pants. Her eyes are pink.

'Was that Dad?' you ask, clambering onto the bed next to her.

'Why are you still awake? Were you listening?'

'Couldn't sleep. Winston, I guess. Did you ring him?'

'No – he rang me.'

She looks through the open curtains to the night sky. Her room seems dingy with its peeling paint and op-shop dressing table. Georgia's scrappy bouquet of lavender and jasmine is wilting in the vase.

'You might as well know,' she says. 'He asked if you'd like to go and live with him. And Cady and the little ones. Become part of their family.'

You're surprised at the excitement, even joy, rising inside you. Joy with a seam of dread. It's like someone's opened a door to let in a fresh breeze. To live with him! You take a deep breath.

'It makes sense, really,' Molly says, rubbing the skin of her forehead with her thumbs. 'You're becoming a man and I don't know how to help you with that. Your father could.'

*

Years later, you reflect that Molly sent you away at the very moment your body grew stronger than hers; strong enough to crack open drought-dried earth with a spade. Now a grown man, you can see how such strength could have genuinely helped her maintain the house and guard the children. Had you stayed, she might have come to depend on you. Did she know she was protecting you from her own neediness, when she encouraged you – against her own feelings – to say yes to your father's offer?

*

Several weeks later, you say your goodbyes to Stefan and Georgia at the house. Molly's arranged for Bridget to mind them rather than go to the airport: they've been crying a lot about you going. Closing the front door, you catch sight of Stefan's little sheepskin Ugg boots left where he stepped out of them in the hallway. The toes point outwards, the way he habitually stands.

The two of you drive to the airport. After you've checked in your luggage, she waits with you. In her usual way, she keeps the conversation light and funny, teasing you about the American accent you'll inevitably acquire and the pretty teenager she's spotted that you could 'chat up' on the plane. When the boarding call comes, she gives you a jar of mandarin marmalade.

'Give it to your dad,' she says, and grins. 'Be sure to tell him I've been *making jam*. I'd love to see his face.'

There's a long, awkward hug, and then she holds your shoulders and looks into your eyes, and out of love for her you strive not to squirm.

'You're the best thing that ever happened to me, Mathew.'

Her eyes are bright with unshed tears and she swallows. 'Good courage, son,' she says, and laughs. 'I'm telling you what *I* need! Now remember, if you feel down just go and chat with that girl.'

Courage *is* what you need hours later, when the first real wave of homesickness hits you. Through the window lies a vast mass of sky and ocean. Your tray is flipped open in front of you with a packet of sweet biscuits, tea and the empty dish that held the lasagne now lodged like cardboard in your stomach. The stricken face of the girl who killed Winston floats towards you, as it does sometimes; it would have been nice to talk to her about it once the shock had passed.

You stack the mess into a pile and fossick in your bag for the marmalade. Your hand closes around the cool glass jar, still sticky from where the old label has been soaked away. Drawing it out, you place it in front of you.

The jar beams on the tray, an orange beacon. Twisting the lid till it pops, you take a spoon and dip it into the marmalade and listen to Molly and Bridget, their voices coming as though from long ago, a piece of history running through your head.

'Put the jam on this frozen saucer and we'll see if it gels.'

That's Bridget, followed by Molly: 'Oh my God, it's too runny – what will we do?'

'Keep boiling it. Just keep boiling it.'

Holding the spoon, you check the texture of the jam and find it quivers and drips in gelatinous globules onto the empty packets. She did it! A thin twist of peel dangles and glistens. Taking another spoonful, you taste mandarins transformed by sugar and heat. Marmalade coats your tongue, thickly golden. How sweet it is, and how bitter.

Bearings

Forging Friendship

Karen Hitchcock

Hannah replied to my Facebook request for friendship by email.

Hey Keira, she said in the email. What's it been, one year, two?

She was no longer with Thomas, had moved interstate, was making a short film and she'd prefer – she wrote – not to use Facebook. She would close her account any day now, it was a nightmare, she knew way too many people, and they all wanted to friend her. Nothing personal; she hoped I didn't mind. She hoped she'd bump into me one day. We should catch up sometime, when she was in town and wasn't so crazy busy.

Which to my mind was a fancy way of saying: Please fuck off.

So I wrote back: I totally understand Hannah, thanks so much for finding the time to respond to me, because I do appreciate how extra precious your time is. I know that you really should have a PA to handle all this Facebook rejecting for you; how horrible it must be to tear yourself away from your city-slicking, vegan-shoe-and-blood-red-lipstick-buying, la-de-dah filmic machinations just to compose little Facebook rejections designed to make everyone else feel like a piece of crap. I mean, HOW TAXING for you, Hannah.

*

Switching pages, I see that Xanadu658 is selling a silver crochet evening purse lined in pale-blue silk. It is 'no longer suitable, due to a change in lifestyle.'

What kind of lifestyle precludes evening purses? I check the other items Xanadu has for sale: three diamante belts (all size XS), red kitten heels (a bit scuffed), a six-pack of baby booties (NWOT).

I'm watching a couple of dresses, their prices creeping, I don't need them, I probably won't wear them, and yet … Maybe I should invest; maybe I need an evening purse. Who knows what the future may hold. Maybe this evening purse holds my future of evenings out clutching purses against perfect frocks over flawless skin, all clutched tight by a companion.

*

Hannah has dark brown eyes. We were once friends. Now we are not even 'friends.'

I have a lot of 'friends.'

I mean, we all know, or knew, or knew of, or wished we knew, or the-guy-from-the-bookshop, way too many people, don't we?

I'd even found my dad listed on Facebook: the first time I'd seen him since I was eight. Late one night, call it the bottom of the barrel. He looked fatter, smaller and dumber than I remembered. Barrel bottom or not, I didn't ask him to be my friend.

What I really wrote to Hannah was this: Cool, Hann. Give me a call sometime if you're passing through town and we'll have a coffee and catch-up. Ciao xx

I don't need to tell you; she'd never call, kiss kiss, how are ya babe.

*

Hannah moved from South Africa to my school in year eleven. Something about the end of apartheid and its impact on cattle farming? Her dad – despised, pined after – went to New Zealand. Hannah and her mum came here.

Her first week at school she caught me smoking by myself, behind the woodwork shed. She asked for a light and said my tobacco was grown in Zimbabwe. I looked at my burning cigarette, then back at Hannah, unsure if she was taking the piss.

She lit up, blew smoke out of the corner of her mouth. 'I'm Hannah,' she said, as if I didn't know.

I made no assumptions, but from that moment on she'd find me each lunchtime and peel me away from my book. We'd nibble our crappy sandwiches, make fun of the other students and smoke our guts out. We never hung out on the weekends; she was seeing some older guy named Frank who took up all her time. But in year twelve they broke up and Hannah and I made the transition from smoking buddies to out-of-school buddies and she started sleeping over at my place.

Weekday, weekend, it made no difference to us, we'd stay awake half the night, gulping hot chocolate and leaning out the bedroom window to smoke. Hannah's appetite for hot chocolate was insatiable; we'd go through a litre of milk each night, at least. Hannah's mum would only allow cocoa made with water and a splash of skim milk, so when she got to my place – where my mum slept heavily and didn't give a damn what we drank – she'd cut loose, heat the full-cream milk in a saucepan till it boiled, add half the box of cocoa and an avalanche of brown sugar. Each week I'd scrawl cocoa and milk on the shopping-list notepad on the fridge.

'The amount of cocoa you girls go through,' my mum would sigh in her distracted way as she tore the list from the pad and rushed off to the supermarket on Friday night.

Hannah's hot chocolates. Her mother was one of those petite, pointy-nosed women for whom eating nothing was a sign of refinement. The world was a great and mysterious place where nothing was certain except the superiority of looking like an old bag of bones. Hannah inherited her father's large frame and appetite and made her mother look like an icy-pole stick. As far as I could tell, Hannah's mum had spent Hannah's entire life trying to whittle her into a twig.

One morning towards the end of the school year we were walking to the bus stop when Hannah told me that I held her in my sleep. I would – she said – wrap my arms around her waist, press my head into her chest or her back and hold on tight. She said she didn't mind, but wondered if I was aware that I did it.

No, I told her, I was not aware.

Then I said: Jesus Christ, how embarrassing, I'm so sorry, I'll try to stop.

She said not to worry about it, she didn't much mind.

She sort of liked it, she said.
She found it sweet.

*

I once read that the reason we are able to walk down a crowded street without continually colliding into others is because we detect subtle movements in the eyes of the people coming towards us – movements that somewhere deep inside our brains we understand as an intended direction and make the necessary adjustment in our trajectory. We make way for each other through a mutual understanding. Perhaps this is why we can feel comforted by a crowd.

Our eyes send signals so we avoid the barest touch. Perhaps this is why we can feel so lonely in a crowd.

Hannah? It had not been what, one year or two. It had been twenty-eight months plus three weeks. And Hannah? Never mind.

*

Facebook makes me sick. Hannah and I used to meet up in the flesh and walk along a real street and enter real live shops, staffed by fragrant, embodied individuals who – if you reached out and touched them – would feel warm and smooth, as human beings do. In such establishments we would try on clothes that were new and available in most sizes, including ours. And we would choose a frock from a rack and slip it on and spin for each other, our backs to the cool, hard mirrors. Then Hannah and I would sit face to face, look across the table into each other's eyes, and lips, and down into our coffees, slowly stirring the froth in, as we spoke words with pitch and waves that hit each other's tympanic membranes and sent physical signals of chemico-electric form zinging through each other's brains.

'Keira?' she'd say.

'Hannah?' I'd say. And we would answer each other – 'yes,' or 'yes?' – without the use of emoticons or excess punctuation. Without the need to ruminate over the difference in meaning of 'ooooooooo' and 'oooooo!!!' and 'oooohhhhhhh.' We used gesture and eyes and sounds. We sat face to face, and a single look transmitted the equivalent of three hundred posts on Facebook. None of which rendered me sick.

That saying 'catch-up' makes me sick.

That saying 'I hope you don't mind' makes me sick.

Sometimes, people streak so far ahead that there can never be any catch-up and too bloody bad if you mind.

Other things that make me sick: hot chocolate, long macchiatos, catching buses, the smell of burning fabric, dark brown eyes.

One time with Hannah I bought a pale-blue silk dress from the Vintage Clothing Shop. It gripped my tits like a cold fist but made my arse irresistible. Around the neck was a ring of pearlised sequins. It was cut at just the right length, highlighting both the bones of the knee and the curve of the quadriceps, which for some reason always screams vagina. Hannah made me buy it, although its price was such a stunner that I had to pilfer money from my mum's purse to pay. But I wore that frock dressed up with fish-net stockings, and down with bare legs, with scarfs and brooches and belts, depending on whether we were going to a club or a show or a café. I wore it with jackets on top and skivvies underneath, I wore it with hats and long socks and gold sandals and gloves. I wore that dress with Hannah.

Also, eBay makes me sick. And spastic and insatiable for things just out of sight. It fuels something frantic, then leaves me gutted. Without getting out of bed, with the rhythmic twitch of one finger against the return button on my keyboard, I can have frock after frock. None of which, poured out of their post-packs, caught warm in my fingers, satisfies anything. Although, according to the vendors' descriptions, every dress on eBay is 'stunning.' They are stunning with tiny flaws, or stunning and unworn, or they are stunning and would look fabulous with heels and golden eyeshadow or equally so with ballet flats and a leather jacket; they are NWOT and stunning. You don't need to ask why the vendors are auctioning off their stunning crap because – like a con man – they tell you before you ask. There are three stories: wardrobe clearout; fluctuation in body weight; change in lifestyle. No one ever says that they are auctioning their kids' toys because they need a carton of fags or a crate of VB, or because the bank's about to foreclose. No one's selling their shit to raise funds for a holiday or to build a herb garden or a gazebo or buy a pet dog. No one's selling their shit because it's shit. They all regret horribly the necessity of the sale. They expect us to look at this detritus and be stunned.

Nothing to lose, I sign in.

There are currently seventy-four thousand, five hundred and thirty-one dresses listed for sale. Five thousand six hundred and twelve of them are pale blue. Seven hundred and forty are pale blue and vintage. I survey the capacity of my room. I turn back to my computer, flip pages.

Nothing to lose, I sign in.

I have a friend request from Nicky Winch, the guy in grade four who had the set of seventy-two Derwent pencils in a tin. I wonder if that's enough to forge a friendship. Nothing to lose, I accept, and the face of another stranger joins my library of friends.

*

So the pale-blue silk dress I bought and wore with Hannah was sleeveless? And it started to unravel under the armholes? At the part they call a gusset? I sewed the edges together, but I'm not much good with a needle and a gusset is a triangle of reinforcement that can only bear so much reinforcing. And then I ran out of pale-blue thread, used up all my white, moved on to pale green and et cetera until the underarms of the dress looked like psychedelic spiderwebs. At special events or where the light was quite bright, I tried to keep my arms pinned to my sides. Someone might flick a glance at my armpit during conversation and this served as a reminder for me to clamp that arm back down. Hannah told me to relax. She said the mass of threads were scary-beautiful. Those were her words: scary, beautiful.

Then, a few weeks later, she said the mending seemed desperate, overly optimistic, why didn't I just get another dress? Desperate, overly optimistic; a cause and its effect.

I'd seen Hannah ruin two striped tops from her prized collection: one with blue-black hair dye; one behind the bus stop where a rusty nail stuck out of the fence. Both times she did the exact same thing, no threads involved: she just chucked them in the bin, like wet tissues.

*

There are three hundred and seventy-three pale blue + vintage + sleeveless dresses for sale on eBay. Forty-four are 'Buy it now!'

The rest are up for auction. All bids end between one minute and eight days from now.

*

The plan was that we'd both do nursing and then volunteer as aid workers abroad. That's what we called it: abroad, which to our ear was far more sophisticated a term than overseas. We enrolled – and then spent the summer around town, me in that dress, Hannah in ballet flats, red lipstick and one of her striped tops. We talked about moving in together as soon as we got part-time jobs. Meanwhile she stayed over at mine. Full-cream milk and cocoa. I held her warm body at night and pretended to sleep.

*

I log in, compelled by the old What if?

Nicky Winch the Derwent boy has sent me a message.

Unusual. Normally you accumulate ancient artefacts and never exchange a word. Befriend, read their inane and desperate and overly optimistic daily updates, voyeurism, despair.

The Westgate sucks, sooooo happy Masterchef's back, shiny, happy, kid topped the class.

But here in the stream was a message just for me. For a fraction of a second, a tiny boy in a crowded school photo, his pursed little lips, calling across years.

Kieiria wots up? Remember the day you fell from the monkey bars landed on me and stuffed my knee my knee still kills me and I might need an op. Work in a sign shop which is pretty shit. Usual stuff, 2 kids, don't have much contact tho. How goes?

He'd spelt my name wrong and I did not remember that monkey bars incident.

Then I did remember the incident and the attending ambulance and the fact that it was a girl called Sonya Murne, the netball champion of the school, who landed on his knee, not me. I hated the monkey bars. I hated netball. I liked coloured pencils in tins, and books and other quiet stuff. Hello? You think you know me? I'm not fucking Sonya Murne.

*

Somehow that summer between school and uni, bisexual had emerged as the new normal, so unless you were a Nazi Christian you said you were bisexual. We discussed it. In theory, Hannah said, she could definitely be in love with a woman; love was love, after all; male, female, what's the diff? Keep in mind that it was me she was sitting with when she said it. She said it to my face, looking into my eyes. Then she said, 'And woman on woman avoids all the problematics of submission that go with penetrative sex, the prescribed male/female dynamic, et cetera, you know?'

I nodded, heart thumping, palms sweating, cheeks probably fucking purple, though I had no idea what she was talking about. All I knew about penetrative sex I had learned at fifteen from Jason Campbell. Over four weekends we'd exchanged a dozen words max and a few buckets of bodily fluids, mostly mouth-to-mouth, and he did penetrate me. If pressed I'd say it was neither pleasant nor unpleasant. Mostly I was on my back, thinking, 'This is penetration. I'm being penetrated. He is penetrating me.' Probably I thought 'fucking' rather than 'penetrating,' but you get the picture.

If penetration was a problem for Hannah then that was no prob for me. And how I leapt to agree with Hannah on the question of loving a woman. Oh boy, that was something I knew all about.

*

I study the eBay pictures one by one with an attitude forensic. My neck stiffens, my eyes ache, and none of the three hundred and seventy-three pale-blue vintage sleeveless dresses resembles mine in the slightest.

*

Then one day Hannah and I were in Degraves Street, drinking double macchiatos because we liked the way they made us look – sophisticated glass, black ink, dense white foam. We were drinking them even though we would have preferred massive mugs of cocoa, cream, sugar, a half litre of milk, and a boy called Andre Devonport (and what sort of name is that, anyways?) comes over to our table and goes, 'Hannah?'

To which the only possible answer was, 'Yes?'

And then he asks if she recognises him.

And she does recognise him: he's a guy from her high school in South Africa. A great looking guy, with flopping-in-his-eyes soft hair and you-are-the-only-person-in-the-world-Hannah eyes. He pulls up a stool without taking his eyes off her and they start exchanging relevant demographic data – me feeling increasingly uncomfortable, then left out, then grumpy – and when Hannah says the word 'nursing' Andre's face expands in surprise, then contracts, and what's left of his eyeballs direct their suspicion at me. He turns back to Hannah, 'But you were so ... clever. So artistic.'

Call it the beginning of the end, if you will.

*

When an auction has less than sixty seconds to close, the timer switches to red numerals and you can watch the countdown in real time. This never fails to scramble my mind and shrink my world. Do I want it? Should I bid? How much is it worth to me? I am held in a 59-, 58-, 57-, 56-second fist where I am without past or future, where I have no idea what to do. I pounce and feel sick. Or I move on and feel sick. Uncertainty, desire and lost opportunities. It's all there in the countdown.

It's a bit different with Facebook. Less intense. Needless to say, I immediately deleted Nicky Winch from my list of friends.

*

We'd be meeting less frequently and Hannah would be saying things like, 'Oh Keira, you're so ...' and finishing off with adjectives that sounded a bit South African to me. A bit male South African with floppy hair and an eye for the particular. This 'you're so ...' made me feel disappointing and small. And when someone starts to point out what you're like with a decrescendo sigh, it's a sign to get ready 'cause they're shrinking you down flat into a face in an old album that can be snapped shut with one hand. And pretty soon, you just watch, the act of misrecognition will be complete.

*

Things I had not contemplated: flats without Hannah, summer-time without Hannah, nursing without Hannah, developing nations without Hannah.

'We can still hang out!' she said, grinning fluoro from the lips but not the eyes, after she informed me that she'd landed a job at the food co-op, was switching from nursing to film studies and moving into Andre's share-house.

Andre this. Andre that. 'He's so ...' Eyes heavenward. Crescendo sigh.

'I'll have my own room, though. At least ... at the start ...'

It has often been noted that catastrophes take place in slow-motion, hyper-real time. I can add that your body sucks inwards. Major arteries slap the underside of your skin like untethered hoses and in the face of all this you can remain surprisingly polite. You can, if you wish, find air for something small and inane: oh, gee, wow, congratulations. Then you can flee.

*

EBay. Facebook. Twitter and chat. Send, comment, respond and reply. I'll buy stuff I wouldn't touch. I'll comment on your post though I wouldn't cross the street to say hello. Things that are not acts will pretend to be acts; they will take the place of acts. I will search and I will trawl and I will neither catch you nor be caught.

*

What I did was walk home, into the house of my childhood, into my bedroom, and close the door. I lay still on my bed for a long time. I peed once, in a milk-crusted mug abandoned on the windowsill. My mum knocked, said my name with a question mark and then went away. The sun rose and set twice. Soon after the second setting, I had a small thought, call it a plan. I stood up, went to the kitchen, gathered a glass of lemon cordial and a cigarette, a lighter, my blue mended dress. I opened the back door and stepped out into the cool night-time breeze. I sat cross-legged in the backyard as standing made me dizzy, and I watched the threads catch and smoulder to a fine grey ash.

*

I read something else: your life has a single story that gets repeated over and over, with a succession of understudies playing the role of your first co-star.

Let's say it's true. My story might go like this: a beautiful dress held my chest in her fist, and when she started to unravel I incinerated her remains. Make way for the understudy, you might say. Let's get this story restarted, you might say.

I log in, check the new pale-blue listings. I log out, I log in, see if anyone wants to befriend.

But the problem is this: you can't force her out of the story. You can't delete her or incinerate her or send her to your trash. She's your co-star, after all. And she might be a tenacious fighting bitch.

I log out. I log in. Out in out in.

Try whatever you like. I wish you all the best. But believe me when I tell you: that bitch has to leave for your first story to end.

(Favoured by) Babies

Tim Richards

While cradling Natasha, Sam automatically croons a song his mother sang to him, having learnt it from her own parents. How can he recall the words to a song he hasn't heard for three decades? He continues to sing through a breaking wave of nostalgia. If the child notices this mood-change, it doesn't curb her delight. According to Sam, Natasha has his mother's eyes.

*

Having disagreed about most things since their wedding day, Stavros and Brittany suddenly find themselves in accord on a serious issue. Parenthood. This agreement represents a major change of position. When Stav wanted her to help with the business, Brittany chose to keep teaching, and when he took the view that children should be their first priority, she argued that family would require an upstairs extension.

Each imagined the other would rush to the police in a situation like this, but they agreed to wait. They would act only if they heard a media report of a lost or abandoned child. In the meantime, the boy would be Michael. Despite their confusion, the couple couldn't stop smiling.

*

Karen and Marie had each entertained sperm provided by a mutual friend. When the turkey-baster failed Karen, she blamed

Jason for shooting blanks, but Marie became pregnant first try. Conceiving was no problem. But after the older woman's third miscarriage, the couple chose to take a break, which may have been their way of making a decision they couldn't make. The lovers couldn't allow their feelings for one another to be swamped by an endless tide of grief.

At first, Karen thought Eamon was a cruel practical joke. A misogynist neighbour trying to set them up.

Stuck behind a funeral procession on their way to the police station, Karen saw Marie gazing deep into the child's eyes. Eamon needed them. They decided to take their chances.

*

None of these individuals, or others yet to be introduced, would describe themselves as careless when dealing with important matters. Yet all chose not to mention these children when speaking to friends or relatives, and none chose to contact authorities. Instead, they began to shop in distant suburbs where no acquaintances would see them purchasing cots and nappies, and the foods favoured by babies.

*

The babies were transported to their doors by a discreet tsunami. So far as the recipients knew, their baby was the only such child, a fluke of divine providence, an infant to be loved by those who hadn't known how much their lives were missing that love.

Even now, no one can say for certain how many babies there were, since recipients remain cautious about coming forward. Some headed overseas the moment they obtained a false birth certificate.

So far as we know, the phenomenon was peculiar to the bayside suburb of Hampton, though one should be careful about inferring too much from this geographical coincidence. Seers versed in ancient knowledge of the earth's energy zones might be less hesitant. Childless couples have now rushed the area, paying above-market rates, desperately hoping that Hampton hasn't seen its last foundling, but these hopes may betray a need to misinterpret the facts.

*

When little Trish became feverish, Kylie and Nick resisted calling a doctor, fearing that she'd be taken from them. Finally, they drove forty kilometres to a clinic in the outer east, and fudged when Dr Wendt, a mature GP who'd encountered most situations, asked about the child's medical history. The parents didn't know their daughter's blood type. Nor could they answer questions about immunisation or childhood illnesses. Aware that the hospital where they said Trish was born had no maternity ward, Dr Wendt notified local police. Two detectives soon discovered that none of the personal details Kylie and Nick gave the doctor were valid.

*

Hampton traders would notice an unaccountable downturn in sales as Beachcomber mothers and fathers took their business to people who couldn't know that they weren't the natural parents of the babies they so clearly adored.

Whenever someone asked Ross and Ingrid too many questions, they made excuses and decamped. If a parent on television began to speak about the distress of having lost a child, they changed channels lest they discover that Jeff was the child in question. Ross and Ingrid found it impossible to believe that Jeff's natural parents could love the baby more than they loved him. This gift was no accident. They had been chosen because they had the exact qualities of love Jeff needed.

*

Many resentments attend this episode.

Allie and Martin had been desperate to have children for more than a decade. They'd tried everything known to medicine, interventions humiliating as they were costly, but it proved impossible for them to conceive. Allie's sister Robyn even offered to carry a child for them. If ever a couple deserved to receive a foundling, they were it.

More than anything, they resented the secretiveness of friends like Sam and Beth, who'd often said they never wanted children, friends who'd pretended to be sympathetic to Allie and Martin's plight. If they'd been sincere, the couple would have given them Natasha. People like Sam and Beth had no right to a baby. Their dishonesty made them undeserving. For all the talk of miracles, these events have been unspeakably cruel to couples with no outlet for the love they wish to offer a child.

*

We now know of thirty-seven incidents where Hampton residents woke on the cool morning of June third to find carefully swaddled infants waiting on their doorsteps. Only three of these foundlings were left at homes where there were already children. Among the recipients were four single women, two single men, three lesbian couples, two gay couples, and two elderly childless couples. Not one of the chosen said a word to anyone until irrefutable assertions were put to them, or until certain that mention of their find would not threaten the loss of their child.

*

Dinner parties were impossible to plan. Overnight, Hampton became a suburb of dodgy excuses, of sudden illnesses and unexpected urgencies. Habitual entertainers put up the shutters. Mothers complained of daughters-in-law who'd polluted their sons' affections.

Loving a child so much that you'd lie to safeguard that love involves difficult trade-offs.

Local sporting stars announced sudden, unexplained retirements. Fiercely resolute businesswomen like Harriet Song withdrew so abruptly from their regular activities that associates suspected cancer. Harriet said nothing to curb these speculations. She needed time with her baby. Hamptonians became weekend stay-at-homes. Some discovered the pleasures of cooking.

*

We should hesitate before speaking of miracles. None of the recipients had prayed for a child to be delivered to their doorstep. Inexplicability doesn't make an event miraculous.

Nor is seeking an explanation the same as expecting to find one. The novelist Manuel Primm describes a similar episode occurring in a small Spanish village during Cervantes' time. Half a dozen foundlings appeared, and no one could ascertain the identities of the infants' parents. These babies, and the middle-aged couples who received them, would later be put to death by the Inquisition.

*

We'd considered having kids, and not having them. If Annie was hankering, or if starting a family had been a major issue, I might have gone along with her, though I was always the one who said, Why add another hungry mouth to a fucked-up world? I meant it, too. It really pisses me off the damage we've done to this continent in two hundred years. Everything: the forests, rivers. Fish are disappearing, and the water's full of shit ... Annie can be pessimistic too, only she says that if sensitive, thoughtful people give parenting the arse, we'll end up fouling the gene pool. She thinks we take ourselves and our business on the planet too seriously. And maybe that's the deal, for us to go on playing Chinese Whispers with the genetic code and let entropy take care of itself ... Before the Pill, you didn't have the luxury of thinking like this. If you wanted to get your tail in, you had to face the consequences ... This stuff is confusing as fuck. If someone had asked me what I'd do, I would've said that I'd be onto the cops in a flash. I mean, the days when you dump unwanted kids on a doorstep are long gone. And there must be a distressed young mother out there who needs help ... I dunno. It's impossible to rationalise the emotions. When I picked Jules out of the basket, he started crying, but then I jiggled him, and he went straight back to sleep. It was like something I'd always done. Something I was meant to do. After that, right and wrong didn't come into it. Annie was the same. Neither of us mentioned what it would do to our career or travel plans, whether we could afford to raise him, or if we might regret it ten years from now. Jules looked just like Annie in her baby photos, and the sky could have caved in for all we cared. Nothing else mattered.

*

These babies are too perfect. They don't challenge the recipients to prove their mettle as parents. Always grinning and gooing, good sleepers. They were, are, healthy, even-tempered and adorable. Everyone's idea of what a baby should be.

If the envious couples who'd spent half a lifetime wishing for babies ever knew just how undemanding the foundlings were to their undeserving finders, their resentment would turn psychotic.

*

P had been about to tell S that he was leaving her for a sales manager at work, that he and this colleague had been having an affair for six months. He felt certain that S already knew.

Did he still love his wife?

When S stopped laughing at his jokes, P stopped asking what she felt or cared about. If you'd told him that a baby held the solution, he would have jumped on you. The very worst thing a couple in crisis can do is have a baby.

As finder of the child, S chose the name, Chrissie – this before she'd even checked its sex, or informed P. But when she told him, something opened up inside the man, as if a wizard had shot helium into his chest. When his wife asked what they should do, P told her to say nothing to anyone. *Chrissie had chosen them.* This man, who'd never lifted a finger to clean, now tore through the junk room like an uncorked genie, creating a nursery fit for royalty. That night, he told S about the sales manager, and agreed to his wife's terms. She would forgive him provided he never saw the temptress again.

*

Were we selfish? Absolutely. But we didn't know how to be otherwise, and weren't capable of understanding that selflessness brings its own joys.

Our selfishness was also the product of something much bigger than ourselves. Fear, mainly. We were too conscious of our place in time, too aware of the difficulties the future would hold, unable to see trade-offs as anything other than negative. We were terrified of showing fear, or need. Winners are never needy.

So we let time paint us into a corner. You don't schedule a nappy-change in a diary, or trade up to the latest model in model sons. If the jargon describes child rearing as basic task-orientation, that task defines itself as demand at any hour of the day or night, till time, and your consciousness of time, become re-calibrated.

You are not heroic because of what you've done, or intend to do, you are heroic because you are present when these instinctive demands are made of you. *The present.* When you finally learn to live in the present, with the soiled nappies and shrieks that mightn't go away, you begin to appreciate that the big game we've been signed up for is geared toward optimists, persons fool enough to believe that no crisis is more challenging or inevitable than a succession of nappy-soiled, chuck-stained immediacies. Trapped in this present, the only sensible course is to insist that you are generating a future where happiness will remain possible.

*

When Major Crime Squad detectives questioned Nick and Kylie about baby Trish, both swore they were the child's natural parents. The lies they'd told the doctor were purely to keep the baby's existence secret from hyper-religious grandparents.

In order to buy time, Nick played a bluff hand, volunteering his blood for DNA analysis. Since the right to grant permission for a sample to be taken from the child was germane to the issue at hand, police had to proceed with caution.

Releasing the pair without charge, the inspector warned that there would be further investigation, and Nick and Kylie should expect to be contacted by Hampton detectives.

*

Though some recipients imagined themselves to be chosen, they understood that God's elect tend to be vilified by those who can't imagine a deity that would exclude them. Knowing that it never pays to advertise a special relationship with God, the recipients smeared Vegemite on rusks, and pushed discretion to the limit.

*

Danielle was too young to know what she was taking on when she married Tom, a man left paraplegic by a head-on smash that killed his father and sister when he was nineteen. There was a hole in her life that not even Tom's charm could fill. If Tom had said that she couldn't keep Ingrid, Danielle would have left him on the spot; but Tom knew, from the moment he gazed into the child's eyes, that he needed to love her more than he needed anything else in the world.

*

Sooner or later, police were bound to ask Kylie's sister Fiona if she knew about an infant niece named Trish. Detectives thought Kylie's oddness about the child might pertain to a surrogacy pact.

The sister was extraordinarily nervous when the police arrived at her door. Once they said that Kylie had a child, Fiona couldn't contain herself. 'My God, it's happened to her as well.'

*

The early theories linked these babies to cult activity. The detectives thought tests would reveal the foundlings had the same father, an ego-monster who'd brainwashed his sex-slaves. Extortion or madness would prove to be the motivating factor.

The DNA tests on Kylie and Nick's baby, Trish, and Fiona and Greg's child, Declan, did uncover genetic commonalities. But the last thing police analysts expected were commonalities stemming from the fact that Kylie and Fiona were sisters. So far as science could establish, the recipients were the natural parents of their foundlings.

*

Once rumours of this story began to leak to the press, more recipients gained the confidence to introduce their babies to the world. Grandparents were notified, and christenings arranged. When the Bayside Council wanted to list baby epidemics among Hampton's distinctive features, the finders lobbied against publicity. Believing these children to be aliens, troubled types had already threatened to abduct them. Bad seeds. Sleepers. Incubi … Everything a disturbed mind could imagine.

All the while, these babies looked and behaved just like babies.

*

Lisa and I couldn't love Stephen any more if we'd attended his birth, or spent six years trying to conceive him. I'm not bothered that the boy resembles his mother's father more than he resembles me. I'm sure he'll have the good grace to adopt my personality flaws as his own.

We're thankful Stephen keeps us so busy. Otherwise, we'd have time to consider questions of justice: why we received this blessing when so many more deserving couples didn't. My mother-in-law, Pam, has a theory that the babies bypassed the people who knew they wanted them to find people who had no idea how much they needed them.

According to Lisa, Stephen and his miraculous cousins embody the Control Paradox. The more choice we have, and the more we strive to preclude accident and error, the more we stand to be subverted by contradictions at the heart of orderliness. Since vulnerability and conflicted emotion are essential to our humanity, control alone can never make us superior beings.

If I look closely, I see my face reflected in the boy's eyes. And maybe my one hope of seeing myself truly is through those eyes. Or through the eyes of an equally miraculous sibling.

Lisa didn't need to speak for me to know that she was expecting our second child. We kissed, smiled broadly, and wondered where the money would come from. We then promised to remove the words convenient and inconvenient from our vocabulary.

*

The babies are settling down, settling in. They're just a little unsettling, too. All through Hampton, you can hear the babies bubbling and burbling. Becoming.

Thought Crimes

Look Down with Me

Jennifer Mills

There's one swinging tonight, but only one; it's all they could catch. In the stable I water the horses and I take my time about it.

I stop with Queenie. I want to cut the sores from her hoofs. She lifts them for me when I think it. I scrape pieces from her feet with the sharpest knife and check her shoes are all intact. When I'm finished I touch her side, gentle, and she puts her foot down. Horses trust me. I fold the knife and put it in its place on the beam above the horseshoes and the brands.

There's a wind up, a chill from the south, and it moves the branches, but the sack hangs limply, as if it has been painted onto this picture. Painted blue from the moon, which is swelling to full like the gut of a dead kangaroo filling with maggots.

The moon will burst when its skin gets too thin and all the flies will spill out of it. They will come down out of the sky and crawl all over us. They try to get in at the mouth, the ears, the eyes. I can squint, dig my pinkies into my nostrils and my thumbs into my ears, but eventually I have to breathe.

The house is full of troopers and syrupy air smelling of port wine, fat and tobacco. There aren't enough chairs so the troopers stand against the walls and my sisters seem to take up all the rest of the house. They seep out of it like honey poured into a sack. I want the men to leave so I can get in and embed myself in Mother's lap and hear her say, *Look at this boy* to Father, the way she says about the sulky dogs.

But they won't go until they catch them.

I want to paint the swinging sack out of the night but it peeks in at me from every gap and crack in the stable which is only a shack no better than a lean-to, and gives splinters wherever you put your hand.

I put my hands down on the horses. I lean into a neck that leans into a basin of water. I put my nose into the place the mane starts and smell horse-sweat like rotten straw. I stay there until Queenie finishes and lifts her head and then we lean against each other, saying nothing. Neither of us could speak even if we wanted to.

I could stay all night and sleep standing like these animals. When the stable is full there's a space the right size for me. There are four of ours brought in tonight and the four the troopers came with. I've watered them all now. Tomorrow they'll be taken out again, taken by those troopers and the two trackers who are resting on the porch on the other side of the house, tobacco for them and a little fat but no port wine.

I hear my father's voice and I can't stay. He says *Alfie* and just as loud *Where is that idiot boy.* They all know I know my name, but they think because I don't speak I am deaf. I touch the horses in the loving way of a mothering mare, wiping my hand down over their eyes like their mothers licked them at birth. It calms them like it calms me to bury my face in my own mother's skirts.

I step out of the stable and move toward the house. My feet as silent as my throat. I walk slowly across the dark dirt yard, looking at my quiet feet. I walk in my own blue shadow. If I don't look up I won't see it and it won't be there.

But it is still there. When I reach the porch the tree creaks. The sack will be turning.

The trackers see me, they are watching. They're only cigarette ends under hats in the shadow but I can feel their eyes on me. I go into the house, wanting to press myself into its warm honey.

Alfie will have watered your horses, he's so good with them. Might have made a trooper himself, Mother tells the policeman with the white moustache. There is a space where they think about what I could have made if only. The moustache twitches but the lips don't move. He's troubled by me, so I give him my reassuring idiot smile. I know she means to tell them I am good, so I don't mind that she talks like I'm not there. They all do this, and also to the horses.

Long day tomorrow, says Moustache, and tips the sweet red liquor into his mouth. The glass looks tiny in his hand. He pats the barrel of a rifle that leans against the wall like a stiffened snake.

*

The troopers sleep in my room. I sleep on the porch with the trackers and the dogs. Mother and Father offer their bed to the men but are refused. My sisters sleep in their own room. They file into bed like obedient children but I know they will dream of troopers riding, dream with their delicate honey-hands pressed between their legs. I've seen them like this before. They whimper gently in their sleep like dogs.

I can move as quietly as a snake in this house at night on my mute feet.

I slip into the hammock that's hung on the stable side of the porch. I can hear the horses snort themselves to rest and the troopers snoring in a rhythm. I close my eyes and make myself still and small and shapeless.

The tree creaks. The tree creaks and the sack will be turning. The moon is bright over the edge of the roof. I can see the painted-in shadow of the hanging sack. I can hear the dogs breathe, alert, knowing they'll be called to hunt. The tree creaks and sleep won't come.

I slip out of the hammock and pad barefoot to the stable.

I walk from stall to stall and touch each of them on their eyes, and when I have seen that all are held fast by sleep, I stop and lean into Queenie and I take my knife from the beam. I return to the beginning of the line and start with the troopers' horses.

I keep one hand over the horse's eye. I press hard, expecting thick skin, but the knife slices easily through the soft place under the chin. I am calm and I stroke each of them like a mother and they do not bark with pain. Blood slips over my hand, warm and thick, warmer than my own. It smells good, like wet metal.

Queenie is last in line. When I reach her, I think I should just let her go. They will only catch her again. I look down the row of stalls, at the steam rising from the floor, and through it, through a crack in the wall, I catch the movement of the sack.

I know what to do. I wipe the knife on my sleeve, and I work it into Queenie's neck. She sighs as she slips and falls.

I don't fold the knife. I have one more sinew, one more thread to sever. I step out into the chill night, walk across the dark dirt yard on muted feet. I hear the tree creak and I face the sack.

It is not a sack at all, but a man. I feel the man-sized weight of him as I stand close. The knife slices through the rope and I let him fall.

Look down on his body, meek against the earth with me, moon, I think. But the moon doesn't answer. Its belly is beginning to split.

I fold the knife and go to my hammock. The tree doesn't creak anymore. I sleep sound through the night, until the flies wake me.

Bruno's Song and Other Stories from the Northern Territory

Visitors' Day

Mark Dapin

For eighteen months, all I thought about was my baby girl, and how I was never going to miss another minute of her sweet and precious life. I was going to teach her at home until she was twelve years old. I would have to start with the subjects I already knew, like spoken English and art – because I can paint, I was going to be a painter, I had a man who was a painter, but he was a drinker, as well – and I would learn the others, like history and geography and chemistry and science, by reading books the night before then reading them back to my baby in the morning, and explaining to her about everything in the world and how it is in books and how it is in real life. Except I wouldn't tell her how it is in prison, because she wouldn't need to know.

I was going to get us a place with the housos in Waterloo – a tower in the sky – and move my bed into her bedroom, or her bed into my bedroom, or just have one room and it could be our room where we would have both our beds from the beginning, so neither of us would feel like an intruder, or a guest, or a cellmate.

I would stay up all night watching her sleeping, stroking her liquorice hair, holding her caramel hands. If she was having a nightmare, if she was making fists or screwing up her eyes, or grabbing the sheet and pulling it over her chin and pushing it into her mouth and biting down so hard her gums bled and her jaw ached in the morning like she'd been punched, I would whisper, 'It's OK, baby, everything'll be fine,' and I would climb into bed beside her – or take her into my bed – so I could smell her and she could smell me and she would know she was not alone in the world with only her own breakable body to draw strength from, and her own soft brain to understand things.

I taped Polaroids of my daughter to the ceiling of my cell – nothing else but photographs of my baby girl in her pink dress with pink ribbons in her hair – so I could see her smile when I woke up in the morning and before I fell asleep at night.

One day last winter, the screws charged in and tore them down – and tore down everybody else's pictures of their baby girls in their pink dresses with pink ribbons in their hair – because prison isn't some kind of five-star holiday resort where you can go horse riding along the beach and put up pictures of your family, which you might be using to hide razor blades, or works, or your baby's kisses drawn with crayon on the back.

Auntie Olive looked after my baby for eighteen months, like she looked after me for eighteen years. When I told her I was getting out on visitors' day, she said she would meet me at the gate in Lenny's shitbox, with my baby in the back seat strapped into a plastic chair.

Fat-pig Screw came into my cell to check that I hadn't stolen any government property, such as the bed that was part of the wall, or the bowl that stank of other women's piss and blood, or the noticeboard that said '1958' and 'boongs R a bunch of food theef.'

Sweet Caroline, my cellie, turned over in her bunk to face the wall. She'd seen her boyfriend in the morning, across a table in the visitors' room. Fat-pig Screw pulled on her gloves and stuck her pork sausages into every dip in my mattress, every crack in my brickwork, then she jammed her hand inside my pillowcase and pulled out the smallest foil of yani you've ever seen.

Janelle, who had strangled her baby in its little pink dress, stopped in the corridor to say goodbye, because she was getting out today too. If you take a life you gave, you are only stealing from yourself, so five years is all you owe to the cops, who have to make sure the books balance at the end of the day and nobody is thieving minutes from the till.

'She's loaded me up,' I told Janelle, whose lips shone with the gloss she had painted on for the pimp who wouldn't live with another man's daughter.

Janelle shrugged – because what can you do? – and blew me a kiss made from the curls in her baby's hair. Big-arse Screw steered her away.

'That your girlfriend?' asked Fat-pig Screw, crinkling her snout, snorting a kiss. She wanted me to slap her, so they could keep me another month – my yani was only worth a week, and where was the fun in that, eh? – but when I lifted my hands all I could do was push them into my eyes. I cried, because my baby was waiting for me in a plastic chair in Lenny's shitbox outside the gate.

'Where'd you get it?' asked Fat-pig Screw.

'It's mine,' said Sweet Caroline.

Fat-pig Screw looked at me like I was potato peelings.

'So *she's* your girlfriend,' she said.

Sweet Caroline did that thing with her hips like she was bucking a mug, and touched me tightly on the shoulder, to give me muscle for the afternoon.

The funny thing is, they call her Sweet Caroline because she is such a sour, twisted bitch.

*

Nineteen months ago, I tied my little girl to her cot with a big buckled belt, and she was lying in her own dirt, hungry and screaming, and my auntie found me on the pavement outside Derek's pub, chatting up some mug through the window of his Falcon, and she said if I ever used again, she'd never give me back my baby. She'd change her name and take her to Queensland. Nobody would come to my funeral.

Fat-pig Screw wrote up Sweet Caroline's charge while I picked up my property. I had to count twenty-five dollars and sign for a miniskirt and a denim shirt and a wide belt – not the same one, not the same one – broken heels and a handbag. The screw at the main gate queried the signature on my pass, just to piss me off.

When the gate screw let me out, Janelle was standing in the car park, smoking through strangler's fingers.

'You seen Auntie?' I asked.

'I told her you'd been busted,' said Janelle. She crushed her smoke into the wall. 'Sorry,' she said, then her pimp drove up and pushed his buffalo head out of the car window, and it hung there like a trophy that some mug had shot and stuffed, until Janelle kissed him like a mad, murderous lady buffalo, with no horns to show what she was.

'You wanna ride?' her pimp asked me, and he made it sound as if he was offering a disease.

I tried to ring Auntie, but there was no credit on my phone.

I crossed the road with cars shooting past my ears – I could feel their speed on my legs – and I froze. Drivers shouted at me to move on, get out of the way, shave my legs, find my auntie, see my baby.

Between McDonald's and KFC, there were two hotels, a bloodhouse for visitors and a sports bar for screws. I knew the screws' pub would be empty until shift change. I walked through the burning lights and accident noise to ask the barman if I could use his phone, but he didn't like my skin. I've got the name of my baby's daddy tattooed across the knuckles of my love hand – he has my name on his neck, I have my name on my neck, I would break his neck if I saw him again – so the barman threw me out, and it was no use crying or threatening him because he'd heard every story before.

I didn't want to go into the bloodhouse. I'd already lost enough blood – I'd seen it fly up and fill my works like a fat mosquito – but I had to phone Auntie and tell her to wait with my baby, and not change her name and carry her to Queensland, and keep her from my graveside when I died.

There was a user hanging from the payphone saying, 'OK, OK,' and I wondered if he was buying, because this was the pub the visitors came to hook up.

Sweet Caroline's pirate was sitting at a table in his earrings, signet rings and chains. He said, 'Hello, beautiful.'

Oh, I used to be pretty, and I haven't lost it all – it's going, I know it's going, heroin took it and used it for itself – but I'm not beautiful. It's nice to be called beautiful. The young mugs all told me I had nice eyes – a drunk copper blacked them with a sucker punch – and my skin is still smooth, you wouldn't take me for a user until you saw my arms.

Sweet Caroline's pirate – I can't say his name, but you'd know it; you couldn't spell it but you'd recognise it – managed Hemispheres in the Cross. I asked to use his phone, but he said the battery was dead, 'beautiful.'

I waited until the junkie was finished, then tried the payphone, but you couldn't use it without a card. Eighteen months ago, they didn't have those cards.

Sweet Caroline's pirate was drinking with a wog, and the wog bought me a Bundy.

It was my first drink for eighteen months. I swallowed it whole and it made my feet shake. The wog laughed and bought me another, then Sweet Caroline's pirate bought me another and I bought a packet of Holiday, and I bought Sweet Caroline's pirate a Bundy, and the wog a Bundy, then we moved up to doubles.

It was good to be with men again.

The wog was wog-handsome, with skin like hash. Sweet Caroline's pirate had a soft voice and gentle fingers on my thigh.

I told Sweet Caroline's pirate how I was going to read all the books to my baby, how I was going to be a real mother, how I was going to get square and keep off the street and stay off drugs – maybe a little smoke now and again, eh? – how I was going to meet a nice guy and clean the house while he fixed the car, and we were going to move out of the city and live on a farm – I once grew roses on a prison farm – where my baby could grow up safe from dope and dealers and mugs and pimps.

The wog said I should live my dream. Sweet Caroline's pirate gave me a hug – oh, it's been a long time since I had a hug like that one, wrapped in arms as hard as house bricks; smelling rum and aftershave and sweat and smoke – and said, 'I hope it comes true for you, beautiful.'

'But you're going to need some money first,' said the wog. 'Why don't you come back to work at Hemispheres?'

'We could pay you in dope,' said Sweet Caroline's pirate.

'I've got to phone Auntie,' I said.

Sweet Caroline's pirate and the wog were the same type. I don't mean they were the same type of wog, they were the stripclub type. They wore their Rolexes loose, as if they didn't care if the watches slipped off their wrists, and laid their wallets on the table, stuffed with fifties, like they might slip one into your bra to buy a feel.

The wog let me use his phone, but I couldn't get through to Auntie. I thought maybe the hotel roof was blocking the signal, so I took the phone into the car park. I dialled another number, talked quickly to a machine, sat back with the wog and waited.

I could hypnotise the wog with my tits. They were part-covered, half-secret. I brushed his arm with a cup of my bra while I scooped his wallet into my bag. Because you are what you are, and prison can't change that.

'I need to try Auntie again,' I said, then picked up the phone and walked slowly to the car park. I could feel the wog's stare on my arse. I kicked off my lame heels and ran – when I was a little girl, I could run like a horse, I used to run barefoot to Auntie when she picked me up from school – and I waved down the cab I'd called.

I was pulling on the taxi door when I heard Sweet Caroline's pirate galloping behind me. I swung my bag into the front seat, but the cabbie saw two waving beer bottles and he slammed the door and drove away with everything inside.

The wog threw me into the wall. My shoulder blades scraped down the brickwork. 'Where is it? Where is it?' he shouted, running his hands through my clothes while Sweet Caroline's pirate held me upright. I pointed to the cab, which was gone, and he started punching me in the stomach and kicking at my legs. You're hurting me, oh stop, please stop. Sweet Caroline's pirate held me with an arm twisted behind my back, whispering filthy ideas, biting my neck with his ugly gap teeth, and the two of them pushed me into their car. I'll kill you. I'll kill you all.

They said I was going to have to compo the wog by working at Hemispheres, to pay him back for the money he'd had in his wallet and the business he'd lose without his phone.

I said, 'Youse can compo your fucking arses.'

They drove me to the club, where the wog grabbed at me, took hold of my blouse and pulled me towards him, bursting the buttons and ripping the cotton, snatching the petals from a rose. I tried to bite his nose, but he butted me with the side of his head.

Dizzy, now I'm spinning. I've got to stay on my feet.

The wog dragged me upstairs, past the stage and the bedrooms and into the filthy room for users – there's my blood on those walls, thin red trails like tears – where the wog wanted to beat me up some more. But Sweet Caroline's pirate said he shouldn't mark my face, and shouted for another man to help handle the mad bitch. It takes three of you plastic gangsters to hold down one girl. I'll come back with a crew of Tongans and they'll tear you to pieces. A young kid came in with a shooter and passed it to Sweet Caroline's pirate.

Now I'm scared, really scared, like this is where I die for a wallet I didn't even get to keep, for a thieving cabbie's phone.

Sweet Caroline's man held it near my mouth. He said, 'You do fifty mugs, and the money goes to the house.' I smiled inside, because I could do ten mugs in a night, and there were only fifty drunken footy players and lonely uglies between me and my baby girl.

First I had to do it with Sweet Caroline's pirate and the wog, but that was for free, so it didn't count. Afterwards, they gave me a cheeseburger, then locked me up until the rain washed the first mugs in from the street. I did it six times with a mob of mongrels on their way to a bucks' night. They all wanted to watch – oh let him finish, please let him finish – so I charged them each a bit extra and stuffed it in my bra. When they left, I curled up sore in a corner and I didn't cry, but I wished I was back in prison and I hurt in my body and my head and my heart because I was a thief and a whore and I got caught.

A blonde walked in – swollen sunglasses hiding pinned eyes in daylight – and I asked if she had a phone, then I saw she was a user and she only had one thing. She sold me a cap for twice the street price – all the money for letting the retards watch their mates – then ran out to get herself two more.

After that, I loved everything: breaking open the cap, the smell of flame on the teaspoon, the feeling of cord tightening around my arm – I've still got veins there, yeah I'm not so bad. I loved the blonde girl and her maybe-clean works, and the world closing down around me.

Two men came in and did me while I was stoned. They did the blonde, as well, and I don't think she was even a worker. She took their money and said she was going out and did I need anything. I had to ask Sweet Caroline's pirate for a sub to buy dope.

'Of course,' he said, 'beautiful. We're not monsters.'

I was thinking of my baby in her little pink dress, and I wished I had a photograph of her. I would have put it up on the wall in the room and looked at it all night long. It would have been like I was watching over her, keeping her from harm, even though I was not there with her. Sometimes in the night I wake up and I know she has woken up, too. She is afraid and alone and I can hear her cry. I close my eyes tightly and concentrate hard, and I send my spirit across the city to her bed.

She can feel my love, and that makes everything all right.

Shelter

Kate Rotherham

You're not supposed to like willow trees anymore. They're not native, they choke the river and crowd out the natives. They're best bulldozed out so the creeks can breathe more easily. It's the best thing for the creek ecosystem. They told me all this in the council newsletter. The thing is, though, when I sleep under one, it doesn't feel so terrible. I like that the green is more emerald than the surrounding natives. I like those long fingers that hang like hair, a dreadlocked chandelier traipsing down to the ground. I like the play of dappled light when I'm looking out, encased in my own pocket of cool, airy shade.

My sister's kids have a cubby under a willow tree, the long slender branches shade it completely and fall cheekily through the red-checked curtains my sister made. I had endless cups of tea with the littlest one in there the last time I visited. (*Anuvva cup, Wobbie?* her blue eyes blinking intensely with the concentration of pouring imaginary tea. *Oh, yes please, Lily, mmm … that's delicious, thank you very much,* all the while trying to keep my balance on the tiny chair). It had gone pretty well, the 'reunification process.' Even though I felt her husband's eyes boring into me and I heard the dull rumble of his complaints from the cubby. I winced at the pity in her voice when I heard her sigh and say, *But he's my little brother.*

We'll be away for three weeks. She writes down the dates on the back of her business card. *The house is alarmed,* she says, avoiding my eyes, *but the cabana isn't.* She hands me the card and her eyes are pleading with me now and I know she wants promises of responsibility, of appreciation, of something, but she doesn't say. I take the card and meet her eyes for half a second. *Thank you, it will be OK, thank you.*

Cabana. I'd never even heard the word. But I follow her nod to the whitewashed structure adjacent to the long sparkly pool. *It's so they don't have to walk back up to the house for anything when they're down by the pool,* I explain to Jacko over lunch.

Well, we all need one of those! Gawd, imagine the hardship of walking all the way back to the house just to get another beer! His yellow-stained sausage fingers start shaking invisible maracas and his thick gravelly voice is surprisingly tuneful, *At the Copa-co-copacabana, the hottest spot north of Havana.*

*

She's left books, magazines, enormous towels, sunscreen, insect repellent, jigsaw puzzles of European villages, board shorts and T-shirts. The mini fridge is packed with milk, juice, margarine, yoghurt, chocolate and sliced peaches in a see-through container like a hundred smiles squashed in a little swimming pool with a lid. There's bread, muesli and English muffins in the cupboard with a note tucked in between them, Robbie, make yourself at home. Please take your medicine. I love you, Mich xxx. Two crisp fifty-dollar bills are attached with a paperclip.

The shower is tiled with long rectangles of swirling sandy-grained marble. There's an hourglass bottle of electric-green shampoo promising my hair more life and energy. I swish the thick white goop all over myself and imagine an electrified tingling. I watch the stream of soapy bubbles slip away beneath my cracked feet, bury my head in a thick fluffy towel and breathe in my new self. I smell like apples and honey.

Lying back in the deck chair, a bowl piled high with muesli, yoghurt, and peaches in my lap, I watch water silently lapping at the terracotta tiles in mini-waves, a seamless transition from water to land. A series of fountains spray in gentle arcs from the sidewall, like liquid rainbows. I have a flash to us as kids, Mich at the kitchen table cutting delicate paper patterns and minia-ture floral cotton prints for Barbie's next outfit. Me, restless and hovering, *Mich, how many more minutes till you'll play with me?* Mum shooing me outside. Feeling a shimmer of heat from the pavers as the flywire door slams behind me.

Today on the tram I saw a bumper sticker saying, *Practise random acts of kindness and senseless acts of beauty.* Reading it felt like sliding into a warm bath. I suddenly can't wait for my next form; no longer will I write *undecided* in the religion question, now I will write PRAOKASAOB. I wonder if maybe it's too long but it's two letters shorter than PRESBYTERIAN and lots of old people probably write that.

I still have my lunch at the shelter. The volunteers, mostly older ladies with short silver hair and Homeyped shoes, always smile when they serve me and today I smile too. One lady whispers a kind secret to me each day to chew over with my food. *You're not like the others here. You'll get well again, I just know it. You have lovely manners. I'm saying some prayers for you.* I wonder if she's practising a random act of kindness or maybe she's Presbyterian.

The fellas ask, *You found a new place, Robbo? Any room for me?* I stare at my hot lunch and stir the peas through the mashed potato. When I think about sharing my Greek Island cabana little prickles of sweat form on my face and multiply down my neck and spine. I chew on my lip, then scoop in big salty mouthfuls and swallow them slowly. Perhaps I should offer, just for a few nights. I shovel a few more loaded forkfuls into my mouth to save myself from a reply. Would that be a random act of kindness? Then I remember Mich's hesitation, her eyes darting with unspoken fears. *Naah,* I shake my head, swallowing, *It's nothin' special.* Afterwards I offer to sweep the floor, hoping everyone will be gone by the time I leave.

Jacko's in hospital, the co-ordinator tells me as I'm leaving. *He went on a bit of bender. But he'll get there.*

I nod but am not sure anymore. Get where exactly? Get sober or get housing or get old or just get dead?

You're looking good, Robbo. Everything OK?

I borrow one of Jacko's favourite replies; it fits nicely. *Never better.*

Good for you! Thanks for sweeping. God bless.

I look over my shoulder all the way to the tram.

Out the rattly window, I see hot and bothered mothers placating their kids. I imagine my sister on the beach, her three kids sticky with sand and sunscreen climbing on her, all wanting her to build sandcastles and take them for ice creams. I picture him, oblivious, his new iPhone clipped to his designer boardshorts below his pasty paunch, pouring over the tiny writing on the financial pages and snorting in disgust at fluctuating share prices. One time when they left Mum's, Mich was in pack-up mode and asked, *Got your blueberry, hon?* and I didn't like the way he scowled at her. *It's a Blackberry and yes – thank you – I have it.*

*

I garden in the mornings while the sun is low and gentle. I just pull weeds out and snip the runaway climbers back. Sometimes I press my weight on my hands, pushing them down deep in the earth, willing some healthy life source to seep through my skin and pulse up my veins. When the lady next door collects the mail I give her my friendly I'm-just-the-gardener wave. I'm pretty sure gardening is a senseless act of beauty.

I try to swim three times every day: before my breakfast, when I get back from lunch, and late at night. Sometimes I do laps of freestyle, trying to remember all those things from swimming squad a hundred years ago, *Bend your elbows, reach out, cup your hands, keep your head still, small turn for a breath.* Other times I just swim breaststroke under the water, propelling myself forward in a silent world of bubbles and swirling ripples, smiling at the Kreepy Krauly on my way past. At night, when the summer moon is fat as an orange and close enough to touch, I imagine a great white is hunting me down, endless rows of shearing teeth snapping at my desperate flutter-kick while my skinny arms thrash around like a cartoon character. Finally I scramble out, my heart pounding and my lungs bursting, and drape my towel around me like a shipwreck survivor, not daring to put my toes back in.

One night the clouds rumble and I soak in the shallow end, watching milliseconds of white electricity flash across the dark purple sky like giant scissors. When they finally come, the raindrops are fat and heavy, drumming down on my head like a marching band. I am cocooned by water for hours. When I finally emerge my hands look different, my nail beds have soaked themselves new.

I lather myself in the spray-on repellent and sleep in the brightly striped hammock, which the tag says was handmade in Guatemala. I wonder if there are many cabanas in Guatemala. Is that where they invented guacamole? Guacamole in Guatemala. The hammock is suspended between two whitewashed pillars by ropes and carabiners. Carabiners in the cabana. I don't know how anyone ever learns English. When the mozzies are especially fierce I try to drape beach towels over every inch of me without tipping out, which is harder than it sounds.

I buy a tray of pansies from the gardening place on the main road. Some are butter-yellow flecked with deep purple, others are navy velvet, there are a few white ones and some electric-sunrise orange ones. I buy some pea straw too, so I can mulch around them. I read about that in one of the gardening magazines my sister left for me; it helps retain the moisture after watering. The guy at the gardening place tells me I'm on a winner with pansies. *It's nice to be a winner,* I say. He lets me wheel it all 'home' on a trolley. *Just drop it back when you're done, mate,* he says, like I am a regular Saturday morning, muesli-eating, pool-cleaning, pansy-mulching kind of guy. Back home, I upend them carefully, spread out their thread-like roots and plant them gently in the spare spaces of the garden beds and along the cubby-house window boxes. I water them with Lily's tin watering can and then stand back and admire their colour and promise. Maybe they will make my sister smile. Maybe she will say, *He's my little brother* in a slightly different tone next time.

They are due home tomorrow. I fold my towels and wipe the bench down. I tuck Mich's note in my pocket and sit for a while dangling my feet and listening to the rhythmic spray of the side fountains. Circadas throb in unison from next-door's towering gum. The sun is sharp and the air smells of fresh eucalyptus. I'm definitely more spring than summer today; new ideas ricochet around inside me as I stride up the road with my new trolley. I feel tall and light, almost willowy.

Island

Ten-day Socks

Marele Day

At lunchtime on the third day I wash my socks then hang them over the clothes horse outside the room.

The gong sounds. I trail up to the hall, along with my fellow meditators. Along the path, in amongst the scribbly gums, are anonymous works of art – discreet arrangements of stones and pebbles, circles of leaves, a flower, a button. Except for meal breaks we meditate from four-thirty a.m. till nine p.m. For twenty-four hours a day we observe Noble Silence, not communicating with each other, avoiding eye contact, better to focus our gaze inward.

The meditation mats are arranged in neat rows, men on one side of the hall and women on the other, with a wide aisle down the centre. Everyone has a shawl and at least one cushion to sit on. Some people have backrests or sit in chairs at the end of rows, but the practice isn't encouraged. With backrests and chairs, the quality of the meditation is dulled.

It takes two or three days for people to settle down, to find the one position they can maintain for an hour without wriggling or fidgeting. It's not easy being still and quiet, even for an hour. In the silence we collectively hold aloft, bodily sounds are clearly audible. The scrape of fabric against fabric if someone moves their legs or adjusts their shawl. Joints creaking. Coughing, burping, nose blowing, sniffing and sneezing. Sometimes even the odd snore or gasp. The slightest sound pierces the silence, causing it to fall to earth like a spent parachute.

Afternoon meditation begins. The recorded voice of the master speaks of impermanence. It is the nature of things. All sensations arise and sooner or later pass; there is no point dwelling on this or that. If you experience agitation or mind wandering, focus on the breath, the area below the nostrils and above the upper lip. Remain calm and equanimous.

The voice stops and we are left on our own. It's warm in the hall but my feet are cold. I try to focus on my breath but my mind is preoccupied with the area below the ankles. That's not all. It has developed a fascination for the word *equanimous* and keeps repeating it. I'm not sure it even is a word. Equanimity, yes, but the adjectival form? I need to consult a dictionary, but we were advised not to bring any potential distractions such as reading or writing material. As well as repeating *equanimous* like a mantra, my inner voice is also singing 'You Picked a Fine Time to Leave Me, Lucille,' both verses of 'Don't Fence Me In' and riffs from David Bowie's 'Starman.'

Accompanying the vocals are random images – snow-capped mountains, a country gate, children playing on a see-saw and people lining up to get their cars registered. Forehead, cheeks, chin. The area below the nostrils and above the upper lip – how come this part of the face doesn't have its own name? My mind has fragmented into a scatter of jigsaw pieces. Is this what dementia feels like? Fortunately, someone coughs and my mind becomes momentarily still.

The respite doesn't last long. I now see my socks, black with a trim of white, slumped over the clotheshorse like two dead magpies. Socks inevitably lead to feet but where have mine gone? I try wiggling my toes. No sensation arising and passing, no sensation at all. My feet have disappeared. It is very difficult to remain equanimous with body parts missing.

When we are finally released from the hall, I hobble out on a mass of pins and needles.

*

The weather in March changes from one hour to the next. Day four begins with a grey misty dawn but by breakfast time the sun has come out. I move the clothes horse into the slim streak of sunlight along the edge of the veranda. By lunch it is pouring and my socks are soaked.

All very well for the master to talk about being calm and equanimous; I bet he never had a sock problem. I do however become alert and vigilant, spending every non-meditation moment observing my socks. I dare not leave them outside unsupervised.

*

On day five when we break for lunch the sun is shining but not on the veranda. My socks, although no longer soggy, are still a bit damp and cold. A half hour in a sunny spot should dry them nicely. I step off the veranda into the natural environment and head for a sunlit tree a few metres away. Birds twitter, insects fly about. Would I be interfering with nature by hanging my socks in a tree? Inadvertently killing some microscopic sentient being? Along with the vow of silence we have also pledged to abstain from killing. With the utmost care and reverence for all life, I place my socks on the sunniest branch.

Then I notice something on the soles – ALL DAY SOCKS in brilliant white letters against the black. This could possibly be construed as reading material and here I am, placing it in public view. I quickly turn the socks over but there's more, this time in bold red: Womens Size 5–8. I try not to obsess about the lack of apostrophe.

The gong sounds for afternoon meditation. I return to my room, hang the socks over the end of the bed and join the line of people making their way to the hall.

The first hour after lunch is a period of 'strong determination.' Be vigilant, observe objectively, sit without moving, do not leave the hall. It is common to experience mind wandering and agitation but perseverance will bring success. Impermanence. Every experience is impermanent. The socks will not be wet forever; eventually they will dry. Now I start to think about having to stay in the hall. What if I want to go to the toilet, feel nauseous, have an aneurism or a heart attack? I scan my body – no chest or head pains, no loss of sensation except in my feet. I do have a dry mouth. What does that mean?

All around me is silky silence. Under the meditation shawl I'm pinching my fingers, trying to divert my multitasking mind from its repertoire of songs, images and medical problems. Does anyone else have a tribe of chimpanzees in their head, swinging from thought to thought, shrieking wildly? Very slowly I raise my eyelids a fraction, look right and left through the curtain of eyelashes. Everyone is still as stone, row upon row of perfect little Buddha statues.

What is the collective noun for chimpanzees – a gang, troop, parliament, colony, unkindness, murder, party? A paddling of ducks, an ostentation of peacocks, a crash of rhinoceroses, a kindle of kittens, a pod of whales. A shrewdness of apes. Ah. But it doesn't quite seem right for chimps. Ground control to Major Tom.

*

Day six. Perseverance has brought success. The socks are dry! Liberation from suffering. In the wisdom gained over the past few days I know that my slip-on shoes flick up moisture and debris, so I do not put the socks on till I am safely inside the meditation hall. Clean dry socks. I can dedicate myself totally to strong determination, with no cravings or aversions.

I am at one with the group, feet warm and cosy, at one with all sentient beings. The air in the hall is warm and nurturing. My mind is alert and vigilant. I am equanimous. The word doesn't bother me anymore.

After a while I notice a smell. Occasionally, as well as small sounds, there are evanescent aromas in the hall. Pleasant smells – shampoo, moisturiser – that give delight and harm not. This one is unidentifiable, a blend of old goat cheese, straw, stagnant water, dead rat and a hint of possum pee.

Is it a test? Are they piping something into the hall to see how equanimous we really are? It's stinging my nose, getting into my lungs. Very soon I am going to have to cough.

Someone beats me to it. The cough sets off a cacophony of sneezes, nose blowing and throat clearing. The woman beside me, obviously not perfectly centred in her lotus position, lurches backwards. I hear a series of soft thuds as the entire row behind goes down like dominoes. I try to maintain strong determination.

When I put my head under the shawl so as not to be diverted by the goings on around me I get a good strong whiff and nearly fall backwards myself.

At the end of this excruciatingly long hour everyone makes a rush for the door.

Back in my room I fill the sink with hot water, pour in liberal amounts of rosemary-scented shampoo, add a shot of lavender oil for good measure and throw the socks in.

I have enough underwear for ten days; why did I bring only one pair of socks?

Instead of going to breakfast, I walk past the rooms of other students. There are not only socks and underwear hanging out to dry but T-shirts, jeans, a skirt and even a jacket. I'm having trouble with one small pair of socks, yet here are entire wardrobes. How come everyone else is coping? What do they know that I don't?

*

Evening of day six. I lift the socks gingerly out of the water. Still a faint odour of cheese. Are protracted periods of meditation distorting my senses? Is it an illusion? I'm a very clean person. I don't smell. How come my socks do? I drop them back in the water, add more lavender oil and clean my teeth in the shower.

*

Lunchtime, day seven. I wash and scrub the little buggers. Rinse them over and over. When I wring them out the lettering on the soles contorts into Day Sucks. I try not to take it personally.

I go for a walk, gaze at the artworks scattered in amongst the trees. Near the boundary fence is a new addition – an abandoned sandal. Then I see its mate in the bushes about a metre away, the strap hanging loosely. What is the point of one sandal if the other is broken?

There are a few people on the path, prowling like lions, but they are all wearing shoes. The abandoned ones are women's, size seven. I imagine a muddy-footed woman silently weeping in her room.

*

Day eight. Socks still not dry.

*

Day nine. The retreat is almost over. Socks improved but still not dry. Tomorrow is the last day.

*

Day ten. Noble Silence is replaced by Noble Speech. We can talk. Silent anguish is now given voice. One woman left her towel out in the rain and had to make do with paper towelling. 'Drying my hair was the worst,' she adds forlornly. Another had a spider scurry out of her hoodie and onto her face. One man, a sleepwalker, got into bed with his room mate. Imagine the room mate coping with that in Noble Silence, trying to keep attention on the area below the nostrils and above the upper lip.

'How about that weird smell!' says a man with a shaved head. 'When was it, day five?'

'Day six.' Everyone turns to me, wanting more information. How much of it am I willing to share? Eventually I say: 'I think it was someone's socks.' Everyone nods thoughtfully, as if I'm terribly wise. I feel like a liar, a fake. I'm not wise. I did not remain equanimous, I was subject to cravings and aversions, obsessions. I take a deep breath. 'Actually, they were my socks.' I expect everyone to get up and leave but no one does. Several people appear to be on the verge of saying something but instead sip their tea.

Finally, the man whose room mate got into bed with him says, 'You've no idea how grateful I am to those socks. I'd been holding on to a fart till I thought I'd burst. When that smell wafted over I was able to let go.'

Then others start owning up to coughs, belches and grunts. One man reveals that he'd smuggled in a fitness magazine and some sudoku puzzles. Another confesses to keeping a diary, writing his thoughts on toilet paper.

*

End of the retreat. The socks are dry. They don't smell.

While packing, I realise that I have managed most of the time without them. Sockless feet took me to and from the meditation hall each day. I have the memory of cold but can no longer feel it.

One last walk. To the boundary fence. The abandoned sandals are still there. Unobtrusive as a butler I lay my socks down with them, then quietly step back.

The outside world. At the train station we equanimously observe the newspaper headlines. Even though the news is a week old and now focused on the aftermath, it seems beyond belief. On the day I first washed my socks, the earth shifted along a fault line in the north Pacific; a wave gathered momentum and monumentally made its way towards Fukushima.

Shooting the Fox

Marion Halligan

Would you like to see the fox I shot this morning, he said, as he opened the gate in the wall.

This is a particular form of words. It is not a question. You do not say no. It appears to be polite – would you – but it leaves no room.

I went and saw the fox. Exquisite red creature. It does not know yet that it is dead. Its eye is not dim, its brush is defiant. Soon it will droop and decay and know its own mortality.

*

His name is Malcolm and he wishes to marry me. I am a 43-year-old virgin and my name is Gloria. An unsuitable name. Except when I sing Gloria in excelsis Deo. Not that I can sing. I lift up my head and open my mouth and pretend to be part of the glorious harmony of the choir. I open my mouth and no sound comes out, but the choir's sound fills it. We are very proud of the choir at my school, it is one of the things we are famous for.

The girls are cruel. Generation after generation they come and flourish and go. They can take all sorts of forms, and one of them is tropical flowers, growing lustily on their vines, their preening tendrils twining and prying, threatening to crush the frail trellis of the school between their vigorous thighs. Flowers that are creamy, rosy, dusky, thickly petalled, with long fleshy throats full of pollen. Even when they sit demurely in class, their blue-checked dresses smoothed down as far as they will go over these strong thighs, the slit between them cries out, I am open and thickly pinkly flesh, I am filled with honey, my sticky juices are waiting for the protuberances of men to find me out and fill me. It is hard to close your eyes to these shameless songs, it is necessary to say in a clear hard voice the tenses of French verbs, words without sentences to give them meaning, possessing only syntax. Pay attention, girls, it is a matter simply of rote learning, of reciting over and over until you know by heart.

Their hearts beat, the buttons of their dresses rise and fall, they slide undone to show lacy bras and the smooth flesh with these powerful hearts beating.

The verbs though meaningless alone are a spell to keep lascivious scents at bay, otherwise their languid beguiling odour-songs would drive us all mad.

*

Would you like to see the fox I shot this morning, Malcolm said, and I went through the gate in the wall and down to the kitchen garden, where the fox hung, its tail bushy, its pointed little face open-mouthed as if to draw in air.

I could shoot a few and make you a fur coat, he said, and I remembered women of my grandmother's age, wearing fox stoles with beady false black eyes and a little chain joining sharp-toothed mouth to legs, bony legs with padded paws. I always wondered how they could bear having a dead animal hanging round their necks. Even flattened out and lined with shiny brown satin.

Why do you shoot them? I asked Malcolm. Don't they keep the rabbits in check?

I shoot the rabbits too, he said. I am cooking rabbit stew for dinner. You'll enjoy its gamey flavour, not bland like farmed creatures.

He is a hunter. He wants to marry me. His name is John Malcolm Crape Pembroke. I saw it in a book. I would be the third Mrs Malcolm Pembroke. Though I could keep my own name. Gloria Jones. When the girls ask me for an example of bathos I am careful not to offer my own name.

The girls call me mademoiselle. I met Malcolm when his daughter was in the boarding house. He came to see each of her teachers when he picked her up at the end of term. She was a good French scholar. Now she lives in Aix-en-Provence, studying translation. She has a brother who is a merchant banker in London.

Malcolm lives deep in the high country in a tower. It's old, built by convicts who first made the bricks. You can find arrows and marks like birds' feet, which ask you to think of the men who made them. It's like a medieval watchtower, designed to keep an eye out for marauding tribes. It is wide and tall, with one round room on each floor. In the basement is a studio, with presses and machines. Then a room with books and a harpsichord painted with blue-grey landscapes of weeping-barked eucalyptus trees. This floor is surrounded by a rim of rooms he calls his offices, a kitchen and scullery and pantry, a laundry and mudroom and storerooms, opening through arches and doors into the main room.

Upstairs is a room arranged for me, and then on the top floor his bedroom. A staircase zigzags round the walls to each floor and up through his bedroom to the battlemented roof. Last year the second Mrs Pembroke fell from this roof and died. He was away at the time. Was it an accident or did she do it on purpose? Who knows? She liked the roof and often sat on its turreted rim. She could see the bones of the garden from there, she said. So he told me.

How can I marry you, I said. I am a schoolteacher. I cannot live here and teach in my school.

I am a rich man, he said. You do not need to work.

I thought of the girls, blooming so tropically and self-regardingly, new ones year after year, hardly paying attention to the elderly virgin who teaches them French. Though they do learn the French, mostly, and pass their exams, and blow the air round my cheeks with kisses and thanks when they leave to truly blossom in the real world. Heedless they are, and cruel by nature but without malice. Could I give them up?

I did not find out then what he did for a living. Maybe I thought he was a rich man by inheritance, that the curious garden and the tower were not earned by him. I am used to rich parents at my school. Later I asked him.

I'm a writer, he said.

What of? I asked, because mostly writers I know are not rich. When we are married I will show you, he said.

I asked if I would have seen any of his books. No, he said. I asked if he wrote under his own name. Two of them, he said. John Malcolm Crape Pembroke: I supposed his pen name would be John Crape. A strong and simple name.

I said, I am a 43-year-old virgin. How can want to marry me?

People think it is difficult to manage to be a 43-year-old virgin in this day and age, but it hasn't been for me. It is something that happened quite naturally, and there I am sitting in my school like a rose hip on a branch, tight and firm and yellowish brown, contented. Slender, slim, thin, and that's hard work, but who could expect otherwise?

Malcolm told me about being married to him. How we would live. The fruitful life in the tower. The delicious meals we would eat. The fine red wines. The garden. The seasons. The reading and music. The trips to cities. The trips overseas. The art galleries, the plays, the restaurants. It occurred to me that I would not stay slim in such a life. So rich, so full of event. Wonderful narratives, like a book he was giving me, inviting me to enjoy.

The thing I did not consider then is that a book is for reading. It is not a life. For the space of its turning pages you may believe you live in it, but sooner or later you must close it up. Put it back on the shelf, and look at the room you are in, a room which will say sternly to you, this is where you live, what are you making of this? The life that Malcolm had written for himself, was offering to write for me, it didn't occur to me that it wasn't my life.

*

My bedroom in the tower was like all the rooms, big. It had a bed with tester and curtains. In the middle was a bath in the shape of a marble boat. It sat on a carpet of pale turquoise wool ruffled like water. There was a table with a lamp, set up for writing. On it was a fat notebook, with marbled endpapers, opened at its first page, blank, and resting on it a pen with a marbled pattern to match. All this is yours, said Malcolm, and I took him to mean the book. I sat at the table and wrote in it. A woman who comes to live in a tower should keep a journal of her days. Of course I wasn't living here then but visiting, and I was hardly the maiden who ought to inhabit such a story, or rather I was a maiden but not the beautiful young one the context expected. If you squinted, looked sideways, glanced at my childish figure against the light, then, perhaps, but is that a true story? All of these things could be written down, the gold nib of the pen sliding across the silky paper of the notebook, making words with perhaps no more intent or trickery than the fine black tendrils of the quince tree gazebo against the winter white sky.

The first morning he woke me to come and see the frost. He came walking down the winding stairs into my room. There were no locked doors in this house. No hidden rooms, no passageways. No desks with secret drawers. The staircases curved openly round the walls, and you entered each room on your way to the one above. It said to you, I am a house without secrets. No doors that must not be opened. No keys indelibly staining themselves with blood.

We went out into the grey morning, through French windows, on to a terrace and across meadow grass to a maze. Everything was powdered blue with frost. When you looked closely there were frail encrustations of ice, holding the cold morning light in their blue refractions. See how beautiful it is, said Malcolm. The hedges of the maze were so far only waist height, but you could still get lost, he said.

So you could get trapped, I said.

I think patience would find you a way out.

At the top of the slope was the quince-tree gazebo, a dome made of arches of iron, over which were espaliered bare branches, to replicate exactly the shape of the dome. There were spaces so you could walk inside and stand in a small house of intertwined branches. In summer, said Malcolm, the quinces hang upon it, golden globes of fruit.

At the bottom of the slope was a pond, or dam I suppose, with reeds and a punt and a small wooden shack. There are birds to be watched, said Malcolm.

When we got back to the house we found a pile of long white boxes on the terrace table. These are for you, he said. Inside were nests of tissue paper and in them stems and stems of red gladioli, every kind of red, crimson, scarlet, vermilion, rose. Malcolm fetched tall glass vases and we put them in, the green thick stems under water through the glass and then the red flower buds just beginning to open. I felt surrounded by tallness and redness.

*

My room, Malcolm calls this bedroom. Gloria's room. The bath like a boat. The wide fireplace. The table with its marbled notebook and pen to match, inviting writing. The bed with tester and hangings in dark turquoise and indigo, the same heavy brocade at the windows. There is always a movement of air in the tower. The candle flames shimmer, the hangings stir, as the air moves through the rooms. As though the building were a creature who breathes, silently but heavily. Every now and then heaving a huge mute sigh. Draughts, I suppose they are, but not cold; the fireplaces are large and log fires burn intensely, but somewhere there is a furnace that pours hot air through the house. I lie in bed wondering if I shall wake to the faint grinding road of machinery, to find the tester a finger's width from my face, or even not wake up at all because it will have wound its way right down and suffocated me.

But I slept, and woke to the sound of shots. Another fox. What do you do with them? I asked Malcolm. Until now, he said, I have given them to Anne the gardener, she buries them under the trees she plants. And last summer we had some fine vegetables grown over dead fox. But now – and Malcolm pulled the fox's brush between his fingers so it sleeked down and then sprang out – now I am going to have them made into a fur coat. It will match your hair, he said.

For that is the colour of my hair. Reddish, russet, foxy coloured. By nature once, these days less so.

So, will I walk through the maze spangled blue with frost like a large dainty upright fox? In the borrowed pelts of a dead animal? Perhaps I will.

After breakfast Malcolm played the harpsichord, such gentle intricate music. You listen entranced to its melodic entwining and interleavings, it belongs to a world that is safe and ordered. Anne the gardener brought in wood and stacked it by the hearth. I sat and read. Malcolm went out again, in boots and coat and taking a gun. I didn't go. I sat and read. I sat and looked at the room.

By the staircase was a big wooden sea chest, old, worn, polished. It had brass clasps and a lock with a key. After a little while I got up and turned the key, but the chest had not been locked, I had to turn it again. Inside were folded pieces of fabric, smelling of peppermint. Ikat, and batik, brocades, embroidery. Most of them were old, some ancient, most had had another existence. I sat on the edge of the chest and lifted them out, unfolding them a little to look at them.

Malcolm came back and I started, so engrossed was I in the chest's contents, and nearly fell in. I remembered the story of the bride who disappears on her wedding day and is found decades later, a skeleton in a marriage dress, in a great chest. But Malcolm is here to save me. Unless it was the husband who shut her in. But Malcolm is not my husband yet, and he was saying with delight, Ah, you have found my treasure.

He shook out several pieces and held them up. It is a pity not to display them, he said, looking vaguely round. Perhaps, one day … though they are fragile.

He draped a piece of gossamer silk ikat against me. They are not for wearing, really, he said, not anymore, but please, look at them sometimes. They need looking at. All beautiful things need looking at.

*

I did marry Malcolm. You may wonder why. Out of a desire to be married, you might think. He did not actually speak of love, but of the delights of marriage. Perhaps because I had been for many years a schoolteacher, and for my girls their time at school is such an interim. It is a stage where they alight, birds with beautiful bejewelled feathers, preen briefly and then fly off to their real lives. I saw the chance for a life of my own, not of other people's interims.

So, I married him. He chose a date in the spring. The ceremony was in the gazebo, which was covered in fresh green leaves and the starry flowers of the quince blossom. I wore a dress of greenish white satin – white because I was still a virgin, but greenish as well, to signify time – like a lily it sheathed my body and at wrists and neck unfolded in bias-cut furls edged with pale green piping. A graceful dress that followed the languid movements of my body.

I carried a posy of lily of the valley with a wreath of it in my hair, and walked across the meadow thick with daffodils and blue-bells, to the piping music of a recorder. Afterwards we spent the afternoon feasting at the long table; Malcolm and I sat together and watched and listened as people drank toasts and laughed and talked. The food was prepared by Gareth, the husband of Anne the gardener, who is a painter but sometimes cooks for Malcolm and cleans the house. He is not a very good painter, Malcolm says, but he can spend nearly all his time at it, which makes him happy. A trio played harpsichord and various recorders and viola da gamba, the lovely intricate slightly melancholic music which is the leitmotif of this house, and is in music what the delicate complicated espaliering of the quince trees is in gardens and my lily-sheath with ruffles at neck and wrist is in dresses.

At twilight Anne drove the guests back to town in the bus Malcolm had hired and we went up to my room where the fire was burning and champagne sat in a bucket, beside a large book covered in fine-grained red morocco. The candle flames shimmered in the warm draughts of air. Malcolm poured some wine into flutes and said, Now that we are married I will tell you what I write.

What he writes is pornography. One volume a year. Produced on his printing press in the basement, illustrated with etchings, or woodcuts. Limited editions of a hundred, selling for five thousand dollars each, more if he hand-washes them with water-colour. A lot of money.

What kind of pornography?

It varies, he says. Any kind, really.

Children?

Of course.

But that's paedophilia, it's disgusting.

No. It's graceful and delicate, small pretty creatures. Remember, they're not people, they're not photographs, they're drawings. No one is harmed by them.

The eyes that look at them are.

He shrugged.

And you, making them.

Do I seem damaged?

What else? I asked. Homosexuality?

He nodded.

Bestiality?

Yes. And harems. Orgies. Lesbians. Nubile schoolgirls. And the intercourse of beautiful ardent lovers.

I knew what he was talking about. The antique style of pornography. For rich men, whose wealth and honourable standing in the community was presumed to protect them from corruption. Not the vulgar cheap effects of television and movies. They use real people, said Malcolm, that is where corruption comes in, they are degrading their bodies for our delectation. But me, I am drawing lines on a page. No one is endangered.

He took up the red morocco book. It had nothing on the cover but the number ten tooled in gold. I opened it. It smelled of ink and rich paper. The pages were creamy and thick, the ink had that satisfying faint unevenness of hand printing. It was in the Japanese style, with woodblocks of lovers, entirely explicit. Had I been as ignorant as I was virginal, it would have been handy. As it was I had not quite considered that people could make love sitting up like that, opening themselves like flowers to one another's gazes and fingers, looking into one another's eyes as much as at their vigorous sexual parts. They were lewd, but tender and delicate as well.

My tongue felt thick in my throat and my skin was hot. So I had married a pornographer. I suppose I might have thought that it was not too late for an annulment, that the marriage had not been consummated. I think I thought, he will know what to do. I stood up. Malcolm unzipped the long sheath of my dress. Underneath I was naked, no lines of underwear to mar its fluid lines. I stood there in my white satin shoes. Dressed I had been a flower, elegant and languid, undressed I was my dry tight pod-like self. He took my hand and led me to the bed, tucked me in under the doona, took his clothes off and was soon white and naked and just a little chubby in the bed with me.

Taking off the dress was my true deflowering. What followed was … it was like acid, corrosive and rough. He dipped his fingers in a bowl of scented oils and anointed himself and me but still there was the tearing and piercing and stinging. His weight. The reluctant sticky brown blood. Is this what lies in wait for all the cruel innocent cheerful girls?

Malcolm said, It is hard, the first time. It will be better. He rolled over and went to sleep. I wished I were a delicate etching in a book, in hand-set type on creamy paper for a connoisseur to read.

He was right, of course. It does get better. And soon I think I shall begin to enjoy it.

*

I asked Malcolm if he would prefer me not to go up on the roof. If it was so dangerous. No, he said, why ever should that be? I said, your late wife, and he replied that it was hardly the roof. It was like a railway line, he said, not at all dangerous, unless you happened to lie on it when there was a train coming. Then of course it was lethal, but it was the train, not the line. The same was true for the roof; it was quite safe, it was the ground that had killed her.

I was not sure about this argument. There seemed some twist or bend in its logic, but I could not quite discern it. But then that is the thing with metaphoric language, it persuades you to see connections and parallels where there are none.

*

I wondered if the second Mrs Pembroke was up on the roof look-ing for marauding tribes. There never were any. Building a tower in this place against marauding tribes was like building a tower against ghosts, they melted through the landscape and you only saw them if they wanted you to. The beat of drums and the glint of sunlight on cuirass and helmet: they belong to the tales of other continents, other civilisations, they never translated here.

I am still Gloria Jones. When we go to Paris in the northern spring for our honeymoon, then I will be the third Mrs Pembroke.

*

I wondered about the first Mrs Pembroke. What she died of. Maybe she drowned in the pond. It is quite deep, and treacher-ous, Anne said, be careful not to fall out of the punt. Anne and Gareth are not chatty. They speak when necessary, but they do not converse. They go about their work quietly and say things like, We need some more toilet cleaner. Or, Mind the pond.

Your first wife, I said to Malcolm. How did she die?

I'm planning to have lunch with her, next week probably, he said. She's not dead, we agreed to part, it's amicable enough. Why don't you come and meet her? It's time we had a trip to Sydney.

I didn't go. I didn't care about meeting the first Mrs Pembroke; there could be time for that. I decided to stay in the tower. To go up on the roof. I sat on the crenellated parapet and looked at the bones of the garden. They were fleshing out with the spring growth. Maybe I could learn the pattern of the maze from here.

I felt but had no trouble resisting the pull of gravity, that seductive invitation to jump off, see what it's like. People are supposed to be charmed by heights such as this and allow themselves to fall; they don't want to die, they just can't resist the pull. At least, people speak of this pull, but they don't do it, they live to tell the tale.

Perhaps the second Mrs Pembroke was pushed. Not by her husband, he was elsewhere, so he said, and must have been believed. But maybe he hired a hit man. For not many thousands of dollars, I believe, you can hire somebody to kill a person for you, and Malcolm has a great deal of money.

I suppose a question is, why would he want to kill her? Why did Bluebeard kill his wives? Because that's what he did. It's a given. It's the plot. Until the lucky one, who is saved.

The even more interesting question is: why did Mrs Bluebeard feel utterly unable to resist opening the door? Don't we all think, when it comes to these stories, that we'd have made it work? So much freedom, and one tiny forbidden thing. Not important, a token in fact. So easy to obey so small a prohibition. We think, if I had been Eve I wouldn't have picked the fruit of the tree of the knowledge of good and evil, I wouldn't have given a piece to Adam. I and my progeny down the millennia would still be multiplying fruitfully in the Garden of Eden.

How crowded it would be. For there would be no death. And there of course, when you think of it, is the answer. Eve had to do what she did. She was following the script. That was the story. The fruit must be picked. The room must be unlocked, and the lady turns the key, staining it with tell-tale blood. The pomegranate seeds must be nibbled, and Persephone complies. The box must be opened, and Pandora obliges. Otherwise there is no narrative, it is just endless shapeless vegetable calm.

And it is in the hands of the women that the narratives lie. They are the ones who must make the stories happen. All through history, they have been depended on, and never failed.

Malcolm is away, but he forbids me nothing. There are no locked rooms whose key I am not allowed to employ. No boxes I must not open, I am enjoined to look at everything. No fruits I must not eat. When the quinces are ripe, he will cook them for me himself, with honey and verjuice.

I am waiting for him to tell me what I must not do.

Shooting the Fox

What Love Tells Me

Nicholas Jose

Climbing up and then down, they found their seats in the front row of a box overlooking the orchestra. James took the inside seat and ushered his son Joe to the empty seat beside it. The boy hung his head over the parapet to check the musicians as they threaded their way through the music stands to their places, the strings tuning up, the drums, the gong, the giant clam-shell cymbals, readying themselves almost directly below. He turned excitedly to his father, who rubbed his neck as if to confirm that they were in this together.

On their way in they had gone to the narrow viewing plat-form at the front of the building where James wanted his son to see the panorama of bridge, boats and islands, and the brows of the opposite shore, receding in dusk. But he felt tense and distant as they stood there, peering, as if he were a vessel too, chafing on the surface against a rope that tethered him deep to the ocean floor. And the boy had not looked at anything except the swell as it approached and retreated, over and over.

The seats were the same ones that James and the boy's mother had occupied the first time they came to a concert, when there was nothing else available. They had enjoyed watching the activ-ity of the orchestra close-up, from that acute angle, its inner work-ings, its heaving heart. They asked for the same seats at the next concert, and kept them for the next season when they became subscribers. They liked to see the striving of the individual players, and the rubbery contortions on the conductor's face, and hear the occasional scrape or knock of wood and metal. They could spy on the players checking their mobile phones for messages. From the vantage point of those seats the orchestra's sound became three-dimensional. You could feel the time between eye and ear, a lagging reverberation as wind, brass, percussion and double bass travelled through thick space to join the leading strings up front.

That was where James's and Cindy's courtship took place, as if the particular vector of those seats on the rich harmonics of the symphony had aided and abetted their relationship. At first it was an awkward, non-committal acting out of an interest that two work colleagues discovered they shared, something they could do at the end of the week, from time to time, instead of heading for the gym or going home alone. Then it became something they looked forward to, even depended on. It turned romantic one night, as they walked back beside the water's black sheen after a performance of Brahms, so snugly arm-in-arm that they stopped in their tracks and stared at each other in wonder, before attempting a first deep kiss. Cindy let James see her home that night, and invited him inside.

By their second subscription series they were married and by the third Joe was born. It all happened so fast. Cindy went part-time, James was promoted, and they had moved into their four-bedroom family home by the time baby Charlotte arrived.

The orchestra was tuning up now, the leader craning her neck as notes hopped from one instrument to another. Horns blurted and were upended, draining their tubes. Patrons edged along the rows to their seats, some with hair up and out, with opalescent flashes against the gold of their bare skin, others more cropped, covered in dark suits and sharp accessories, lithe youth and stiff age alike. James and his son looked out at the hall, its tiered caverns almost full.

'He's too young,' the boy's grandmother had objected. 'He's only four.'

'It will be an experience,' James said.

'But Mahler, my God! Those things go on forever. So grim. Which one is it? The Third! You can't expect a little boy to sit through something like that. It'll be midnight before he's home in bed.'

But James was determined. He could not bear his son not to be there for the first concert of the season. Cindy had always said they should introduce the children to music as early as possible. Joe rocked to Vivaldi in the womb. Charlotte, who was two now, went for *Carmen*. Of course *she* needed to stay at home with grandma this time and be a good girl, James explained, hoping to calm his little daughter.

'Didn't you start Cindy on music at the age of three?' he reminded his worried mother-in-law.

'That was *The Nutcracker*! That's magical.' The woman's lip trembled with the memory. Her daughter had grown up wanting to be a ballerina. She had always loved music.

This was the sixth year of their subscription and James would not let Cindy's seat be empty for the first concert. Their ritual place, where they had felt the orchestra's rumble in their faces. Cindy had renewed the subscription not long before she died and James knew what she intended.

It was six months now and James wondered how that eternity felt on the boy's time scale. The absence that would last forever was still as raw and warm as the prickly red cover of the seat where Cindy had sat less than a year ago. He gave Joe a cuddle, a little too tightly, with a tight grin to match.

'Try to sit still, mate,' he said, as his son wriggled away. 'Be as quiet as you can. No clapping until everyone else claps. Just sit there quietly through the quiet parts. OK?'

The boy looked stern with the responsibility. There was to be no intermission in the six-movement symphony. The conductor, a compact, boyish-looking fellow with carrot-coloured hair and apple cheeks, raised his baton and set his mouth in an agonised pout. They were off, into Mahler's Third, the longest work in the symphonic repertoire. *Langsam. Schwer*, the opening mark. Slow, heavy. With low thunder and the twisted restraint of funereal brass, the fanfares of musical descent began.

*

What happened to Cindy was the worst possible thing. The tests picked up the cancer through a routine blood test, the doctors pleased to have got it early. The operation, though radical, was deemed a success. But when she went on to treatment, they found that it had spread. More difficult surgery ensued, and further treatment, none of which made her feel any better. They missed things in the subsequent procedures and it kept spreading. Then Cindy just came home and waited. She was heroic throughout, and always protective of the children, calm, strong, loving, as loving as anyone could be.

James on the other hand was blown apart by anger that misfired in every direction. He overloaded himself with compensatory tasks. Eventually he was sent home from work, a jangling wreck.

There were pools of peace that might almost have endured. So they were able to believe. They laughed at how they had been taken by surprise. It was not fate, but a trap. Son and daughter, wife and mother, husband and father, they tumbled on the sick bed together holding each other, laughing. Cindy suffered, and smiled, with a benign whisper. Then she was gone.

On the stage, a grand dark woman stepped forward in a ballgown and started singing, her voice round and low. Joe smirked to his father at the sight of the woman's bare back, her cream skin squeezed by straps of crimson silk that stretched as her volume expanded. Into what space was she headed, rising there like the prow of a ship?

The boy had growing pains in his legs. He wanted to kick the barrier that kept them from toppling headlong into the throng of brandished instruments. He cast his father a defiant glance. It was going on so long. But his father sat rigidly fixed. He might not have been hearing anything at all.

At last there was a break. Coughing and shuffling burst out, unstoppered. Joe felt his father's hand clamp down hard on his arm. He fidgeted some more. Then the music started again. The dishevelled conductor swayed like seaweed, imploring, reaching wide to draw the sound forward in mighty waves. *Nicht mehr so breit.* It was torture.

With teasing slowness, a melody unfolded, gathering in all the forces of the orchestra, building without shame. James recognised it as the song of longing that a songsmith from Tin Pan Alley picked up later and turned into a trashy tune to tear your heart out. *I'll be seeing you* ... Such yearning for the reunion of souls across time and place ... *in all the old familiar places* ... *I'll be seeing you.* Such passionate need. He shuddered. Joe felt his father's grip gouge his arm. He writhed to get free. Now his father was shaking, invisibly. The boy could feel it. Tears were running from his eyes and over his stubbled chin.

Then James emitted a choking sob that caused people to turn their heads, as the music rose to a crescendo of blasting and pummelling and smashing that must surely drown all grief.

The boy was scared. 'Daddy,' he whispered. 'Stop it.' There was nothing he could do to shake his father's manacling hold. James was somewhere else.

*

It was as if James were Joe, the boy blocked out by his father. He was back in the country town where he grew up, in his father's study, in their weatherboard house on the edge of town, the winter light pale through the square windows and thick curtains half-drawn. His father sat in the corner armchair near the teak veneer of the new phonograph. He had headphones on, like Mickey Mouse ears, a brace around the brain, making any sound that came from the turntable inaudible to the boy who stood at the door.

The cold, high-ceilinged room was dark and orderly with neat bookshelves and a four-drawer filing cabinet. Pens, folders, a bottle of ink, a slab of blotting paper for the signing of documents, were set out on a desk with the slight degree of disarray that suggested work abruptly ceased. There was always enough business in a lawyer's practice in a country community, but never too much. Work was passed on through the family, like the practice itself, like the house they lived in. Lawyers for three generations in the town, they had prospered into respectability from their first pioneering publican entrepreneur ancestor whose disreputable past was now a gauzy legend. Others in the family may have gone off the rails, possessed by demons. Some had been hopeless or merely lazy. But in that country world of endless hard work and low horizons no one was ever cast out completely for such failings.

In James's father's family the upward aspiration was steady

and firmly directed. Their law degrees, their time away in the city, gave a modest warrant for wider interests – books, music, politics even, and an expected civic-mindedness towards the town library and School of Arts. In James's father's case the tradition extended. The World Record Club sent him LP records in boxed sets to be played at home on the latest equipment, music he wouldn't share with the town nor even with his wife, who had no taste for it. She preferred to be outside in the garden for all to see, working in the fragrant thickets of flowering shrubs and greenery that set off their bone-white house so amiably. She joked about her husband, in his dim study with his headphones on, climbing the peaks of classical music. He was no different from other men, she laughed, who gave their Saturday afternoons to the track or the football on the radio. She tended the garden lovingly, leaving its corners deliberately wild.

Beyond the garden was a fence with a gate to the vegetable patch and the hens and the cows that the neighbours milked each evening. Patrick, James's elder brother, had recently taken over the old shed there as his own space. He moved his things out from his bedroom, put his posters on the walls, his clothes in a pile, and a mattress on the floor for a bed where he slept all day. Because he was awake all night, his mother worried, listening to the music that he played so loudly she could hear it all the way across the yard in her own room, where she lay awake too, in the darkness. Patrick would come and go to the shed through the paddock at the back, or down the pathway beside the house, without coming inside to say hello. The loyal dog that had been his puppy never barked at him either. Barely stirred in its sleep. So you never knew whether he was there or not. For that reason it was almost a comfort to her to hear that discordant music through the quiet night and know he was safe home.

She did not know why her first-born son was so unhappy. She did not know why he stopped speaking to them, first to his father and then to her, or what he did to his younger brother to make James slam the door and stay away, hurt, fearful, warned off. Why was Patrick so angry? When she saw him in town sometimes, hanging out with other kids his age, he looked away from her, avoiding her eyes as if to order her to walk on. She heard how he was bashed one night outside the pub. And Father Kenna told her that the police were on to the drugs being peddled among the young people in town, and mentioned her son.

She wondered if her husband thought about this when he put his headphones on and listened to those massive symphonies. No. 3, no. 5, no. 9.

She had pruned a rose bush within an inch of its life and was on her knees digging around its root ball to enliven the soil, when the horror happened. She heard the shot from the shed. A cry came from her, as if in reply, and an instant after she was running, falling through the gate to the shed to throw open the door on the body of her son, slumped backward on the floor by the makeshift bed, a bloody mass scooped out where his face had been. He had put the gun in his mouth. The rifle his father had taught him to shoot. The spatter of blood and stuff – bone and brains – everywhere on the walls and ceiling, speckled like stars across heaven, spinning in her head as she moaned.

He was warm as she held him, covering herself with his blood as her fluids had covered him at his birth. Then she came shouting for her husband who was in his study with his headphones on and had not heard a thing.

*

A year later, on the anniversary of his brother's suicide, James came into his father's study wanting a ride to a friend's house on the other side of town where there was a party and he was invited to stay overnight. He was carrying his bag, ready to go. His father was sitting in his armchair with the headphones on, listening to a record. Gustav Mahler, James saw, on the side of the box, though he had no idea who that was. The man sat rigidly fixed, staring out the window at the dull winter afternoon, the half-drawn drapes obstructing the light. His mouth was firmly closed, his face grey, his eyes dry. There was no expression on his face of any kind, nothing that could be called an expression except what the passive set of a face's habitual incised lines might suggest.

Grief enclosed the man impenetrably, preventing any wave of communication, any current of shared emotion, any touch of catharsis. James stood in his father's angle of vision and his father could not see him. There was nothing in the room but the silence, and an entirely private music on the inside of the headphones, into which his father had disappeared, engulfed in loss.

James took his bag and turned away down the hall. Outside in the damp silver day he found his mother fondling in the soil for new potatoes, laying them in a wicker basket that was like a nest for her dirt-smeared earth eggs. She was crying. James paid no heed to the tears that blotched her face as he hugged his mother clumsily, an embarrassed boy. He asked if she could drive him to his friend's place. She nodded and brushed herself down, and trailed after her son into the house to look for the car keys.

*

'Daddy!' Joe demanded, shaking until James let go of his arm. The din of the orchestra would drown out any noise the boy made or any reaction he provoked in his father. He was determined to make his presence felt.

The long last movement returned to its opening tempo, yet all the time the music was straining upward, aching for the sublime. The brass blared its demand that heaven should open. The two harps rippled, riding the uplift on golden winds. The tubular bells chimed. The strings quavered ever higher.

James felt Joe tugging against him. He couldn't help the flush on his face, the burning sensation through his body. His ears were ringing. This was the music his father must have heard. He let it come. He felt he was moving closer than ever to the emotion at its source, to the cause. If he could reach that he would understand. He could feel the harmonic resolution, working forward, breaking through.

And he felt Cindy, present in the music, coming towards him, wanting to be there, until she *was* there, as if their love had summoned her. The boy moved his arm from the armrest and squeezed it round behind his father's back in a little hug. James felt the warmth of the boy's body close to him. They were together, the three of them, Cindy's presence interposing itself into the midst of loss, undoing their ties to darkness and grief. He was helpless before that wish, that effect, as the music pulled him into its current, its surging flow, upwards into the light.

Applause broke out in a stamping roar of release. The boy jumped to his feet to join the ovation. 'Yay!' he yelled. 'Yay!' They had got through it, and something had shifted.

'You're a hero, mate,' his father said, blowing his nose on a checked handkerchief, wiping his crinkled eyes.

*

The harbour's equilibrium took the form of a breathing swell that never let its surface settle. The eternal restlessness made lights and stars swim together, elongated, striated, pulsing in oily blackness. Father and son emerged from the concrete carapace of the concert hall onto a platform where the breeze was gusting. It had been designed as a high altar, inspired by ancient ritual, by Mayan sacrifice, where transactions between earth and heaven could bloom like lotus. From there the great flight of stairs descended. Taking wide paces, the boy skipped every second step down to the forecourt, his father following. Above loomed the vaults of the Opera House in lit-up planes and vanishing recesses. On one side the bay curved away into darkness. On the other the city lights bobbed in lapping water, in broken reflection. To reach the car park they pressed through the crowd of late-night revellers who were dancing and shouting to the music that pumped from quayside bars.

Joe let James hold his hand firmly. They had been somewhere different, in the concert hall, and now it was over, the boy would see his father safe home, as his mother had always done.

HEAT

The Index Cards

Louis Nowra

When I found the index cards she had been dead for a fortnight. I was about to put my rubbish in the bin on my landing when I saw the words *Tell Number 14, that I want him to stop that noise.* They were written on a pink index card which had fallen from a cardboard box stuffed into the bin. I pulled out the box and dozens of index cards fell out in a rainbow of colours – pink, green, white, blue and yellow. They all had writing on them, from a single word to a paragraph, in handwriting that was beautiful on most cards but on others was merely a scribble or smudge.

What intrigued me, of course, is that I am number 14. For weeks Gladys had banged her Zimmer frame against my door and when I answered it she would shout hoarsely at me without articulating a word. Then she'd thrust a blue index card into my face. It said, in beautiful cursive script, *Stop that music. Turn off your TV!* I was never playing CDs or watching television when she'd knock on my door. Occasionally I'd invite her in to see my living room, but she'd never believe me. She'd yell incoherently, her spit splattering my face, after which she would thrust another blue index card in front of me that anticipated my reply: *You are a liar! You turned the music off when you heard me at your door!* It was no wonder I thought she was barmy and there were times when I heard her thumping my door that I pretended I wasn't home.

It was probably her relatives who had cleaned out the apartment and gotten rid of anything they didn't want or couldn't sell.

The cardboard box with its index cards was obviously a part of the cleanup. I glanced at some of the cards and saw that they were divided up into colour codes. Yellow cards had written instructions that were obviously daily chores (*Tea. Would you run the bath? Time for lunch? I need to have a nap*) with three cards containing just a single word (*Yes. No. Please.*). Blue cards contained abuse directed at me. White, pink and green were more informal questions and statements that seemed directed towards one person, a nurse called Ken. Curious as to what had gone on with she and the nurse, I put the cards in what I thought was roughly their order and, after guessing what some words were, began to read:

Who are you?

Where's Jean?

She didn't tell me she was retiring.

Jean's husband lives off her like a bludger. He used her money to drink like a fish. Now she has to care for him. She's a wonderful woman.

How old are you? You look twelve.

I have to use these cards. Didn't you see my files? I can't talk. I have cancer of the tongue.

I don't care if you have other patients, surely you should read their files before you visit them?

I don't want a man nurse. I want a woman.

Ring them, tell your bosses I want a female. I don't like being naked in front of a man. Nurse or no nurse.

Yes, I understand that you're understaffed and I'm grateful for these visits as I can't look after myself. I miss Jean. She was more than a nurse, she was a friend.

Do you hear that noise? Like an engine idling.

She'd check my blood pressure, give me painkillers, bathe me, heat up my baby food because I can't eat solids.

How long have you been a community health nurse?

So I'm your guinea pig?

Those photographs on the top of the bookshelf are my nieces and nephews on my sister's side. They're older now.

I used to be quite stylish. See how well cut my dress is. Look how lovely my perm is. It's years since I had a perm.

No, I never had children. Never married. Came close once – a long time ago.

The baby food and soup are in the kitchen. It's the only food I can swallow. Not too hot either. It burns my mouth.

You don't have to tell me – I smell lamp chops cooking in the apartment across the landing and I feel so hungry and want to eat real food.

Those are an original Wedgewood dinner service. My parents' wedding gift. They're worth quite a lot.

Where were you yesterday, Ken? I'm supposed to have four visits a week.

What do you mean you didn't know? Jean was organised. You're not.

Can't you do it right? Jean always found a vein.

You are a flatterer but one of the reasons I don't look eighty is that I didn't smile when I was a girl so I wouldn't get laugh lines.

I want a bath now. I feel clammy in this heat.

(*Waterlogged card*) Not so (*hard?*).

Never married. During the war I dated a Pommy. He did the dirty on me. I've never trusted men since. Are you married?

I wish you hadn't told me that. Men should love women, not other men.

Do you hear that noise?

Take off your shoes. Feel the noise coming through the floorboards.

You must be deaf!

If you won't go and tell him – then I will!

I went down there and the liar said he wasn't playing any music.

Why hasn't my niece come?

Phone again! Phone her again!

I'm going demented with that noise.

You look as though you've slept in a rubbish tip.

Why did your tooth fall out?

Why would you use heroin?

It's a weakness. Take me to the bank. I'll get out $500 for you, so you can buy a new tooth.

He was a Pommy, that's all. Handsome and a cad. I could have sued him for breaking his promise to marry me. You could do that, years ago. Now women are not protected from cads.

No, never. I was not a playgirl. No man for me after the Pommy.

The dentist did a nice job. You don't look such an idiot with a new front tooth.

It's not quite a hum but one with a thump thump thump sound.

I know. I look like a concentration-camp victim.

You can laugh, but old age is dreadful.

Tie my purse to my Zimmer frame. That way muggers won't get it.

I gave you a new tooth, why are you so lazy? Take out the rubbish, please.

YOU ARE A LIAR! You didn't ask him about the noise.

Don't sulk.

THE NOISE IS NOT IN MY HEAD!

Why do you spend your money on nightclubs and a good time? I own this apartment. I went without.

If there's one thing I hate it's your smirking.

That needle really hurt. Jean could find my veins.

Where's my niece?

She's not interstate. She lives in Earlwood.

She would have told me if she left.

She said she did? I don't remember.

Why are you crying?

Nonsense. Maybe you were in the wrong. I've lived alone for sixty-three years. You'll get used to it.

Is yesterday Monday or Tuesday?

I don't want a bath today.

Put that photo of my niece against the wall. I don't like her anymore. She's getting my money and yet she won't visit.

I like history shows. They bring back memories.

I thought you were a fool. Now I know you are. Fancy not having heard of Winston Churchill.

TURN IT UP LOUD. TURN THE TV UP LOUD, SO I CAN'T HEAR THAT NOISE AGAIN.

It's not in my head. Don't be unkind to me, Ken.

I'm afraid of dying and yet I have to. That way I will find peace and quiet.

The lift is broken again. I'm stuck here until they fix it. Last time it took three days.

It's that dirty Egyptian miser. He runs the block and won't buy a new lift.

Where's the Wedgewood serving plate?

I can't have broken it. I never take it out of the cabinet. I must be going mad.

What?

I need something stronger. The pain is terrible.

I don't (*feel?*) so good.

NOISE!!!!!!

I have cotton wool in my ears to stop the noise. It doesn't work.

Don't bathe me. My body is too sore.

Every time I look at the cabinet there is less Wedgewood crockery. What is happening to it, Ken?

I don't remember breaking them.

God take me. I'm going mad. I'm a skeleton.

Your eyes are unkind today.

Don't laugh at me.

I thought I'd die here. I need hospital.

Call ambul ...

Doctor.

I'm dying doc

noise.

noi

no

doc

(*undecipherable*)

The last card was impossible to read. Not so much words as a scribble done by a drunken spider dipped in ink. I remember talking to her nurse only once, even though the cards seem to suggest Gladys sent him down to complain about the noise often. He knocked on my door to say that Gladys was convinced I was causing her intolerable pain by playing my music and TV at loud volumes. Ken was about thirty years old, gaunt with the lived-in and lined face of an ex-junkie. I showed him my apartment and he could see I wasn't causing any of the noise Gladys thought she heard. He showed little interest in anything except for a small silver art deco sculpture of a woman's face. He picked it up, examined it quickly and announced that it was worth quite a lot of money. As he was leaving my apartment he turned back and said, 'She's a pain in the arse. The noise is all in her head. She's driving me mad.' With that he left. It was the first and last time I saw him.

MONUMENT

This Awful Brew

Julie Chevalier

If the sun were out you might have veered off to Maroubra beach and forgotten all about visiting Gav Cooke, justifying your existence and the whole gaol catastrophe, but it is raining. You drive on.

*

A custodial officer in blue appears and the gaol gate opens and just as promptly shuts, excluding you and the other visitors clustered under umbrellas. Someone inside the sandstone walls must be watching a monitor. It's already ten a.m. and you're anxious to prove your work has been worthwhile, that at least one prisoner is continuing to study and isn't using. Hard to believe that until a few months ago you'd been in charge of the education of these prisoners.

Your hand itches to push the buzzer until a man lifts a small girl who relieves you of all responsibility by pressing it. You're paranoid, imagining the surveillance camera swivels. Following you because you worked here? Possibly. One visitor is yelling and waving her bare arms in a jerky backstroke. You're the only one wearing a raincoat. You like to have as much of your body covered as possible.

A car skids and stops. Doors open and young Asians, one with blond streaks, race to the gate. Rain spots their white shirts. Rain drips off the brim of a Koori father's Akubra, drips on the bare shoulders of a redhead who's rolling up the waistband of her skirt. Her legs must ache from standing in those boots.

The gate swings open and the officer orders a man to take the child down from his shoulders. He orders the redhead to pick up her baby and collapse her stroller, ready for searching.

You stand at the sign-in desk holding your ID. The later you arrive, the less time you'll get to stay. The stooped man ahead laboriously prints numbers on a card. A bald officer passes the stooped man's licence to a hirsute colleague. The officers pass the licence back and forth, marvelling at how one way the writing is the right way up and the other way the photo is. They wave the man through, then run their fingers down creased computer printouts, down the food-spotted computer screen itself, before agreeing that Cooke, #899472, the inmate you have come to visit, has been sent to Goulburn. Bugger, bugger, bugger.

'When?'

'Dunno. I saw a crim looked like him going out to run laps,' says the hairy officer.

You look at your watch. The bald one rechecks Gav's number and phones the wing.

'He's there, hanging around,' they chortle, handing you a see-through satchel for your belongings.

Muttering families crowd the entryway behind you. The bald officer upends a stroller and shakes it until a baby bottle filled with orange cordial bounces on the cobblestones. You follow the arrows pointing to the visitors' waiting room, turning around in time to see the redhead pick up the bottle, wipe the nipple on her hip and thrust it at the baby.

One of the officers must say something you don't hear because the redhead screams, 'Search a baby? Piss orf, you sick old pervert. You got somethin' about baby bums or what?'

'Officers found contraband in his nappy at Parramatta ... '

'The filth planted that! I'll tell my guy, youse are all perverts!'

To the right of the corridor a toilet door is ajar. The overhead cistern drips and rust oozes through the pipes. You imagine a sign, *Last place to shoot up before visiting.*

In the waiting room you join gaunt tattooed westies jiggling and scratching in front of a wall-mounted telly. Kids whining for soft drinks fling themselves over and under chairs. To distract them the adults fold fliers about the Children of Prisoners Support Group into paper darts.

Eventually an officer shouts, 'Visitor for Cooke.'

You take a few steps forward. The officer steps close and whispers, 'First time, luv?'

You jump. He must be new. You turn away. The less he knows the better.

'Youse wanna go fer a beer after, luv?'

You cross your arms and shake your head. It's like visiting a foreign country.

'Be at the gate at four?'

You aren't that lonely.

'A bit long in the tooth for young Cooke, aren't youse, but?'

He's right about your preferring Gav. Who wouldn't? You'd confided in each other every day like old friends. He'd had his first shot when he was twelve. He'd fetched beers for men who arrived when his mum still had someone with her. The day he gets out he's going to get a job in a gym. You trust him. Sort of.

'Visitor for Cooke, pro-ceed, please.'

A video camera is mounted at each turn in the corridor. A blue uniform opens the door and you scan the visiting area, willing Gav to be there, waiting. Visitors and prisoners sit hunched over tables like primary-school parents at parent–teacher night. Not that you've ever been to one, or are likely to go for that matter. A woman officer hands over the number nineteen and you wander among the tables looking for Gav.

'I don't care who the fuck he is, you didn't fuckin' hafta let him spend the night, did ya?'

A male voice. Nothing to do with you. Gav is wearing a white plastic bag with no opening in the front. A body bag.

'Table which?' you lip-read him say to the female custodial officer. 'Nineteen? OK!'

He can't find the table with the nineteen on it because you're still clutching the number. You hope he isn't expecting someone more exciting. Finally he sees you.

'Hey, Chalkie. There's a table in the corner.'

What doesn't he want the officers to overhear? He wouldn't ask you to do anything illegal. He unwinds your fingers from their grip on the number. You want him to keep touching them.

'Took a long while to get here, eh?'

'I've been here ages.'

'Me too.'

You smile and tell him about the police planting drugs on the baby.

'Tell me about having an addicted mum, eh? Talk quicker. We'll be lucky to get fifty minutes.'

He looks like he's been working out, but not using is the important thing.

'See Big Max's lady?' He points.

The whole room throbs. You turn in time to see Max's hand move under his lady's skirt. Probably she isn't wearing knickers. Gav says she tapes a sawn-off fit loaded with heroin to her thigh, a takeaway for Max. Are drugs more a commodity than sex? You can never figure it out. That's Berko coughing, the one whose missus claims she got pregnant in this room. You cross your legs and check out what a toddler conceived during a gaol visit looks like. Brown eyes, sticking-out ears and sticking-up brown hair – just like Berko. The air, thick with volatilised juices, wraps around you like a bodysuit of sperm, sweat and sour breast milk. Thank goodness for cotton knickers.

You sit side by side at the low table next to layers of chipped mustard paint, craving a hit of passion, some touching, love – the things everyone else here seems to have in abundance. You're desperate to hear him say something personal – like his release date has been brought forward, and he hasn't had a shot in months, and he's enrolled in a certificate in sports training, and he attributes all this to your excellent work. Just *I miss talking to you* would do.

'Instant coffee with fake milk and sugar?'

The legs of his chair scrape on the cement. Screams and swearing bounce off the high-gloss walls. People intertwine like pretzels – hands down neckbands, hands under shirts, hands up skirts, hands down pants. Berko's clone, snot dripping from his nose, careens into the legs of your chair.

'This awful brew.' Gav places the coffee on the table.

You drain the last bitter drop and dig your right thumbnail into the bottom edge of the polystyrene until crescent-shaped dents ring the bottom, like the moon has orbited for the entirety of someone's lagging, one crescent for each month. He jiggles his legs.

Names are called out as new visitors replace those whose time is up. The crim at the next table leans over to tell Gav that, bad luck, a trannie with a stroller has been barred entry.

Was that redhead a trannie? Bringing in drugs?

'Gav, how's your course going?'

'It's impossible to study when you're two-out. You know that.'

'But you're still submitting a unit every fortnight?'

'You try studying while you're locked up with some arsehole eighteen hours a day.'

'How many units have you sent in?'

'The guy I'm two-out with watches telly until three in the morning.'

Like you're responsible for the overcrowding. 'I suppose you've gone on request for earplugs?'

'No luck.'

He must have done something major to get the super offside.

'You bring some in. Give it a go, Chalk. Earplugs and packets of Drum. Not for me. For yourself. Prove to yourself you're no longer a puppet of the system.'

One earplug inside each cheek? Or in your ears and wear your hair down? 'I could end up in Mulawa.'

'Aw, don't be so middle-class. You can count on me. I'd visit you.'

The hell he would! Suddenly it's quiet. The paint on the cement floor is worn so thin you see the grey underneath.

'Visitor for Cooke, one minute.'

He's looking straight ahead. You keep your chin level with the table, look into his dark smoky eyes. Pinned. Just like the rest of them. He won't even ring when he gets out.

'Doesn't matter, Chalk. I'm being sent to Goulburn tomorrow.'

'Goulburn. Why?'

'Visitor for Cooke, thirty seconds.'

You stand.

'If I'd been able to get enough tobacco I'd have come down easier, but you weren't here.'

'It's not my fault you're using.'

He stands up. 'Shh. Not my fault they urine-tested me when I least expected it.'

'Fuck.'

'Visit me in Goulburn, eh?'

'Time's up, visitor for Cooke.'

'Please, Chalk?'

You touch cheeks.

*

Outside the gate the rain has stopped. Bright straw hats, striped bags and T-shirts replace sandstone, brick and concrete. You join the queue at the ice-cream vendor's cart. No sense feeling hungry at the beach.

Permission to Lie

Beneath the Figs

Mark O'Flynn

Shona and Dean live in Abigail Street, a street that is twenty houses long on either side. It is a short, shady side street cutting between two main roads bludgeoning their way through the suburbs away from the city. Abigail Street is cool and quiet, while at either end, especially at peak hour, there is mayhem.

The shade is the result of a row of Morton Bay figs that buckle the footpaths of Abigail Street. The trees are on death row, having been placed under a council intervention order into their longevity. These trees have proved an ideal habitat for a colony of fruit bats that each year comes to feast on the ripening figs. Every night, particularly during the full moon, the bats swirl drunkenly through the sky like the opening credits of an old Vincent Price film. In daylight they hang from the trees like blackened tumours. In the words of local residents the colony has grown into a plague.

If she happens to leave it out overnight, by morning Shona's washing is a mess. Her uniforms are particularly vulnerable. Dean's car is also a mess. Every car in the street is a mess. A siren is set up in order to scare the bats out of the branches with short, sharp blasts like a ferry's foghorn. It partially works. The bats fly about frantically for a while, then settle again to their gorging. Unfortunately the neighbourhood children are also woken by the sudden noise and the locals begin to see there are pros and cons to this and other solutions.

One evening, after a night at the theatre, where Steven Berkhoff tries to terrify them with dramatised tales of Edgar Allan Poe, they find themselves driving up Abigail Street at bat hour. They are everywhere. Suddenly, out of the distorted moonlight, a drunken bat falls from the sky and smacks against their windscreen. Shona screams. The bat's face is pointed, like a fox's muzzle. Its ears are sharp and, well, bat-like. Dean slams on the brakes and the bat, dribbling rabid saliva and fig juice, slides down the glass and off the bonnet, wings outstretched as if trying to hang on.

Other people have had similar experiences.

There are so many of them that their urine is starting to kill the fig trees. It looks as though the leaves, yellow and withering, have been sprayed with Agent Orange. The botanical gardens are apparently facing a similar problem. This is when their neighbour, Ian Ikin, contacts the council. He demands something be done about the bats. They should be sprayed with a natural solution of python excrement and shrimp paste, he says. The council demurs. Their solution comprises a proposal to get rid of all the fig trees, to pave the entire nature strip with asphalt. There is a chorus of protest.

One of Shona and Dean's neighbours is a family of Plymouth Brethren. Scarf people, the children call them, although not to their faces. They appear to have no opinion whatsoever on the problem of the bats. Dean facetiously likes to think the bats are the agents of Satan come to test the resolve of the Brethren. On the other side are the Ikins. They are the ones who lobbied for the siren. The siren has been borrowed from a vintner friend of theirs who uses it to frighten birds from his vines. When the figs themselves come under threat the Ikins are the most vocal in defending the trees and the amenity they give to the local area. You can't underestimate, they say, the value of shade.

There is bat shit all over the footpaths of Abigail Street. It stinks of sour, fermented figs. Shona has to dodge the lumps as she walks from the car to the front door. Bats squeal in the trees, hanging there like great drips of bitumen. She shivers involuntarily. The invisible *whump* of their wings as they flap up the street is unsettling, especially after a long nightshift during which she has dealt with patients' greatest fears. Nurses often work with the human condition *in extremis*. Her nerves are exhausted and frazzled. The last thing she needs is bats.

In the Ikins' house, music is blaring. She wonders if she should phone, ask them to turn it down. But she doesn't. On the other side, in the Brethren house, all is dark. The Ikins and the Brethren (called the Braithwaites) do not get on ideologically. Shona and Dean are the meat in the sandwich. The Ikins have no children. Shona and Dean have two. The Brethren have eight. The Ikins' yard is messy with straggly native banksias and acacias. Pebble paths wind among them and they have a birdbath, empty now due to water restrictions. Ian Ikin is vocal about his lack of a lawnmower, which he offers as a measure of his small carbon footprint.

The Brethrens' yard, by contrast, is clipped and shorn and barren. An expanse of couch lawn, bordered by a couple of pot-bound buxus shrubs. In their windows the lace curtains are never parted.

Mr Braithwaite owns a muffler-repair shop in an outer suburb. *Owns* is perhaps the wrong word. The Plymouth Brethren (Inc.) are probably the owners and Mr Braithwaite just manages it. Dean took his car there once when it sounded as though it had a chest infection. The most unusual thing about the Braithwaites' muffler shop is that they have no credit-card facilities. There is no EFTPOS machine. There is no computer. There is a sign on the wall behind the receptionist's head that reads: *No cheques. Cash only.* Dean recognises the receptionist and realises that she is Braithwaite's daughter. One of the eight. He also realises that she is pregnant. Dean has to catch a taxi to the bank to withdraw the cash in order to deal with this primitive system of doing things. Do they have some religious dispensation from accepting cheques? What a crock, he thinks. They have hydraulic lifts, don't they? They have pneumatic spanners.

Later that night Dean vents his innocuous spleen to Shona over the inconvenience.

'I had to get a taxi all the way to the bank and back. You'd think they'd give me mates' rates, being neighbours and all, but no.'

How dare, he wonders, they refuse to take his money.

How, Shona wonders in return, did he not know the girl was pregnant?

'It was pretty obvious once she stood up.'

'No,' Shona corrects herself, 'I meant how is it that we live next door and never even noticed? What sort of neighbours are we?'

'Ones who respect their privacy.'

Shona doubts this. She worries about the breakdown of community values, how neighbours are becoming clusters of strangers, wary of each other.

Later she says, 'I wonder what hospital she's booked into?'

'Probably yours. That's the closest.'

'I wonder who the father is?'

'One of these other hanky-heads,' Dean says, 'There's cars pulling up there all the time.'

'I would have thought,' says Shona, 'that a group like the Brethren would be pretty vigorous about knowing who the father is.'

'Hanky-panky,' says Dean for no other reason than it is there to be said.

*

Shona and Dean actually like living next door to the Brethren family. There is no noise. There is barely any sign of people living there at all. Occasionally cars do gather and people stream into the plain, besser-bricked house and not a sound comes out. Dean imagines that the interior walls must be made of egg cartons, like the makeshift sound studios of his youth. But of course he has no idea. He has never peeped inside, though he has looked over the back fence. It is just as barren. Not even a sandpit for the kids. Isn't there something about them rejecting activities associated with fun? Fishing, for instance? Well what are pneumatic spanners if not fun?

'I wonder which one is the grand pooh-bah?' Dean asks one day, peering through the kitchen blinds as the cars begin to arrive.

'I don't think they have any ministerial order,' says Shona.

'Then why don't the men have to wear hankies on their heads?'

'I don't know.'

*

MARK O'FLYNN

Shona is a nurse at the Prince of Wales hospital. She has just finished a stint in oncology and a few months ago moved to maternity. She likes the maternity ward as it always gives her a feeling of hope. One day she notices a young girl in the Tresilian unit. Actually it is the scarf wrapped tightly across the girl's head that makes her look twice, and she recognises one of her neighbours. The girl's shoulders are hunched forward, as if she is trying to take the weight of the smock off her breasts. Shona recalls that awful sensation. She makes some congratulatory noises, but is embarrassed, not only by the girl's rejection of her interest, but because she does not know the girl's name.

'Did everything go well?' Shona asks.

'Yes, thank you.'

'Did you have to have stitches?'

'No.'

'It's just that you're here in Tresilian.'

'We're just trying to find some alternative feeding method.'

'Oh, well, good luck,' says Shona, not wanting to intrude, 'And congratulations.'

'Yes. Thank you.'

Shona walks off on her sensible rubber soles thinking: I could rot in my house before this girl came in to check on me.

*

Otherwise they would not have known there was a baby. There is no fanfare. No cots or prams or newborn paraphernalia wheeled into the bland brick house. No relentless midnight screaming. The Ikins want to take a bottle of champagne in there. By force. Shona says she does not think it would be a welcome gesture. So they drink the champagne themselves. Wetting the baby's head by proxy.

'I wonder what they've got hidden in their garage?' says Dean, 'I bet they've got fishing rods in there.'

After a few bottles they hear themselves getting a little raucous, but from next door there comes nothing but a stony silence.

*

As a trial run the council comes with a cherry picker and half a dozen men in hard hats with chainsaws and cut down one of the fig trees. Admittedly it is dead, but that does not stop the Ikins working the phones. The tree-preservation officer is called to Abigail Street and work is put on hold. He detects a small contradiction in that the residents want the grey-headed flying foxes gone, but not the habitat to which they are attracted. He'll have to think about it.

*

As part of her duties Shona is always pleased to be rostered on to home visits. It gets her off the ward. Unsurprisingly, according to the logical sequence of events, one of her visits is to the house of the Braithwaites. Maddeningly, Shona has to travel all the way in to the hospital only to be given the address right next door to her own home. She drives back, happy to think that afterwards she might be able to steal a cup of tea in her own kitchen, put a load of washing on. The street looks different in the middle of the day. She cannot believe how much sky there is above her yard. Sawdust from the amputated stump of the fig tree blows across the road.

She knocks on the Braithwaites' door and it is some minutes before the lace curtains flicker and an eye peers out. More minutes before the girl, a crimson scarf tight over her head as if holding down a haystack, opens the door. Beneath the scarf her long hair hangs free, brushed and electric down the length of her back.

She stands back and ushers Shona inside. Shona, entering slowly, lets her eyes adjust to the dimness. She blinks. She has never seen a room like it. In the main room (it can hardly be a room for lounging in), there are about thirty hard-backed chairs lined up side by side around the walls of the room. There is no other furniture. No pictures. No table. Just the rectangle of chairs. In the middle of the room on a mauve bunny-rug, like some sacrificial offering, lies the baby. There is some whispering from the far end of the room. Shona glances up to see the door quietly close. She coughs, trying to break the ice.

'You worked at the muffler shop, didn't you?'

There is a whispered snort from the far room. Shona can sense there is not a man in the building.

'How do you know?' asks the girl.

'My husband … Oh, never mind. What seems to be the problem? I saw you were in Tresilian.'

Shona feels as though her voice is too loud.

'My baby won't feed properly.'

Shona can see she is young. Perhaps nineteen or twenty.

'Let's have a look.'

She goes to the tiny, swaddled bundle on the floor and kneels beside it. Carefully unwraps the soft blanket. She peers closely. She starts. The baby is yellow, but not jaundiced. It looks tiny and withered, pixie-ish, with pointed ears and, Shona sees, a pointed muzzle. Like a bat.

'What's wrong with her?'

'They say it's something called Edwards disease.'

Shona has never heard of it.

'The doctors wanted to keep her, but my mother said it was time to bring her home.'

'Edwards disease?'

'It's chromosomal.'

Shona stares at the shrivelled baby, then asks:

'I'm embarrassed to have to ask this, but what's your name?'

The girl balks. 'Susan.'

At that moment the door at the far end of the room opens and the mother, Mrs Braithwaite, and two other women who look just like the mother bustle in. They all wear identical crimson scarves and ankle-length skirts. One of them holds a tray rattling with teacups. They fuss around Shona and the girl and the baby, which no one picks up.

One of the aunts – they can only be the mother's sisters – asks Shona to take a seat, any seat, over by the wall.

'Will you take tea?' asks the aunt.

'Yes I will, please.'

The aunt pours from a plain pot and for a moment that is the only sound.

'Milk?'

'Yes, please.'

A cup of tea is thrust into her hands. They sit in silence for a moment with hot cups in their laps.

'The issue,' says Mrs Braithwaite from across the room, 'is that the baby won't take the breast. It is too large for the mouth.

The teat of a bottle is also too large. So what are the alternatives? We were thinking of an eyedropper. Or there is formula, and perhaps a siphon.'

'Well, premature babies need all the colostrum they can get—'

'The baby is not premature. She went to full term. She is five weeks old.'

The baby, Shona looks again, is small enough to hold in one hand. She has seen zucchini that are larger. The eyedropper is not such a silly idea.

'It's the chromosomes,' says Susan.

'It is not the chromosomes,' snaps Mrs Braithwaite. 'It is God's will.'

'They say she will not live past two months,' says the girl to Shona, her eyes pooling with tears.

'And so now we have brought her home,' says Mrs Braithwaite. 'Christina. To her home.'

'Is she taking any milk at all?' Shona asks.

'As soon as she takes a sip she perks it back up,' says Mrs Braithwaite.

'Your flow might be too fast for the size of her stomach. We can look at that. But really, Susan, this baby would be better looked after in the hospital.'

'Thank you for your suggestion,' says Mrs Braithwaite quickly. 'We shall consider your advice. But for the present we shall pursue the idea of the eyedropper.'

Suddenly there is a scarfed aunt on either side of Shona, helping her to her feet. One of them removes the unfinished teacup from her lap.

'But—' protests Shona.

'Thank you again,' says Mrs Braithwaite.

Shona looks at Susan, who says, 'If she goes back to hospital she'll die.'

'God will prevail,' says the aunt who has not yet spoken.

The aunts steer Shona towards the door.

'But—' Shona thinks rapidly, 'You'll need a breast pump.'

'Thank you for the suggestion,' crows Mrs Braithwaite.

'Do your breasts hurt?'

Susan glares. She gives a sour little nod.

'For the mastitis put cabbage leaves in your bra,' Shona says.

'Thank you,' trills the mother, turning to her daughter.

'This is too much,' laughs one of the aunts. 'Cabbage leaves!'

The other one squawks, 'Breast pump!'

Shona finds herself outside the plain, wooden door at the top of the steps. The security screen snicks behind her. The couch lawn stretches to the fence. Not a weed. Next door, her own unkempt garden seems somehow foreign from this odd angle, as if appearing in a dream. She can see inside her own dining-room window. Realises that if she forgot to draw the curtains she would be plainly visible. Or that her children would be plainly visible. She walks numbly out to her car. Behind her the lace curtains are so still they might be made of concrete. She does not even think about detouring into her own house. The washing can wait. She notices the postman riding past on his motor scooter. He skilfully pops some letters into her box without even stopping. Shona sits in her car for a moment. There are some forms she should fill in. She is aware of the dark, sleeping shapes of the bats high in the fig trees, hanging on for grim life.

Going Down Swinging

The Anniversary

Deborah FitzGerald

I jump the low brick fence at number seven and bang on the screen door. The flat, blue sky is unnerving; it's painted on, brash and claustrophobic. My phone beeps. It's the third text from Craig in as many minutes. 'Jesus, give me a chance,' I mutter. I turn the handle and enter gloom.

The house is closed against the heat, blinds and curtains drawn. I squint as I make my way down the hallway and past the tiny kitchen, following my mother's voice.

'I'm back here,' she calls.

Mum is down on her hands and knees cleaning the bath. She squirts Jif on a cloth, leans into the tub and rubs. I lean on the doorframe.

'Hey, you,' I say. 'Got a sec?'

The bathroom is oppressive. A drizzle of sweat is visible on her neck and back.

'It won't clean itself,' she says.

Mum has lived on the Gold Coast for seven years. Having emerged from the sand five decades earlier, the city carries none of the burdens of history. People come to catch their breath, worn down by failed marriages, boredom, the cold weather, death. And when it is their turn to die, far from their home towns and small familiarities, they are enshrined in sparkling, smooth-lined crematoriums.

She stifles a groan as she puts a foot out in front of her and uses the bath to haul herself up. I grew to her height – five foot two – but she has been shrinking this past year. She hustles me out of the doorway into the hall. My hair is pulled back in a rough ponytail and I redo it now, pulling the strands quickly through the band and back again, twice. I try to catch her eye. She walks past me with purpose, past the kitchen and living room to the largest of the three bedrooms at the front of the house.

I follow her, hovering.

Her pale green eyes narrow with concentration as she kneels before her dressing table and begins the ritual of unpacking and repacking it. Craig says she is performing this task with alarming frequency. It has grown worse over the years.

'Got everything you need for the barbie?' I ask.

'Yep. I'm all ready to go.'

She is wearing a light cotton dress and her grey-blonde hair is tucked behind her ears. Watching her, I am a child again. She leans into one of the drawers and then twists her head towards me. The lines on her face draw me back.

'Hairspray,' she suddenly announces.

'Hairspray?'

'If you've got biro marks on your clothes, hairspray will do the trick. Just spray it on the stain and it will lift right off.'

'Cool!' I say, bemused.

She has tidied her drawer but lingers over the white box tucked under one of her slips. She lifts it gently, sits it on top of the Queen Anne dresser and wipes it with a soft, dry cloth. She draws it to her lap. Inside are my sister's ashes.

'We could sprinkle them over the ocean,' I say.

'She was scared of sharks.'

'Maybe in a park overlooking the sea?'

'She didn't like to be alone, especially at night.'

'A rose bush, right outside in the garden.' I say it forcefully as if it has all been settled.

'She didn't want to be buried. She needs to be with her mother.'

Screw my brother and his superior skills in rock, paper, scissors.

Reen bustles up the hallway shouting her arrival. She fills the room as she gives Mum a kiss and flops on the bed. She is flush with life, in a large, fifty-something, ripened kind of way. It's the mouth you notice first, wide and pouty, always bleeding with bright lipstick. It's a little too generous for her face but her dark brown eyes rescue her.

Reen lives next door in a one-bedroom unit with Roy. He has emphysema. Their son Cliffy sleeps on the couch in their living room. He has schizophrenia. She says he's OK when he takes his medication. Sometimes she gets a phone call from the cops saying they've locked him up. She says he's bloody strong when he's having one of his turns.

'Can you tell her, Reen?' I say, emboldened by the prospect of an accomplice. 'Tell her the whole "ashes in the sock drawer" thing is getting a bit creepy.'

'I'll do no such thing,' she says. 'Your Mum'll scatter 'em when she's good and ready.'

Mum takes the white box and nods at Reen, who follows her. They walk down the hallway to the kitchen door and Mum places the box on the side table opposite. I follow behind, feeling like an afterthought.

'I want Rachael out here with me today,' Mum explains to no one in particular.

In the kitchen she takes vegetables from the fridge and places them on the table of the small breakfast nook. Reen miraculously slides into one of the seats, tucking her ample proportions into a seemingly impossible space. I go to the sink and start rinsing the lettuce. Mum is chopping onions for the salad and tears appear. I have never seen her cry, not even when Rachael died. Even at the trial of the drunk who killed her daughter, her face remained smooth and expressionless, as if she was waiting for a bus.

Mum's other half, Bob, is at the back door taking off his boots. He has been mowing the lawn before the barbecue. Mum says it drives her mad that he leaves it till the last minute. He pokes his head around the doorway and chuckles.

'What's going on here? Secret women's business?'

'You betcha,' Mum says, winking at Reen.

Bob is wearing khaki shorts and a black singlet stretched to breaking point over his huge stomach, which looms larger due to his lack of height. He has a grey moustache and is wearing his favourite hat, which rarely leaves his head.

DEBORAH FITZGERALD

'I'll clean myself up and then I'll fire up the barbie,' he says as he heads towards the bathroom.

My phone beeps. Craig again. The text reads, *All sorted*. Shit.

'Mum, you know I mentioned a bush?' I try again.

The screen door at the front of the house bangs and we can hear voices in the hallway.

I finger the silver cross hanging around my neck. It was Rachael's and I'm hoping Mum notices I am wearing it.

Roy and Cliffy appear in the doorway. Roy is huffing and puffing. He leans his small body against the wall, overcome with the exertion of walking from next door. Cliffy is his polar opposite, tall and twitching with nervous energy.

'OK,' Mum announces. 'Officially too many people in the kitchen.'

She squeezes past everyone, carrying two bowls of salad, and we follow, emerging on the small porch. It is a concrete slab with a green shadecloth awning that offers some respite from the Queensland sun. A sea breeze teases us with bursts of cool air. Mum places the bowls on the table, its lace covering flirting with the wind. The esky holds the Fourex on ice, minus the one Bob's nursing in a Gold Coast Titans stubby-holder. He is provoking the sausages on a large home-made brick barbecue over by the paling fence.

I try calling Craig to warn him. It goes straight to voicemail and I swear under my breath.

'Craig, it's me. Call me when you get this.'

'Where is Craig?' Mum asks with her back to me.

'Not sure. He's not picking up.'

Cliffy is sitting on an old wrought-iron chair he has placed on the lawn. His foot taps the ground in quick, insistent beats as if he is primed and ready to run when given the signal. He pulls off his T-shirt and tosses it over the back of the chair. He has strong shoulders and a surprisingly taut stomach. A tat on his left pec announces, *I am God*. I wonder if he has stopped taking his medication.

'Want a beer, Cliffy? One won't hurt,' Mum says, handing over the small brown bottle.

'Cheers, Mrs D.'

Roy and Reen sit side by side in the shade. He rattles with

the effort of breathing and she is vigilant, ready to take over if needed. Mum disappears inside and re-emerges carrying the white box. She sets it carefully on a small bench below the laundry window, retrieves her beer from the table and makes a toast.

'To Rachael.'

'Hear, hear. To Rachael.'

Everyone sips their beer, including me. Then I take a couple of gulps but it doesn't help. I text Craig, *Abort! Abort!*

The gate creaks open at the side of the house and my brother's face pokes around the corner. He is wide-eyed, his curly brown hair matted with salt and sea. He shuffles forward, dragging a skinny bush, its disappointing foliage wilting in the heat.

'Ta da!'

Everyone is silent. The barbecue crackles as another sausage pops its skin.

'What?' he says.

Mum edges forward on her seat, ready for a fight.

I walk over and try to put an arm around her shoulder. She shrugs me off.

Craig glares at me. 'I thought you had cleared it with her.'

'I said I would talk to her.'

'For God's sake, Mum, it's been ten years.'

'Your point?' Mum folds her arms and leans back in her chair.

'Look, I'll dig a hole right here, we'll scatter the ashes and you'll have beautiful roses all year round.'

'I'm not ready.'

Mum jumps up and grabs the white box.

Craig walks towards her and begs, 'Please, Mum, give me the ashes.'

'Back off.' Mum is sidling towards the door.

Reen is on her feet, covering some of the ground between Mum and Craig.

'Now, now, she's your mum. What she says goes!'

For a minute, I think my brother is considering a reluctant retreat.

Instead he says, 'Reen, stay out of it,' and walks over to Mum.

He tries to take the box from Mum carefully, gently loosening her grip, but she jerks it back and it falls from her hands. The lid bounces away, the ashes spill out. A sudden gust takes the silver tailings and throws them in the air, lifts them in a shimmering dance and showers them over everything.

The remains of Rachael are in our eyes and up our nostrils and coating our hair. Roy struggles with the new hazard, wheezing and rocking. Reen flaps her hands dangerously close to his face as she tries to clear the air. Cliffy jumps onto the seat of his rickety chair, all elbows and knees, like a giant praying mantis. Bob eases back to the barbecue, tongs in hand, retreating from the menacing grey mist.

Craig and I scream and jump around, flailing our arms as if spiders have fallen from the sky and are running through our hair and across our skin. He leaps from foot to foot, rushing his fingers across his scalp and shaking his head. I frantically wipe my face and arms.

'Fuck. This is freaking me out!' Craig calls from beneath his upside-down hair.

'Jesus, I don't want her on me!' Cliffy sprints to the back fence.

Reen shows superhuman strength by lifting Roy off his chair with one hand and turning it 180 degrees before dropping him back onto it. Convinced his fragile airways are safe, she turns her attention to everyone else and, sliding her sleeves up her arms, she lurches towards the swirling debris.

A noise emerges from beneath the cries and the curses. It's Mum. Laughter trickles out of her as she kneels before the little white box, trying to scoop up what's left of the pile. She is scraping and laughing and looking at me and I hold my breath, partly because I don't want to suck my sister into my lungs and partly because I want to remember the sound.

The Life You Chose and That Chose You

Strawberry Jam

Penny O'Hara

Frank looks at his watch. Eight o'clock. He's been here an hour, no more.

At the next stall, David's already unloading his second batch. Out they come, from the ordinary cardboard cartons underneath the table and into those baskets he's got, in arty, rabbit-dropping piles. The women are the usual free-range crowd, shouldering their way to the front like punters on race day.

Frank eyes the stallholders, with their smiling and nodding, their passing of bags. All *he's* getting are backs and arses. He feels the cat's-bum tightness in his mouth and knows it's his own fault.

He hears Ellen's voice in his ear. *You're scaring them off.*

She's right, as usual. And David – despite the ponytail, the silver eyebrow ring – is a canny bloke. The way he spreads his palms, nods towards the laminated photos. 'Happiest chooks in the world,' he grins. All a bloody show, but it gets the customers.

'They're not buying an egg,' David said once. 'They're buying a story.'

Holy shit, he thinks. *A story.*

In the last hour, as David's baskets have emptied and been refilled, Frank's sold one lousy jar.

'Cheers, mate.' David raised the jam like a schooner. A pity sale.

There's a noise at his elbow. He looks down to see a kid tugging at the tablecloth, eyeing the wobbling jars.

'Hey, kid.'

The boy looks up, gives him the look: the *watchya gonna do* look.

Jesus. He's in no mood. He looks around for the mother. Three bloody guesses. There, in the purple pants. She's lifting an egg, holding David's eye.

'Oi,' Frank says. 'Leave it.'

He sees the woman pass David a note and cock her head, asking something. David gestures his way.

She's coming over.

Come on, Frank, says Ellen, straight into his eardrum.

He pulls his face into a smile. The woman stops at the table, picks up a jar, examines the label. He gathers the words in his throat.

'Home-made.'

Her eyes do a quick dart, taking him in.

'My wife.'

'Ah.' She turns the jar in her hand.

A story, he thinks. *A story.* He should've brought the photos. 'Stop bellyaching,' Ellen had said as she'd snapped him unloading the crates of seedlings. Later, she'd tied on her apron, stood before the big saucepan and told him to get her good side.

The woman's thinking it over and the kid's started jiggling again. *Leave it, Frank. Forget the bloody kid. She's interested. It'll be three jars, maybe more.*

If only he had the photos. That'd clinch it, no question. Only … those shots were a bit out-of-date now, weren't they? Not the full story, the real story. And what would he put in their place?

The answer rushes in before he knows it's coming.

Ellen. She's standing at the stove, holding the spoon. Her face, without the wig, is like a peeled potato. Her mouth is open. She's telling him she's had enough. She's chucking the bloody chemo and there's no use trying to talk her out of it.

'I'll take three,' says the woman, but he's not listening. He's seen what's coming, knows it's been coming, suddenly, since the day started, since he stood in the cool morning and slid the rattling boxes into the back seat of the car.

'Kid!'

He lunges forward, but it is too late. The jars are rolling and toppling like skittles. They're crunching onto the floor, one by one in quick succession, a rapid vomiting cascade of glass and strawberry jam. There's a slow leak across the concrete floor.

Frank finds himself standing with his hands by his side, helpless as a child holding the pieces of his mother's favourite teacup.

He feels the gentle pressure of Ellen's hand on his arm.

*

He walks out of there four hours early, a schoolboy with an early mark. He leaves David and the others to smile smile smile until the crowds trickle away and the bottom of the boxes show.

He'll drive home, he thinks as he walks across the car park, with the window open. Let it blow away, the whole bloody lot.

'Fuckin' ratbag,' he'll say. And Ellen, sitting in the passenger seat, will try to look disapproving.

Only he won't, and she won't.

The last of the jam has gone, one way or another. The last batch, just like he'd promised her.

And now it's gone, she's going too.

She used to do that, when she'd had something she wanted to say. Hold her thumb down on the remote, making the sound plummet. 'Oi,' he used to say. 'I was watching that.' Only now it's *her* voice that's fading.

He walks to the car, opens the door, slides into the driver's seat. He rests his hands on the wheel. After a while – minutes, hours – he puts his key in the ignition. Going, going, gone. Nothing to hear but the sound of an engine starting in an empty car park.

Fifty Years

Stephanie Buckle

'Pamela's here,' says my father, as if I am all the emergency services rolled into one. As if I will save the day. 'She's flown from
Perth this morning.'

I put my arms round him, and as soon as I feel his familiar
stubble on my cheek and breathe his tobacco smell, I start to cry.
He was the one who was supposed to save the day.

He clings to me, his hug uncomfortably tight.

My mother lies on the hospital bed as if cast away. But she
turns her head towards me, and her face changes. Her eyes fill
with tears and she reaches out her still-good right arm to me. She
does not say my name. She does not say how glad she is that I've
come. But she still knows how to hug; she still knows how to hold
hands. I sit on the bed and she lets her good hand rest in mine.

'What a relief,' says my father. 'She knows you!'

My mother moves her mouth strangely, as if she has been
asleep for a long time; but words are beyond her. Through the
window, a hot air balloon drifts slowly across the rooftops beyond
the hospital and she points to it, like a child who is seeing for the
first time.

'I knew you'd perk up,' my father says to her, 'once Pamela got
here.'

For the moment, I'm spared from having to find words for
either of them, because a nurse comes in to adjust the drip. She
regards my mother's innocent wonder at the drifting balloon as

she might look at a wound and she tells us, 'With a stroke, a person can be a bit emotional, you know, like cry for no reason, or be rude when they normally wouldn't dream of it. They can lose their inhibitions.'

'Oh, I can't see Gwen doing that,' says my father. He leans on the bed rail and knocks the medication chart onto the floor.

For goodness' sake, Jim, why don't you sit down? my mother would say, if she could talk.

'She's not the sort to start being rude just because she's sick, are you Gwen?'

And that's when I see it, the first time. It's the expression you make when you think no one's looking. The one you make to yourself with your back turned. It's the one that makes all the others look like masks, as if all the cups of tea and all the ironed shirts are just pretending. She turns from me and regards him quite steadily, but as if she sees him down the wrong end of a telescope, or as if he's a fly buzzing still against the window, which she briefly thinks she might stir herself to deal with, but then can't be bothered. *Are you still here?* it says.

But my father's fond and anxious gaze does not waver. 'Don't worry; we'll have you out of here in no time. We need the Christmas pudding making, don't we, Pamela?'

She turns her eyes back to me. 'You're going to get better, Mum,' I say to her, softly, wondering if she can hear me. 'I'll take care of you.'

'I took her a cup of tea,' says my father. 'Seven o'clock, she never wanted it earlier. She reached her arm out, and I thought, that's funny, she never does that. That's when I realised, something's not right.'

He's told me this twice before, on the phone. It's as if there's a piece missing and if he keeps telling the story, he might find it.

While he's telling me for the third time, I imagine her waking – only yesterday morning! – unable suddenly to make her body answer to her and praying that he would come sooner. She would have tried to call out to him and found that her words had gone too. She would have heard the kettle whistle and the cap blow off, and the back door creak, and then the silence while he had his first cigarette and let the tea brew, then the creak of the door again and he'd be back inside, stirring the pot, pouring the tea.

Then she'd hear him coming down the hall, and the knock at the door – he always knocked, since they'd had separate rooms – and then, at last, he'd be there, the cup trembling in his hand as he put it down on the bedside table.

Now, he pauses his story, and leans over the hospital bed so that his face is close to her, and he smiles encouragingly.

'"Wake up, Gwen, here's your tea!" That's what I said, isn't it? Same as I do every morning.'

She's not looking at him.

'Did she say anything?' I ask him. Even one word would be precious.

'She was trying to,' he says. 'I didn't catch on at first. She's never been much of a one for talking first thing in the morning, have you, Gwen?' he jollies her. We wait, smiling, for her response, but of course there is none. Her face is stone. 'Then I realised,' my father continues, 'something wasn't right. She was making this strange noise and struggling, trying to move, but nothing was happening, like when you slam the accelerator and clutch together in a bogged car and the wheels spin.'

'What did you do?'

'She'd half fallen out of bed,' he says, 'so I lifted her back, propped a pillow behind her and tried to get her to tell me what was wrong, but she wouldn't speak.' His eyes fill with tears and I reach for his old man's wrinkled, dry, tobacco-stained hand. 'I said to her, "I'd better call an ambulance, Gwen, what do you think?" But of course, she couldn't answer. In the end, I called the ambulance anyway, because I could see I wasn't going to be able to get her into the car by myself.'

How long was it, I wonder, before he called the ambulance?

*

A neighbour, Margaret, has come with flowers, which lie in their vivid orange and purple cellophane, untouched and unlooked at. My mother's eyes are closed, her body limp against the pillows. The nurses have dressed her in one of the nighties I brought in; the frilled neck of it cups her desolate, sunken face.

'She's not very well this morning,' my father says.

'I can't believe it,' says Margaret. 'Gwen's always been so fit and active.'

'We've been married fifty years,' says my father.

The shadow of a fresh concern passes over Margaret's kind, plump face. 'I know, Jim. Des and I were there for it, at the club, remember?'

'She didn't want a fuss,' says my father. 'She didn't want anyone going to any trouble.'

'It's something to celebrate, though,' says Margaret, 'being together for fifty years.'

'We've stuck together through thick and thin.'

'It's an achievement,' says Margaret.

I want better words than these for my mother's life. I want essential truths and real meanings; I don't want to hear these platitudes.

My mother gives no sign that she hears anything.

*

'We're going to put a catheter up,' says the nurse on our third day of watching. 'Why don't you both go down to the canteen for half an hour?'

'You go,' my father says. 'I'll stay with Mum and hold the fort.' He's sitting on the window side of the bed, between her and the sky.

I take my hand slowly from hers. 'I'll be back in half an hour,' I say to her from the door. Her hand lies where I left it and her expression does not change. There's no mothering in it at all. Nothing that might go with, *Go on dear, you go and have a break, I'm fine, take some money from my purse for your coffee and a magazine.*

'Don't worry Gwen, I'm not going anywhere,' says my father.

But she is still looking at me. *Don't leave me,* her eyes say.

The canteen is a windowless place crammed with formica tables with chrome legs, families out of their element, toddlers in pushers and a lot of bad food. The coffee is as bad as coffee can possibly be. I check my watch; upstairs on the eleventh floor it is the eleventh hour and my mother is dying and I've left her, although I know she didn't want me to.

Do as you're told now, she used to say to me. *Don't make a fuss.*

Would she want me now to argue with the nurses? Would she want me to make my father go away?

She never told me she was unhappy. I never questioned the solid, dependable habits of her life.

*

When I go back, she's asleep, her head fallen forwards on the pillow. Asleep, she looks as she always has; it's possible to pretend that nothing has happened to her.

'I don't know what it is,' says my father, 'but she doesn't seem to want me here. She doesn't want to look at me.'

'Dad, you mustn't take it personally,' I tell him, taking his arm. 'She just can't express her feelings properly, because of the stroke. We've just got to keep trying to communicate with her, and hope it gets better.'

He takes me at my word, and when she opens her eyes he redoubles his efforts at communication. He reads out the messages on all the get-well cards, holding the pictures in front of her face.

'This one's from Frank and Julia,' he says. 'They say, "Thinking of you, hope you make a speedy recovery. We will be down for a visit soon, but Frank's mother has had to go into the Mercy Hospital for a kidney operation. She is eighty-six." Fancy that, having an operation at eighty-six! What do you think of that?'

She stares, somewhere beyond his arm; her eyes flicker. He reaches and pulls her bed jacket closer across her, smooths it down her chest. She turns her head to look at me and her expression is imploring. I pass him another card to read, so that he has to lift his hand away from her to take it. He begins again, 'Oh this is a pretty one! Look at that! This one's from Mrs Dobson at the post office.'

He takes up the newspaper and asks her which bits she'd like him to read. '"Bus driver had heart attack, inquest told," – do you want that one? What about "Triplets reunited after seventeen years" – that sounds a bit more cheerful, doesn't it?' But she looks at me still. I glance at my father; his head is in the paper and he's reading out about the triplets. *I love you,* I mouth to her.

Every time my father takes her hand, she pulls it away. That's if it's the good one, of course. If it's the paralysed one, it just lies limp and he strokes it. She seems to shrink away, as if her whole arm has betrayed her and doesn't belong to her anymore.

Every time he speaks to her, she turns her eyes away. Sometimes she manages to turn the right corner of her mouth down, as if she says to me, *Can you believe the rubbish that comes out of his mouth?*

He holds a glass to her mouth, pushing a bit, encouraging her. Her lips are useless flaps of skin, and water and saliva dribble down her chin. He dabs her with his handkerchief and she turns her face away again; her eyes seem dead already.

He makes his little jokes. He offers me the change out of his pocket when I go to get the paper and I take a coin from the palm of his hand because I can't bear to do anything that is like what my mother is doing. He wants to help, but there is nothing he can do. He wants to be forgiven, but he doesn't have a clue what he's done – there's fifty years of it, tangled up like the umpteen balls of wool in the pillow case at the back of the linen cupboard, you'd never get the knots out, ever. She's not going to forgive him – the stroke has stripped away all the shades of grey, and left just this one plain black truth.

We ignore it. We pretend. We say she's tired. We say we saw the shadow of a smile on her face when he came in. He sits on her paralysed side and says to me, 'Go on, you sit where she can see you,' as though he is sacrificing precious time with her for me.

She gives it up in the end, all that truthfulness after so many years, and even her own daughter won't acknowledge it – it's more than her little body can sustain. I watch her fade and there's nothing I can do to keep her.

*

After she dies, my father is cut loose, rudderless. He shakes, trembles, has to put down his cup. He can't remember where anything is.

'Gwen would know, Gwen took care of all that,' he says.

He wanders about the house, picking things up and putting them down again. He lets me organise the funeral.

'What music do you think she'd like, Dad?' I ask him.

'One of her piano pieces, maybe,' he says, but he can't name any of them. '"Abide with Me"! That's it, that's the one, she liked that one!'

Among her CDs I find Purcell's *Dido and Aeneas* and I add

'Dido's Lament' to the mix.

He follows me like a child from room to room.

'What am I going to do about the shopping? Do you think I should water the pots on the patio? Where did she keep her pension book, do you think?'

I look for the pension book and find a diary, tucked at the back of the drawer in her bedside table. I sit on the bed and open it.

Went for walk in the park. Lovely sunshine. J wouldn't come.

Made jam. J shouting about electricity bill.

Went to bowls. J took car so had to walk.

Birthday – seventy-six! Don't feel any different. Lovely call from P. J surprised when I reminded him, shot up to milk bar and bought box of Cadbury's Roses, again.

Worried about plumbing, noises very loud, taps dripping, leak in bathroom. J won't get plumber – says he will 'look at it.'

J upset about fish, went out and bought hamburger! Don't know anything about losing weight, apparently.

Played piano all afternoon – lovely! (J out.)

'She's kept a diary every day,' I tell my father.

'Any revelations?' he says.

'No, not really, just ordinary, everyday stuff.'

He doesn't ask me for it.

I go through all her things; everything is open to me now, it's a treasure trove, so many ways to hold her, keep her, I want them all – jewellery, clothes, letters, bowling-club medals, nail scissors, photos. I keep taking things to him, showing him. 'What do you want me to do with this, Dad?'

'Oh, you have it,' he says.

I want to know the stories; there are things I haven't seen before. A beautiful green cut-glass brooch. 'When did she get this? Was it a present?' I ask him.

He turns it over in his hand briefly and gives it back to me. 'I think her mother might have given it to her,' he says. 'I don't remember her wearing it. I can't find the pegs.'

There are letters from a friend, Dorothy, who moved to Melbourne when her husband died.

'She missed Dorothy terribly,' I say to him. He's watering the hanging violet, which died of neglect days ago.

'Missed who?'

'Dorothy. Her friend from the library who moved to Melbourne. They were planning a holiday in the US together.'

'No, she wouldn't have done that,' he says. 'We were coming over to Perth to see you at Christmas, that's the only holiday we had planned.'

'But Dorothy says in this letter,' I say, trying to show him, but he doesn't have his glasses, won't take it. 'She says she's written to her sister in Portland to see about them staying with her.'

'Just talk,' he says. 'She wouldn't have gone all that way.'

*

Across the plates of sausage rolls, surrounded by cards and piles of hothouse flowers, he sits with the unfamiliar whiskey that someone has pressed on him, accepting everyone's attentions. The expression of bewilderment has settled on his face now; it is as if he is always about to ask a question.

'We had our golden wedding anniversary only two months ago,' he says to Bill and Audrey.

'We were there, Jim,' says Audrey. 'We were all very proud. It's a wonderful achievement, fifty years of marriage.'

'The only woman I ever loved,' my father says. His eyes are filling; he puts the whiskey glass down. 'I never wanted anything else. I think she knew I loved her.' He looks to Bill, who realises belatedly that it is a question.

'Of course she did, you were best mates, you and Gwen.'

'You were her rock,' says Audrey.

'I'd have done anything for her, you know,' my father says, as if he must state his case. I put my hand in his rough old one and nod my understanding. He's looking at the piano and the music on the stand, still open at the last piece she was playing.

Silence 1945

Rodney Hall

A man jumped up on the horizon. Quite suddenly he jumped up where nobody had been before. A soldier, with nothing on his head to protect it. In the afternoon. Behind him mushrooming clouds gathered. And above the clouds three parachutes seemed fixed in the sky. The big guns had already fallen silent and every last aircraft had long since flown away. It was on a ridge above some straight shadows that were the enemy trenches. And up he jumped.

And there was one who asked: Do we shoot him, Sergeant Potts?

But Sergeant Potts just spat. On the ground. Because this was something no one could account for; a soldier making a target of himself in full view of the platoon of hidden men in helmets, each one of us with his finger on the trigger and a question in his eyes. Each homesick from too much bitterness and loss. And too much fear felt too soon. Boy soldiers, rookies, with no idea what to do next.

Someone whispered: It must be a trick.

Or else a lunatic, another whispered back and opened the wound of a grin in his face.

Another asked: What will they chuck at us next?

But Sergeant Potts poked around under the rim of his helmet and scratched his skull.

All because a man jumped up where nobody had been before.

Quite suddenly, dark and small in the afternoon, with nothing to protect his head and only clouds beyond. And three parachutists fixed in the sky while we hid, watching him, a platoon of boys in baggy uniforms, with no idea what to do. And this man, who was our enemy, lifted wooden arms. Slow as a broken windmill he started signalling. One letter at a time he spelt a message in semaphore: ICH HABE HUNGER.

Good Weekend

Jumping for Chicken

Sharon Kent

I nudge in close, waiting for the right moment to cut the engine, to let the boat drift in. If I've got it right, the current and the wind will hold the bow back, and she'll just lie there, like a well-trained pup. It's the one I've been looking for all week. The five-metre male. Big daddy. Boss of the river. There – on the sandbar, motionless, jaws agape. I coast in. Four metres, three, two. I hold my breath and my heart skips, and for a second I wonder if I've pushed my luck too hard this time. And then, miraculously, the boat stops. Perfect. No one says a word.

It's always like this, coming up close. Everyone, everything, is silent. There is just the water swirling against the hull, tinking and tapping against the aluminium, little bird taps. No one moves, their Nikons and Canons and long lenses forgotten. The woman in the front leans back so far, she is almost horizontal, her eyes wide with fear.

Afterwards, at the bar, they will all be garrulous and you won't be able to get a word in – it'll be that tight with talk.

Mate, you're another Crocodile Dundee!

I can't *believe* how close we were!

Remind me to bring a spare pair of undies next time I get in your boat!

And they'll laugh and buy me drinks and slap me on the back and drape their arms over me, like I've saved them from something, taken them into the jaws of terror and then delivered them safely home. And I have. It's my job, my life, this river.

I always think it's best to start a tour off with a big saltie. Some of the other guides go for the build-up, begin the day with a juvenile. They reckon you get better tips if you leave the big ones for last. No, I say, you only get one shot, come in hard first up – it's the memory they pay for. And these kinds of memories just get bigger and better by the minute. By the time I drop them off later today, when it has all had time to cook a bit, the croc will be seven metres and we will have been close enough to touch it. Anyway, I usually get a good tip. Most of these tourists are cashed up. At a grand a night, they ought to be. Being a tour guide isn't big money, but then I don't need big money. The shack's paid for, I catch fish, shoot a wild pig now and then and grow my own everything – vegies, dope, fruit, flowers. Everything. The job – it's just money for jam.

You love that job more than anything, she used to say. I know what she meant – that I loved it more than her. And then, later, more than both of them. Well, I did and I didn't. You can't *love* a job. And this one has its downsides – the rubbish runs, maintenance, cleaning dunnies and all that. And talking to tourists all day can get a bit much sometimes. No, I wouldn't say I loved it. But then I wouldn't say I loved her either, not really. Not by the end of it, anyway. By then I felt like that croc the fisheries caught years ago, the one who was causing trouble, clambering up into backyards, eating the odd dog. They brought it in, all trussed up on the deck, its jaws wired shut. The whole town came out to have a look at it, standing around sipping beers, arguing over whether fisheries had done the right thing.

Shoulda left it.

Nah, you can't have a rogue croc in the river.

Yeah, well now we'll have all the males in here – bloody free for all.

Fisheries, what the fuck do they know – at least we *knew* the cunt.

On and on. Opinions and anecdotes and big croc tales. It was like a wake. Someone even brought a fruitcake. People took photos, pushing and poking at its flesh with their boots, kids squeezing in to jab at it with a stick, shrieking with the thrill of it. I looked at that old river croc, five and a half metres long, fifty, maybe sixty years old, destined to spend the rest of its life living in a cage – and I felt sick inside. That was gonna be me. Jumping for chicken.

I didn't think she'd have the balls to go through with it. I stepped right back when she told me. If I could have, I would have held my hands up in the air, to show her how fully I surrendered, all the while walking backwards into my own life. It's your choice, your decision, all yours, I said. When she told me she was keeping it, planning to have the baby, well I kept on retreating, until I hit the wall of my own existence. And for a while, she had me there, pinned up against it, me squirming, with nowhere to go. Having to face up to everything. Even thinking at times that I *could* manage it, that at fifty-three I could be a father, a real one this time. I tried it on, like a coat, shrugged my shoulders into it. Eight months to get used to it. Trying to stretch myself into it, gingerly, month by month, as if I was the one who was pregnant, as if I was the one who had to do all the growing and accommodating. I think I'm really ready for this, I told her. And she prattled on, all earnest and passionate like she was selling me something I couldn't possibly do without. And I let her go on, all the while nodding thoughtfully, pretending to listen, but when it came down to it, I never bought a thing. Just kept on living my life, while she moved further and further beyond it, until she was insignificant. A speck on the horizon.

*

I allow the boat to drift well downstream before I start the engine. Everyone is still silent, just looking around, adrenalin, I'm sure, still pumping. We pass a smaller croc baking in the mangroves. This time I don't slow, just carve in close and the croc startles and lunges out into the water. I call out above the engine.

Speeds of around ten ks an hour – can almost outrun a man and can leap half their body length from a water start.

The passengers nod and I spend the next hour showing them the inhabitants of the river – herons and kingfishers, green tree snakes, mudskippers, archer fish. The only thing we don't see is the sea eagle. I know where the eyrie is, but you've got to hold something back, keep something for yourself.

The boat flies over the water and it feels like the hull is sitting a few inches above it. I manoeuvre it past mangroves and shallows, following the contours of the river back downstream until we are at the mouth. There I slow the engine and look for the bar, idling back, waiting for the right moment to gun it. And then we're through and easing out through ocean chop, around the headland, the jetty up ahead, angling out into the blue.

God, I love this. The boat ride. The freedom of it, being at the helm, shooting skyward and skimming the surface. I don't think about the owners out here, about the job or the money or anything. It's just life. Living. Heat and sun and salt. Sometimes I just want to keep on driving, out to the horizon, the wind in my face, the water slipping past, until there is no land in sight and there is just me, out on the ocean, under the sky. That simple. I want my life to be that simple.

And it was, until she arrived and blew it apart.

We could do six months in each place, she'd say, when I'd fly down to visit. Take a year off. Just be with us. Take some leave, fix your place up and we'll come up. And with every coaxing, every push, I'd pull out the same card, slap it onto the table like the winner that it was. The job. I can't leave the job. I've got to work. That's when the river became more than it is, more like a life raft. I clung on so tight, nothing was gonna wash me off, not even a newborn son.

I tie up to the jetty and help the passengers out onto the wharf. Mike, the American, slips a bill into my pocket. I think it's a hundred and we nod silently, like two conspirators. I busy myself with the boat, coiling ropes, checking the fuel, stowing the life jackets. She is still standing on the wharf, the woman who was sitting at the front of the boat, the one that's been asking all the questions all afternoon.

So, she says.

So, I reply.

We size each other up. Her – English, slim, fortyish, no ring. Me – just turned fifty-seven but fit, always fit and strong in a brown-skinned, nuggetty kind of way.

So, what would a male be doing, after dark? she asks with a smile.

He'd be going back to the river.

He doesn't hang around, then? Doesn't stay close?

I don't even hesitate. Nope, I say, without looking up.

Shame.

Well, he's got things to do.

Like what? She sits down on the end of the jetty, long legs swinging.

Defend his territory.

She bursts out laughing. Is that the croc or you you're talking about?

I stop and straighten suddenly. Look at her directly. My house is on the river, I hear myself say. No one for miles.

*

I walk to the letterbox. The sweat beads on my skin and slides down as a sheet, my whole body drenched and soaked through. January. Worst month of the year. It's not too bad if there's cloud cover. You can work outside if there's cloud. But if the sky is clear, the heat is relentless. You can almost feel your flesh cooking. If I'm off work, I can't even get out into the garden. Just have to sit inside and watch TV, the fan on full, waiting for the sun to go down. Hoping for a storm.

You can feel the build-up of a tropical storm way before you see it coming. There's this kind of static in the air and a peculiar smell. Some summers the weather builds and builds, sometimes for weeks. The tension of it is unbearable. And then, suddenly, it breaks. It's like the whole sky is cracked and torn and you wonder if it'll ever mend, ever be blue and whole again. And it just rains and rains and rains, so hard you can't see through to the other side. That's the wet. That's how it is.

I stop and stand for a moment under the mango tree. Absently I reach up for the closest, tweak its stem and the fruit falls into my hand. Perfect – the skin yellow-green, a bright blush of red across the shoulder. I lift it to my nose and the smell is sweet and strong. It's a Kent, first one of the season. Way better than the Bowens they go mad for down south. I hold the mango to the light, twist it around in the sun and let it drop into my palm. It feels like I am holding a hand, warm and comforting, as I walk down the driveway to my letterbox.

There is an envelope inside. It's her writing and on the top corner, written in neat print, it says, *Photos – do not bend.* It's the letter that I had stopped waiting for months ago – so much worse when your guard is down and you're unprepared. What am I thinking? If the letter had come in August, it would have been different. But January – a man can't be expected to think clearly and rationally in January. I carry the envelope inside and sit down to open it.

Inside is a note, typed, the paper cut neatly across and folded in half. She's only written a few lines.

He is well and happy.

Please send Xmas presents this year to the following address.

PS I've enclosed some photos as requested.

She doesn't sign her name. I push the note aside and reach for the pictures, my guts all strange and tight.

I try and flick through the photographs. The humidity sticks them together and I can't get them apart. I feel like crying, fumbling at the prints, trying to *hold* the fucking things.

And then I have them laid out on the table. One, two, three.

I get my glasses and sit in front of the photos. It's like magic. He's here, in the world, smiling, clutching a toy car. And then this one, his face up close and the blue of his eyes – they're like sea glass, and I'm swimming and drowning in them at the same time. And this one now, tumbling about on the grass with two mates, head thrown back laughing. That's my son! That one there. That's him! I want to go to him now, rush over and pick him up, cover him in kisses, hold him to my chest, take his hand, walk down the street, kick a ball, buy him an ice cream, take him fishing, show him the crocs, the reef. Pick him a mango. I'm in a fever for the phone, for her number, her mobile – does she check her messages now? I dial it – what will I say? What will I say? Then the answering machine cuts in, not even her voice, and my mouth is working but nothing is coming out and I listen to the silence until the recording cuts out and then I hang up. I sit there, staring at the wall until the midges and mosquitoes sting through the pain of it all and I get up and roll a smoke. Suck hard until everything is thick and white and there is nothing to feel at all.

*

There are slide marks in the mud and I know it's the big saltie. I putter past, in my boat now, and then I turn the engine off and drift downstream with the current. Lay back in the hull and light a cigarette.

I quit once. When she was pregnant. And I started again the day he was born. Smoked half a pack, one cigarette after the other, on the drive back from the hospital. Six months on a tightrope and all undone in one lousy fifty-minute drive. I can remember the smell of the eucalypts as I wound my way up the mountain, cold wintery air blasting through the car. When I arrived at her house, I lit the fire and sat there, smoking the rest of the pack, reliving the birth of my son and building the flames up until I couldn't bear the heat of it.

What I remember most, though, is the feel of him in my arms. And his smell, like fresh-cut hay. I have this memory of sitting in half-light, half asleep in the hospital chair, my head bowed down with my nose against his hair, smelling and smelling, like an animal might, as if I could burn his scent into my brain. I could feel the warmth of his foot resting against my finger and in that moment I felt charged with everything that being a father might mean. I held him to my chest and if I could have, I would have licked him clean, like an old wolf, claimed him as my own. Growled at anyone who tried to take him from me. I don't know what happened. I don't know where that feeling went.

I imagine sometimes that one day he might write to me or phone. That one day I'll be in my garden, planting, weeding, tidying the yard and the phone will ring and I'll race in and pick it up, my hands covered in dirt and sweat and she'll say he wants to talk to me. And I'll jump at it. Wherever the bar is, however high she raises it, I'll jump. Like that old river croc. I know I will.

I shift my shoulder up against a life jacket and stretch out. The boat is caught up in the mangrove roots and I can feel the water eddying and pooling around the hull. I'll head in soon, fire up the boat, cruise back to the ramp. For now there is just the river, the fug of a low tide, mangroves creaking in the wind. I give myself over to it, to the sweet river sound, to the whine of the mosquitoes, and tell myself I am home.

The Life You Chose and That Chose You

Izzy and Ona

Favel Parrett

Izzy is wearing his best shirt and long pants. Grandma pressed them hot this morning and the shirt is stiff, the collar tight around his neck. But he does not mind. He is happy he looks smart. He is happy his mother will see him all dressed up.

A big boy now. Just as smart as Ona, his brother.

Only his shoes let him down. His worn blue plastic sandals are covered with dust. Ona has proper shoes. Black leather shoes with laces and as he stands, he shines his shoes on the backs of his trousers one foot at a time. He is looking ahead. He is waiting for the plane to come, just like Izzy.

It is dead and stuffy in the open-door airport, and it is crowded. Just one big room with two ceiling fans that barely move the air. All the seats are taken. All the tourists are waiting for their flights away from here to other places in his country. But Izzy only knows this place. And Izzy does not want a seat. He is happy to stand. He will see his mother and he will run. He will beat Ona. He will be the first to fall into her softness, the first to kiss her, the first to greet her.

He is always the first.

Now Baby is crying. It is the heat, or maybe she is hungry, but Izzy does not look at her. He keeps his eyes fixed on the glass doors that lead out to the runway. The doors he will see his mother come though. The doors he has watched her come through every four months for as long as he can remember.

Grandma is stretching her back. She puts Baby down. Now Izzy wishes that there was a seat, one for her. For his grandma. He wishes that the tourists would leave and give her a seat. Can't they see that she is old and that her back is hurting her? They seem dumb, these people. Melted by the heat – pink necks and pink faces.

Izzy doesn't like to look at them.

Baby walks to him. She falls over but she does not cry. He tries to help her but she gets up on her own, pushes past him with her chubby arms. She walks to Ona. He looks down at her. He takes her hand and she stands quietly with him.

Baby will do anything Ona commands of her. She will listen more to Ona than to anyone. She looks at him like he is the leader, the man of the family. But he is not the leader of Izzy. He is not the boss. Izzy is old enough to have a pair of shoes of his own. His mother is going to buy him some good shoes with the money she has saved and they will go into town. They will go into Maun and get some shoes fitted. Black shoes better than Ona's. Because he will need them for school. He will have good shoes for school when he starts in three months. And then no matter how Ona beats him he will not be bossed. He will stand tall and think, *Don't you even try to boss me with your mean eyes. Don't you try and boss me anymore!*

Grandma walks over. She picks up Baby.

The plane is here.

People are laughing as they come through the doors. And there is shouting and calling. They are happy. They are home. It has been a long time.

Izzy keeps his place at the front, but his mother is not there.

People are hugging, gathering luggage, moving out of the airport and onto the street outside. Many are wearing the same uniforms as his mother. Light khaki pants and shirt, with a little emblem of a steenbok on the pocket, its two tiny horns pointing up to the sky.

Still his mother is not there.

Ona moves forward, as far as he can without crowding the tourists, and he looks around. A man comes over. He is tall and he shakes Ona's hand. He speaks to Grandma.

'I am sorry,' he says. 'Mma Nancy is delayed. The replacement cook took ill and it may be a week or two before another can be found.'

Grandma nods at him. 'Thank you, Rra,' she says.

The man looks down at Izzy. He pats him on the head.

'Do not worry, little man,' he says. 'You will see your mummy in a week or two. She will still have her twenty days. You will not be cheated.'

And the man laughs like it is funny. Izzy turns his face away.

The doors to the runway are closed now. There is no one left to come through. Grandma rests one hand on his shoulder. She is standing behind him, the weight of her there for him to lean on.

'OK. OK,' she says. 'Let's go. We have a long bus ride. Let's go.'

Izzy makes himself walk.

*

The bus stop is crowded. Many people from his mother's work are there. They are chatting with friends, hanging onto family, holding their babies. The man who laughed at him is not there and Izzy is glad.

They wait.

There is no shade and the sun is beating them hard. Grandma drapes a cloth loosely over Baby's head and face. She is asleep again. A concession man walks over, a blue and white cooler box strapped around his neck, and people start buying drinks. Izzy can hear bottles and cans being plucked from the ice cubes. It makes him feel cooler that sound, the sound of the ice clinking on the glass and against the cans.

He listens.

A lady is speaking to Ona. She tells him she knows their mother.

'We are good friends,' she says. 'She is a great cook. We all love her. We all love chef Nancy.'

Ona nods and he thanks the lady. She buys two cans of Coke Cola and she gives one to Ona.

'Share it with your brother,' she says. 'It is too hot for water.'

Ona looks up at Grandma and she nods her head. It's OK.

He opens the can with a crack and takes a gulp. He takes another and holds the can out for Izzy. Izzy can hear the fizzy drink inside but he shakes his head.

'Take it,' Ona says quietly, his eyes wide. 'Don't be rude!'

Izzy can see the beads of condensation running down the can. He wants the feeling of coolness inside him, but he can't make himself do it.

His chest hurts too much and something is wrong.

He stands with his arms by his side and tries hard to breathe. He looks down at the dirty concrete, his dusty sandals. His mother is not coming. She is not coming and he will not see her. She will not hug him and kiss him. She will not be there to make him his favourite cakes. She will not be there to sing him to sleep.

They are going home without her.

*

The bus is already crowded and full when they get on. Grandma and Baby take the last seat. Izzy stands in the aisle and holds onto the seat railing. Through the open window he sees a small plane take to the air – a tourist plane full of those people with shiny sunglasses and matching clothes. And maybe they are going to his mother's camp. Maybe they are going deep into the Okavango, a place he has never been and is not likely to go. And they will eat his mother's cooking, the lunches and the dinners, and she will make them cakes and biscuits, the ones that he should be eating.

Someone taps him on his shoulder. He turns and Ona shoves the can at him.

Izzy takes it in his hand. The outside of the can is already warm but there is at least half left inside. And it is still good. Izzy lets his jaw fall loose with the sweet liquid – the Coke Cola.

He nods his head to Ona, his brother.

Home

Catherine Cole

The government has given Ahmed a house to the west of the city, a stone's throw from Rookwood cemetery. His friend, Bert, brought him here. As Ahmed's official visitor, Bert brought sweets and books to Villawood. He took Ahmed some new black socks once and cigarettes, though neither of them smoked. Bert's eyes are an odd blue and when he laughs, lines fan from them. There is a gap between his front teeth. 'Now we are *unofficial*,' Bert said on the day of Ahmed's release. And Ahmed nodded, grateful to have a friend at last.

'Nothing special about this place,' Bert said when he opened the front door. 'Fibro. But it'll do till your papers are ready. And it's very quiet,' he joked, pointing at the house's only neighbours – two monumental stonemasons with work yards rarely used, two other dingy houses, the dead.

When Bert left, Ahmed inspected the peeling paint, the large garden at the back, the outdoor laundry. Hiding in Baghdad with neighbours he'd read old *National Geographic* magazines. London looked very big, Paris elegant. He didn't like the thrusting New York skyline or Singapore's clipped blandness. He was sorry his house was a long way from the wicked blue of Sydney Harbour, the curve of the Harbour Bridge, painted one end to the next over and over, he'd read, as the great Greek Sisyphus had laboured with his rock.

*

Now he's been in his house a month, Ahmed goes into the city to look at the harbour, returning on silver trains that carry the desperate scents of a long working day, of someone's dinner of precooked chicken or fried potatoes, the callers on mobile phones telling people where they are … nearly home, they say … I'm nearly home.

As soon as he gets home he likes to walk slowly into the cemetery, the visits allowing him time to regain something of himself, some sense of a purposeful past from the rows of neglected graves. Gone are the train trip's greasy takeaways, the sweaty underarms, the sweet plastic smell of school children. All is grass and loam, the scent of decay and sun on stone.

He often worries that the silver trains run too close to the cemetery for eternal rest, the clatter of the carriages pulsing deep into the earth. In his country the dead are buried beyond a city's walls, where it's quiet and too far away for the spirits to walk back into town. Here they mingle with the living and a few times now he has seen a phosphorescent haze above his street, ghosts straying beyond the cemetery walls, he presumes. This is when he feels his difference most keenly. What could he say to these wraiths? In Rookwood the steaming souls like to see smiling faces, he decides, to gather some happy images of the living world to fortify their darkness. What use are thoughts about rich and poor, migrants and generations long gone, the venerated whose mausoleums are dotted here and there?

*

Flimsy or not, Ahmed thinks, the house at least offers a quiet space from which to watch the street pass, the trains slowing for Lidcombe station, the Orthodox church on the other side of the tracks. It is the view from the back of the house he prefers, the garden with its shrivelled old lemon and unpruned roses just like those at home. He lost his wife, Feroza, to cancer in 1996. His son and son-in-law were taken away to be tortured one night four years ago. Ahmed and his friends searched everywhere for the boys while his daughter wept into the hair of her newborn son. Then a neighbour came to say he'd seen the bodies thrown into a trench on the outskirts of town. Ahmed had gone looking for the grave but he never found it.

One day, when his daughter finally comes, they will plant basil and parsley, tomatoes and oranges. They will fill the garden, every inch of it, with grapes and figs and plums. And when all their papers are finally approved, they'll find a beautiful house with brick walls and a red-tiled roof and there they'll live in happiness until they too are dead.

*

Ahmed turns towards the cemetery gates. Walking alone helps to pass the time while he waits for news of his daughter. There are other places he could go, to the big shopping centre in Parramatta or the cinema, but the films are often cruel, the language coarse and brutal. When he buys his groceries afterwards his eyes are still dazzled by the blood and violence. He offers thanks before each solitary meal. Waits. This cemetery gate is always open. Ahmed passes through it and looks across the wide vista, the higgledy-piggledy rows of graves, some with family portraits. The barely discernible mounds of long-dead children. The white crosses. Some of the suburb's migrants are buried in this cemetery. Not under this old angel missing one of its wings or an overturned urn, a residue of soil around its lip like ancient coffee grounds. It might yet sprout the pale blue flowers he heard a woman in the Lidcombe fruit shop call 'Easter daisies.'

The migrant dead are in their allotted spaces – the Chinese and Vietnamese, the Jews, the Muslims, the Christians – each group burying its dead in its own way, aligned as their religions decree. A sheet, thin as filo pastry, might lie between the corpse and the earth. Their ashes might have been scattered to the four winds. They are the lost generations of his new city, some long-dead like the doctor from whom this angel perpetually tries to fly on just one wing, and this woman whose children numbered fourteen, each one of them dead before her. Distant reds and yellows mark the graves of the Chinese. He has walked over to that area a few times now, drawn at first by the bright flowers, red silk carnations mostly, some silk roses. They looked like a child's storybook garden in which the flowers always bloom and the sun always shines, round, its beams radiating from a face as smiling as Bert's.

In one *National Geographic* he'd seen pictures of European cemeteries that looked like ancient cities full of houses, temples, cobbled streets down which the living came with guide books and cameras searching for the famous. This cemetery is nothing like those but it holds something true about death: the dead must be held in stone. Cats, like the skinny shadow walking slowly towards the old western gate, must sun themselves on the slabs. The wind must eradicate the names from the tombstones and subsidence must consume the burial mounds. The dead must slowly disappear.

He knows he cuts an odd figure amid the sandstone ruins of century-old graves, stooping to read an epitaph or to pull out some weeds.

I was a professor in my old country. My son and my son-in-law died fighting our oppressors. I no longer believe in inherent goodness. I still pray though I no longer believe in God.

His clothes are crumpled because he has neither the desire nor the energy to iron. Who is to see him other than the anonymous passengers on a passing silver train? But he dresses up when Bert visits with his pink iced sponges and date scones and they listen to music on Bert's old record player, songs from musicals and country and western, Bert singing along and tapping his feet against Ahmed's second-hand lounge. Bert sometimes asks him questions about his old life in Baghdad but Ahmed prefers his memories silent. When Bert goes home, he walks alone in the graveyard, practising his English on the gravestones.

*

As Ahmed returns to his house a silver train rushes past. He likes the noise the trains make, the way the tracks curve away from Central Station as though someone has taken particular care with their aesthetic. Sleekly silver, they disappear towards Redfern, blending with the grey stones sprinkled between the sleepers. Monotone: the soot-stained walls of the tunnels, the university tower, the slate roofs of the terrace houses, the unforgiving gunmetal of the roads.

The weather was perfect on his last trip into the city, the sky an opalescent blue, then during the night he heard a southerly wind come rattling in, the leaves of the neighbour's gum trees spiralling down and the twigs hitting the roof tiles, then rain, sheets and sheets of it slicing hard against the window. He likes the rain, its Australian intensity always surprising, just as he likes his trips west through Sydney's layers. Two cities – the wealthy one with its million-dollar flats and shining department stores and botanical gardens and all the water, vast oceans of it. It laps at the stone harbour walls of Circular Quay and rustles after the green and yellow ferries, is neon-stained at night when people in their finery walk to the opera or sit under the stars drinking champagne and laughing loudly. But when the lines that divide all great cities are crossed, the roads develop potholes, the trees thin out, leaving only bare streets and littered parks and tired amenities.

In this part of Sydney many migrants have gathered, and the shops offer bread and rice and lentils and oil and dried fish from some faraway sea. Then the shops give way to dilapidated houses, to his house, the monumental masons and the business of burial.

*

Ahmed's gate is hanging on one hinge like a child's milk tooth held only by a filament of skin. The flyscreen on the front window seems to curl in greeting. He runs his hands along a wall. Fibro. That was what Bert called it. What a flimsy house it is too, brittle and thin. It certainly wasn't built to last centuries, not like the houses in his old town where the walls spoke of birth and death through layers of whitewash and dust. A palm tree in his childhood front garden dropped a dried frond from time to time onto rose bushes planted so long ago and so close together they formed a soft melange of red and pink and yellow, each bush weaving into the other, the old limbs thick and thorny and bent.

*

The postman is walking slowly up the street, past the stone-masons' yards, past the blue house with the rotting veranda post and the stripped car in the driveway. The postman's bag is light, not a trolley today, and he has stopped riding his little motorbike. Brown envelopes and a white one for those people, nothing for him. The postman went into the cemetery one day to eat his lunch under a tree, not sitting on the gravestones but on the grass, looking at the graves as he ate, his head moving slowly left to right as he chewed, his bag on the grass beside him.

But no, the postman has turned back. A mistake. A letter now in Ahmed's rusty letterbox, not government-brown but a flimsy, crackling rice paper, all the way from Indonesia. He waits until the postman is out of sight before walking down to the letterbox, taking the letter out, opening it. A letter in his daughter's hand, careful as she has been in every endeavour, each word measured, he knows, to allay his fears. He can no longer say the words 'wait,' 'take small steps.' They have travelled now for three months, on donkey carts and in the boots of cars, by ship and aeroplane. She is closer, she writes. The boatman is paid. *My father. My dear, dear father. We will soon be with you again.*

The flowering trees in the garden next door are bent low with the burden of their damp flowers. Bees buzz around them and the air seems mobile as Ahmed watches from his vantage point behind the venetian blinds. The wind makes snow of the petals and he takes a deep breath. It is honey he smells, strong and thick.

May the sea be smooth. May it be the perfect blue of a freshly planed lapis lazuli. May it be perfumed, as the air is all blossom now in this square, dry house. He knows his family will smell only salt and the fuel of the ship. But this is the olfactory surprise of it – as soon as land is near, perfumes will set out to meet their boat. May the little ones know this: land smells of clay and coffee and oil. Flowers, please, yes, flowers for the girls. And for his little grandson? The loamy promise of acres on which to grow tall and strong and proud of what is new and what he has left behind.

*

Before dinner, Ahmed walks again to the cemetery gates. The rain has made the paths treacherous – puddles, the ground slippery with the ruts of neglect – but he is happy now his daughter and grandchildren are coming and there is so little time to wait. He finds a quiet grave in the sun and sits down carefully on the illegible name of its occupant. He closes his eyes and lets the sun turn his eyelids red and translucent. Far brighter than the red flowers in the Chinese cemetery, the red of his granddaughters' lips, the red balloon he will buy at Paddy's Market for his grand-son. There will be red flowers on the table when they make their first feast, vermilion pomegranates, blood-red cherries and wine-dark figs.

A shadow flits by him and he opens his eyes so quickly he is momentarily blinded by the sun's intensity. The postman has come back, he thinks.

'Good afternoon.'

He lifts his arm to shade his eyes. A young woman walking alone, her hair as long and dark as his daughter's when he last saw her. 'Good afternoon.'

She is gone.

*

An hour later when it is again threatening rain he sees the girl kneeling before the rotting doors of a mausoleum, sketching the timber with the tips of her fingers. He watches for a moment from a distance. She is older than he thought. Her long hair gave her the look of a teenager but he suspects she is closer to his daugh-ter's age, twenty-four, almost twenty-five. Does she also have chil-dren? She seems too engrossed in her touching to notice the return of the rain, but he feels the drops and turns towards home. A drenching might lead to a cold, a cold to pneumonia; silly hypochondria, he knows, now his life has a waiting purpose. Soon he will take control of his family's new life.

By the time he is back in his house the rain is pelting down. He leaves the front door open so he can watch the way the rain forces the overburdened branches of the flowering tree lower and lower, the flowers a sodden carpet beneath it. And there is the young woman running along the street, a cap on her head, an umbrella held high above it. She pauses for a moment as though deciding whether to seek shelter in the second stone-mason's office. No, she has made a bolt for it and disappears down the street.

Now, Ahmed thinks, I am ready to eat – some bread, some olives and fruit. I will read my book and practise ways to speak English slowly, flatly, as the people speak when he walks up to Lidcombe, squinting at him, taking money delicately from him as though his hands are dirty. He must stop thinking like this.

He spends too much time alone, the television his only company. He watches the Special Broadcasting Service at night and if he's lucky he sees a film in a language he knows. And each morning he watches the same news in many languages, the same footage, the same bombs.

As he closes the front door he looks back towards the cemetery gates. The sky has darkened; before too long the sun will set. I must pray, he thinks. Thanks for the living, meditations for the dead. Prayers to take my mind from the images that will descend with the night: sea monsters and pirates and giant waves and unscrupulous brokers and rusty, overcrowded little boats. I am old, he thinks, and the old lose the elasticity of their optimism. Two new generations are coming and my life is good.

Meanjin

Publication Details

Julie Chevalier's 'This Awful Brew' was first published in *Permission to Lie*, Spineless Wonders, Darwin, 2011. Reprinted by permission.

Catherine Cole's 'Home' was first published in *Meanjin*, volume 69, number 3, Spring 2010.

Deborah FitzGerald's 'The Anniversary' was first published in *The 25th UTS Writers' Anthology: The Life You Chose and That Chose You*, Figment Publishing, Sydney, 2011.

Rebecca Giggs's 'Blow In' was first published in *Overland 201*, Summer 2010.

Rodney Hall's 'Silence 1945' was first published in *Good Weekend*, Summer Fiction Issue, 8 January 2011. It has since been published under the title 'Semaphore' in *Silence*, Pier 9, Sydney, 2011.

Marion Halligan's 'Shooting the Fox' was first published in *Shooting the Fox*, Allen & Unwin, Sydney, 2011. Reprinted by permission.

Sarah Holland-Batt's 'Istanbul' was first published in the *Adelaide Review*, October 2010.

Nicholas Jose's 'What Love Tells Me' was first published in *HEAT 24 New Series: That's it, for now...*, edited by Ivor Indyk, Giramondo, Sydney, 2011.

Sharon Kent's 'Jumping for Chicken' was first published in *The 25th UTS Writers' Anthology: The Life You Chose and That Chose You*, Figment Publishing, Sydney, 2011.

Jennifer Mills's 'Look Down with Me' was first published in *Bruno's Song and Other Stories from the Northern Territory*, The Northern Territory Writers' Centre, Darwin, 2011.

Louis Nowra's 'The Index Cards' was first published in *MONUMENT*, issue 100, December 2010–January 2011.

Mark O'Flynn's 'Beneath the Figs' was first published in *Going Down Swinging*, issue 30, 2011.

Tim Richards's '(Favoured by) Babies' was first published in *Thought Crimes*, Black Inc., Melbourne, 2011.

Kate Rotherham's 'Shelter' was first published in *Island*, issue 122, Spring 2010.

Gretchen Shirm's 'Carrying On' was first published in *Having Cried Wolf*, Affirm Press, Melbourne, 2010. Reprinted by permission.

Nick Smith's 'Everybody Wins on Kid Planet' was first published in *fourW twenty-one*, November 2010.

Miriam Sved's 'Matter' was first published in *Meanjin*, volume 70, issue 2, June 2011.

Leah Swann's 'Street Sweeper' was first published in *Bearings*, Affirm Press, Melbourne, 2011. Reprinted by permission.

Chris Womersley's 'Where There's Smoke' was first published in *The Big Issue*, no. 388, 30 August 2011.

Notes on Contributors

THE EDITOR:

Cate Kennedy is the author of the critically acclaimed short-story collection *Dark Roots* and the novel *The World Beneath*, both published by Scribe, as well as poetry collections and a travel memoir. Her work has appeared in many publications and anthologies, including *The Best Australian Stories*, *Harvard Review* and the *New Yorker*. She works as a mentor, editor and judge when not at work on her own writing. She lives in northeast Victoria.

THE AUTHORS:

Debra Adelaide has published over ten books, including three novels: *The Hotel Albatross, Serpent Dust* and, most recently, *The Household Guide to Dying*, which has been published in a dozen countries. She has also been a freelance researcher, editor and book reviewer and is now a senior lecturer in creative practices at the University of Technology, Sydney.

Stephanie Buckle lived in the UK and New Zealand before settling in Canberra. She has been a teacher and a counsellor and began writing in 2003 after the Canberra bushfires. Her writing has won numerous awards and several of her stories have appeared in *Island*. She is currently working on her third novel, as well as continuing to write short fiction.

Julie Chevalier lives in Sydney. *Permission to Lie*, a collection of her short stories, was published by Spineless Wonders in 2011.

Her poetry collection *linen tough as history* is forthcoming from Puncher & Wattmann and *Darger: His Girls*, a poetry sequence about the life of the reclusive artist Henry Darger, will be available in 2012.

Catherine Cole has published three novels (*Dry Dock, Skin Deep* and *The Grave at Thu Le*) and two non-fiction books (*Private Dicks and Feisty Chicks: An Interrogation of Crime Fiction* and *The Poet Who Forgot*). She edited *The Perfume River: Writing from Vietnam* and co-edited *Fashion in Fiction: Text and Clothing in Literature, Film and Television*. She has also published poetry, short stories, essays and reviews and is professor of creative writing and deputy dean of creative arts at the University of Wollongong.

Mark Dapin is the author of the bestselling Australian travel memoir *Strange Country* and the Ned Kelly Award-winning novel *King of the Cross*. His second novel, *Spirit House*, was released in September 2011. He is a features writer and columnist for *Good Weekend*.

Liam Davison has published four novels and two collections of short fiction. He has received numerous awards for his work, including the National Book Council Award for Fiction for his novel *Soundings*. He writes for the books pages of the *Australian* and lives in Melbourne.

Marele Day is the author of seven novels, including the internationally acclaimed *Lambs of God* and, most recently, *The Sea Bed*. She lives and works on the far north coast of New South Wales.

Deborah FitzGerald is a journalist who lives and works in Sydney's inner west. She is married to a remarkable man, Mark Waugh, and mother to two beautiful sons, Mac and Finn. In 2006 she won a Harper Collins/Varuna Development Award for her first manuscript, *Tower Hill*, which is as yet unpublished. She has a Master of Arts in creative writing from the University of Technology, Sydney, and is currently working on a second novel.

Rebecca Giggs is a writer of essays, fiction and poetry. She grew up in Western Australia, in what geologists refer to as the passive margin that runs between the Yilgarn Craton and the sea. Her work can be read in literary journals, in books and online.

Rodney Hall's books have been published in the USA, UK, Australia and Canada and in translation into German, French, Danish, Swedish, Spanish, Portuguese and Korean. His radio and TV scripts have been broadcast by the ABC and the BBC. He has twice won the Miles Franklin Award (for *Just Relations* in 1982 and *The Grisly Wife* in 1994) and was presented with the gold medal of the Australian Literature Society in 1992 and in 2001. His new collection of short fiction, *Silence*, will be published in November 2011.

Marion Halligan's books include *Spider Cup, Lovers' Knots, Wishbone, The Golden Dress, The Fog Garden, The Point, The Apricot Colonel, Valley of Grace, Shooting the Fox*, a children's book and books of autobiography, travel and food, including *The Taste of Memory*. In 2006 she was awarded an AM.

Karen Hitchcock is a writer and doctor. Her collection of short stories, *Little White Slips*, won the 2010 Queensland Premier's Steele-Rudd Award and was shortlisted for the New South Wales Premier's Literary Awards and the Dobbie Award. Her first novel, *Read My Lips*, will be published by Picador in 2012.

Sarah Holland-Batt was born in Queensland in 1982. Her first book, *Aria*, won the Arts ACT Judith Wright Poetry Prize, the Thomas Shapcott Poetry Prize and the FAW Anne Elder Award. She is also the recipient of the W.G. Walker Memorial Fulbright Scholarship, an Australia Council Literature Residency in Rome and the Marten Bequest Travelling Scholarship. She lives in New York.

Nicholas Jose has published seven novels, two collections of short stories, a book of essays and a memoir. He has a chair in writing with the Writing and Society Research Group at the University of Western Sydney.

Sharon Kent has recently completed her second postgraduate writing degree at UTS, a Master of Arts in writing by research. Her stories have been published in several UTS writers' anthologies, in *Southerly* and in national magazines including *HQ*. She is working on her first novel, which has attracted three Varuna fellowships and a reading at the Sydney Writers' Festival. She lives with her five-year-old son and is currently travelling the outback in an old bus.

Russell King was born in England and emigrated to Australia twenty years ago. He has lived in Sydney, Brisbane and the Northern Territory. He currently works as a general practitioner and lecturer at the School of Rural Medicine, University of New England in Armidale, New South Wales. This is his first published story.

Karen Manton lives in Batchelor, one hundred kilometres south of Darwin. She won the Arafura Short-story Award in 2003, 2009 and 2010. Her work has been published in *The Best Australian Stories 2005*, *True North* and *Bruno's Song and Other Stories from the Northern Territory*.

Jennifer Mills is the author of two novels, *The Diamond Anchor* and *Gone*. Her work has been widely published, broadcast and performed and has received numerous awards. A collection of her short fiction will be published by UQP in 2012. She lives in South Australia.

Louis Nowra is a playwright, novelist, screenwriter and essayist. He lives in Sydney.

Mark O'Flynn's stories have appeared in a wide range of magazines. He has published three collections of poetry as well as two novels, most recently *Grassdogs* in 2006. A third novel is forthcoming from HarperCollins.

Penny O'Hara is a Canberra-based poet and short-story writer. Her work has appeared in the online journal *Islet* and in the anthologies *FIRST 2009: Undertow*, *FIRST 2010: Shattered* and

Block. She was highly commended in the 2010 Michael Thwaites Poetry Award.

Favel Parrett's debut novel, *Past the Shallows*, was published in 2011 by Hachette Australia. She is currently working on her second.

Joanne Riccioni's stories have been published in the *Age*, *The Best Australian Stories 2010*, *Westerly*, *Stylus* and *Taralla*, and have been read on the BBC and anthologised in the USA. She is currently working on her first novel, which will be published by Scribe.

Tim Richards is a Melbourne-based writer. The most recent of his three books is *Thought Crimes*, a collection of short stories. He works as a script assessor for Screen Australia and teaches screen-writing at Box Hill TAFE and RMIT.

Kate Rotherham lives in northeastern Victoria. Her stories have won national awards and appeared in anthologies, journals and magazines including *Award Winning Australian Writing 2011* and *2010*, *Island* and *page seventeen*. She is working on a collection of short stories, often finding inspiration in the wide-eyed wonder and fantastic energy of her four young children.

Michael Sala spent his childhood moving between Holland and Australia. He was shortlisted for the Vogel/*Australian* Literary Award in 2007 and his work has appeared in publications including *HEAT*, *Brothers and Sisters*, *Kill Your Darlings*, *Harvest*, *Etchings* and *The Best Australian Stories 2009* and *2010*. He lives and teaches in Newcastle. His memoir will be published by Affirm Press early in 2012.

Gretchen Shirm was born in 1979, grew up in Kiama and moved to Ballina as a teenager. Her first book of interwoven short stories, *Having Cried Wolf*, was published in 2010. She was named as one of the *Sydney Morning Herald*'s Best Young Novelists in 2011.

Nick Smith is working on a comic novel as part of a PhD in creative writing at the Australian National University. He has previously been published in *Westerly, Kill Your Darlings, McSwee-neys, Australian Short Stories, Harvest, Block, fourW, Redoubt* and *Perilous Adventures.*

Miriam Sved's fiction has appeared in journals including *Mean-jin, Overland* and *Strange.* With the help of an Arts Victoria devel-opment grant she is currently completing a series of short stories set in and around an AFL football club. Her novel, *After the Game*, was commended in the IP Picks Awards. She has a PhD from the University of Melbourne, where she teaches creative writing.

Leah Swann lives in Melbourne with her husband and two chil-dren. She is a freelance writer and former public-relations man-ager. Her first book, *Bearings*, a collection of short stories and a novella, was published this year by Affirm Press.

Chris Womersley is a Melbourne-based writer of fiction, reviews and essays. His work has appeared in *Granta, The Best Australian Stories 2006* and *2010*, the *Griffith Review* and the *Age*. In 2007 one of his stories won the Josephine Ulrick Prize for Literature. He won the 2008 Ned Kelly Award for Best First Fiction for his novel *The Low Road.* His second novel, *Bereft*, was shortlisted for the Miles Franklin Award and the Australian Society of Litera-ture Gold Medal and won the Indie Award for Best Fiction.